THIS LAST CHANCE

ANGELS & EVILDWELS BOOK 1

D. L. FINN

ALSO BY D. L. FINN

Evildwel/Angel Series

This Second Chance (Book 1)

The Button: This Only Chance (Book 2)

This Last Chance (Book 3)

Companion Evildwel/Angel Stories

A Long Walk Home: A Christmas Novelette

Red Eyes in the Darkness: A Short Story

I Wouldn't Be Surprised: A Short Story

Paranormal Thriller

A Voice in the Silence

Other Short Stories

Bigfoot: A Short Story

Poetry

Just Her Poetry Seasons of a Soul

No Fairy Tale: The Reality of a Girl Who Wasn't a Princess and Her Poetry
(Memoir)

Children's Books (middle grade)

Elizabeth's War (historical fiction)

An Unusual Island (fantasy)

Things on a Tree (holiday/fantasy)

Dolphin's Cave (fantasy)

Tree Fairies and Their Short Stories (fantasy)

Photograph: D. L. Finn

Cover design by Angie of pro_ebookcovers on Fiverr

Book design by Maureen Cutajar

www.gopublished.com & D. L. Finn

Library of Congress Control Number: 2020936507

eBook ISBN: 978-1-7329662-1-5

Print ISBN: 978-1-7329662-2-2

D. L. Finn

www.dlfinnauthor.com

D. C. Hawk Publishing

DEDICATION

In loving memory of Marissa Bassett.

CHAPTER 1

"My name is Nester. I've been around a long time, way before humans invented their first stone tool. My kind migrated from a distant planet that couldn't sustain us anymore, in case you've been wondering where we came from. Although I doubt you winged ones—that's what we call you angels—give evildwel history much thought. Your attention goes to the humans, including this young woman, Amber. You hardly leave her side. It's an unsettling thought, but I can almost understand your devotion. I feel something from Amber that used to repel me, but now it draws me to her, much like you. Not sure what it is, though.

"I'm attempting to communicate with you, like winged ones do, by thoughts. I can't take the chance of speaking out loud and being over-heard by another evildwel. Anyway, it's my hope you can hear me because my life is literally spinning out of control."

Nester paused and studied the beautiful winged one. Zelina didn't indicate she wanted him to stop, so he continued to push his thoughts to her.

"There was this planet before Earth where we ran out of food. We had no entities like winged ones to stop us, so the planet's inhabitants destroyed each other. We feasted well on their fear and suffering, something we've done since time began. I've heard some voice the opinion that it was even before that, since we only know we are here, not how we came into existence. I've never pondered much on the philosophical part of our presence but considered what we did like culling the weak from the herd, until now.

"Humankind was still new when we arrived, but they supplied us with a feast, much like the banquets spread out for kings and queens. I don't like to admit it to you, but I've dined on the hatred and misery with each blow inflicted through slavery, genocide, torture, burning witches, wars, serial killers, or a man simply abusing his wife or child. Human hatred and fear were delicious food for me."

Nester paused again, making sure Zelina wouldn't lash out at him for saying that. Her face was serene, gazing down at her human. It was as if he didn't exist. His discomfort sharing himself was painful, like a festering open wound, but what other choice did he have?

"Of course, you winged ones haven't made it easy for us evildwels, which is why some of my kind has already moved on to new planets. I've heard winged ones or goodness doesn't interfere with their feeding there, but it's only a rumor. I tend to believe good is as wide-spread as we are, and that last planet we landed on with only evil there was a fluke. Those blue-tinted, one-eyed beings made us feel like we'd won the lottery, much like these humans are always trying to do. It was great for many decades—until it wasn't. Then we were left with hardly anything to feed on after they used their lethal weapons on each other. It'll be toxic for years for those scant few that survived.

"Earth was different, and the population has increased immensely. This has left us the luxury of choosing our hosts. In these so-called modern times, there's been plenty of opportunity for joint feedings, like World War II, when the bombs dropped on Pearl Harbor or Hiroshima and all the pain and fear inflicted by the Nazis. We've gathered in New York, Iran, Iraq, London, Spain, India, Nigeria, and so many other places as large-scale terrorist acts occurred. I was on Air India Flight 182, where over three hundred died. Rape, murder, and massacres have been met with opposition from you winged ones, but you've barely made a dent in the larger-scale events lately, which causes me some concern for this planet's prospects, until recently, that is."

Nester sighed. He didn't know what to do with these new feelings he had, and he wanted answers. He wished Zelina would at least acknowledge he was in the room with her. He knew she saw him.

"But none of this has bothered me until now, and the consequence is I'm rooting for this girl while trying to get my thoughts across to you. My attempted communication with you is taboo and would be my death sentence if another evildwel knew. They would believe I'd gone insane. Maybe I have—I honestly have no idea. All I know is there's nothing I can do about what's happening to me.

"Do you understand how strange it is for an evildwel to observe this golden-haired human without the slightest intention of feeding on her fear? I watch simply because I feel like she's important in the scheme of earthly things. It's an evildwel thing to feel out the bad, and there's plenty of it around her right now, but to know she's important to humans is a completely new thing to me. To see that she's...well, good."

Nester hesitated to say more as Zelina hovered over Amber. He frowned. His dark mist swirled tightly around him as it did normally, but nothing else in his life was normal anymore. All he could do was try to get through to the winged one by staying close and watch.

CHAPTER 2

$\mathcal{T}$he gloomy gray afternoon was framed in the small office window like a dismal black and white photograph. Amber's world reflected this monochromatic existence as her fingers furiously tapped away on the keyboard. Even the rare shimmer of a positive political piece couldn't instill illumination into the murkiness labeled as grief. But how could she feel otherwise after what had happened? The fulfillment her job used to offer wasn't important in her new reality, including this piece about the new presidential candidate, Myles Stroud. The man her sister, Iris, used to work for... before.

Amber choked back the sadness that still threatened to consume her whenever she thought about her twin sister. If she let those tears escape the heavy barrier she'd built up over the last six months, she knew her coworkers would be at her side. They cared, and she couldn't fault them for trying, but their advice was meant for someone who had closure.

"You need to move on, Amber."

That line had assaulted her ears like an eager beginner's drum solo. She was surprised that her eardrums hadn't burst with good intentions. Amber shook her head and stretched out her legs and arms in her small white cubicle. Heavily buttered popcorn whiffed its way out of the lunchroom, but it didn't trigger hunger; instead, it promoted an uneasy queasiness. Amber slowly sipped water from her crystal-infused water bottle, forcing the kaleidoscope of emotions back down into that familiar numbness. Finally, working robot Amber took charge and was able to focus on double-checking facts and punctuation. Her reputation rested on truth. No slanting a story for either side, even for this candidate. Independent Senator Stroud made her job easier, though.

"I think he's the one who will finally fix things," Iris had declared brightly over breakfast one morning. Amber had believed her then, but now?

She sighed and muttered quietly to herself, "He's not magical or capable of bringing people back from the dead."

She pushed back the wavy blond hairs that had escaped from her ponytail. Her current condition could be summed up in that hairstyle: parts kept escaping from her tightly guarded emotions.

She continued to work on her article until she was satisfied there were no mistakes and sent it to her editor. She scanned her emails and responded in meaningless words when necessary. Peeking hopefully over her glowing screen at the clock, she shook her head as disappointment surged through her. Another hour to go. Would this day ever end?

Sighing loudly, she started another article for next week about a boy who was doing good in this world, saving homeless animals. She had a recorded clip from the event.

"Although they need our financial support, they also need hands-on support, which is why I am here to help in any way I can," Senator Stroud had declared to great applause.

Then the candidate that filled Amber with disgust every time she saw his smug face, Bo Wright, successful businessman, spoke up. "Here's an issue we can agree on, Senator."

The two men shook hands and smiled for the camera. She inserted that picture into the article.

Even doing something good, Bo Wright still managed to irritate her. He always had. The man was the worst of humanity—arrogant, pretentious, and something else she couldn't quite place. It might have been his friendship with her less-than-stellar stepfather, Jeb Cadwell. It showed Bo's lack of judgment, like trusting a curled-up rattlesnake not to strike if you got too close.

"Idiot," Amber mumbled between clenched teeth as she hit save.

Another glance at the clock finally granted her the reprieve she'd been waiting for. Without a single goodbye, she grabbed her coat and heavy black leather purse and bolted to the elevator. She knew if she even so much as waved at her coworkers, she'd end up at the club with them again, as she'd been doing for the last few months.

Tonight she had the elevator to herself. With no distractions her palms began to sweat, and her breath came out in short bursts as the claustrophobic vessel thumped to a stop. The silver doors slowly creaked open, offering her an escape into the parking structure that her newspaper shared with a popular casino. Surrounded only by waiting vehicles, she felt the loneliness surface. It was a familiar feeling since her sister's murder. She couldn't stop the anticipated quiver from surging through her with the image of Iris's body tossed away like trash next to the garbage bin. It hit her every time with the same punch as the first time she'd seen the picture. Nothing that happened that night made any sense to Amber. Iris shouldn't have been in that part of town in a dark alley. She was supposed to be at work. The very last conversation Amber had with her sister replayed in her head.

"Hi," came Iris's breathless voice over her cell phone.

"Are we still on for the movies later?"

"Um, not sure if I can get there on time. I have so much to do. If I'm not there, you go without me. I'll get there as soon as I can, okay?"

"We can go later," Amber protested.

"No. You've wanted to see it. I don't mind, honest. Well, sis, I'd better go and finish up here. When I see you, I have something to share."

"What's wrong?"

"Nothing, silly. You worry too much. My news is good—no, great. Gotta go. Love ya."

"Wait! Tell me now," Amber said, but Iris had already disconnected.

Amber hadn't even been able to tell her sister she loved her back one last time—and she'd never learned what the good news was. Since that horrible night, Amber had waited patiently for the police to find the murderer and supply some answers. Six months later, they had done neither. She thought they'd finally caught the killer three months ago.

Britney, a coworker who had taken it upon herself to be her grief counselor, took her to the police station. She attempted to console her afterward. "Just some crazy old man who didn't even know where she'd been shot. Sorry. It was the same thing with my aunt. Never did catch the killer."

Britney's words had rebounded off her that night and now. All Amber had left to think about was the terror and pain Iris must have felt with each blow she endured. What had been her final thought as the bullet penetrated her skull, destroying her existence? Amber clenched her hands tightly as if she could punch away those images as she slipped sideways between two parked cars. Her red nails drew a couple of drops of blood to match, but she didn't feel it.

Her phone buzzed, startling her out of the grim memories. It was Britney, who didn't realize that Amber wasn't as into their friendship as she was. Yes, Amber's best friend was dead, and maybe she did need someone in her life, but she wouldn't choose this needy woman as a replacement. Amber sighed and clicked on the message:

You must be so upset today with it being the six-month anniversary of Iris's death. I can't imagine the pain you are dealing with...well, that's not really true. Since my sweet auntie who raised me was murdered in her house four Halloweens ago, each year on that very day, it's been horrible. No one was there for me, even my ex, Steven. He was only all-in when we were in the bedroom, like I've said before. Anyways, I'm here for you always. So, I thought it would be best to follow me to my house later and drive me over to your house. I know you are kind, not making me drive all that way to your house in the boonies. Even Kyle backs my plans—for once. So, meet me at the usual spot and we'll go from there. Love ya, B.

Amber shook her head, knowing the best thing to do was pretend she'd never seen it. Although it did sound like Kyle might already be on the way out if she was reading between the lines correctly. She didn't like him. He had what her aunt used to call a wandering eye.

"Oh, Britney," she murmured, stopping to pick up a coffee cup someone had dropped.

The first time Britney told her story, Amber had felt for her. It was a lot for anyone to handle.

"It was only me when my adoptive parents died in a car accident. Like you, I went to live with my auntie at twelve years old. Then—it's still hard to say this—she was murdered right after I moved out. While I was grieving my auntie's death, my boyfriend cheated on me. Then I was really alone. Later I realized it was time to start over, and I ended up here." Britney wiped away a tear and shrugged.

After hearing the story over and over, Amber started to realize Britney needed the attention it brought her. If Amber were Britney, she'd ask that therapist she had been seeing for the last two years for her money back—it hadn't worked. A bottomless pit of need no one would be able to fill until Britney filled it herself. That was Amber's diagnosis.

A strong gust of wind cut through Amber's navy wool coat, sending a chill through her. She pulled the coat tightly around her as she suddenly felt she was being watched. She didn't see anyone in the garage, but that didn't mean they weren't there. She was frozen in her fear. Maybe leaving alone wasn't such a great idea, but if she had left with her coworkers on a Friday, she'd have gone out with them to eat and dance and ended up with a houseguest.

She shook her head and frowned. It was just her imagination. Besides, she had to honor the promise she made to her sister right before she scattered her ashes into Iris's favorite place, Lake Tahoe.

"I will live for both of us now. I might even break a rule or two, just for you."

She could imagine her sister smiling down on her at that moment as she released her ashes into the Nevada side of the lake. Amber couldn't bring herself to break the law and do it on the California side. Iris had been the risk taker. As she watched the cremains float away, she could have sworn that she saw her sister's face form in the white ash on the surface of the deep blue water.

"Iris?" she called out, with no reply other than the boat captain's inquiring look. "I will live life fully, as you did. I won't let this...you know...make me bitter or afraid, sis, and I won't add to the world's existing problems, either."

There were many times Amber couldn't prevent the rage or fear from creeping up and threatening to consume her, and she'd remember Iris's words, "Don't add to it."

Amber had almost broken her promise immediately when she considered joining her sister in death, but the need for justice and her sister's words deterred her. Her sister had been her only real family—Amber had to call their mother about the arrangements.

"I'm jusst tooo upset," her mother had responded, slightly slurring her words. "The doctor doesn't think your stepdad and I should travel to the West Coast now. We should take care of ourselves. Maybe take a local cruise or spend some time on the golfff course. There's a highly sought-after golf pro at our club that everyone is talking about, Neil Ramseyyy. Would you believe I can't get a lesson in with him for a year? Anyways, you know how golfing has always relaxed me, and well, that's what the doctor says I need after such a shock. So, ummm...I know you understand why we can't be there. I'll send you a check to cover the costs for the cremation and boat to disperse her ashes on the lake, like you were talking about. Okay? Well, someone's calling. I'd better check. You take caaare now. Love youuu."

Her mother always managed to talk about nothing when she was drunk. Amber hadn't spoken to her since that call. A check did show up. Sure, it made her mom feel better and only cost her $5,000—just an excuse to avoid pain. Her mother had been skillful at that since she lost her first husband, Amber's beloved father. She collected a huge life insurance policy and a payout for the car accident. Amber remembered her aunt talking about her mom winning in court. Her mother had been able to take care of her investments but not her daughters.

Amber shook her head to bring herself out of her stupor. She continued through the parking garage and found an overfull trash can that she topped off with the coffee cup she had acquired. Her thoughts had become like that mound of garbage, and they were overflowing. She cut through a row of neatly parked cars, threw her shoulders back, and took a deep, soothing breath. Time to dump all that trash. Her black ankle boots echoed against the concrete, but it was the silence within that sound that filled her with foreboding. The darkening clouds peeked through the sides of the parking structure, indicating an oncoming storm and adding to her heavy mood.

Amber struggled to rein in her spiraling thoughts. "Sorry, Iris." The only other person capable of pulling her out of a funk had been Aunt Kathy. Breast cancer had taken her two years ago. She rolled her eyes and sighed. "Okay, pity party over."

A sudden light flashed, blinding her for a split second. Her boot landed on a long, round object, causing her to lose balance and slip. She was able to plant her other foot firmly down while her arms flailed about like long hair in a windstorm, but she kept upright. She carefully glanced around, hoping no one had seen her ungainly display. Was she getting a migraine from that flash of light? Fortunately, no other flashes followed, and her vision was clear—none of the blurry, floating colors that preceded a migraine. Maybe a reflection from somewhere? She shivered and massaged her temples. Something caught her eye. A white feather.

"What..."

Her sister had believed that feathers were messages from angels, although Amber wasn't so sure she believed in all of that. Still, she was compelled to pick it up. A small part of her hoped it was from her sister, but her logical side insisted it came from a bird sheltering from the storm in the parking garage. Conflicted, she bent down to grasp the delicate, silky feather when she heard a slight whoosh above her back and hoped it was from the bird whose feather she held. Then there was a slight *thunk* off to her right, but it was the object right in front of her that made her mouth go dry. What she had tripped on was a yellow rope.

"It can't be..." was all she could get out as she straightened back up.

Not today. A short length of yellow rope—the very thing that had been found next to her sister's body. She trembled and stuffed the feather into her pocket as her eyes scanned the parking structure. She didn't see anyone but still felt like she was being watched. Unnerved, she bolted the rest of the way to her vehicle, leaving the yellow rope behind.

She unlocked her slightly used 4x4 silver Blazer with a beep, jumped in, and locked the doors with a sigh of relief. She heard a thump and crash coming from where she'd just been. She spun around but didn't see anything. Was someone hurt? Should she check? Then a car started, and she slowly let her breath out, unaware she'd been holding it. There *had* been someone else in the lot. Sometimes it paid to think like Amber instead of Iris.

An older white SUV, a common sight in Lake Tahoe, slowly pulled out of a tight parking space. The noise had probably been the owner trying to get into the truck. Amber shook her head, feeling a little silly, and turned the ignition. Cranking up the heater and shutting off the radio, she thrust in an old CD so she didn't have to hear any unwelcome news on the radio. A little Tom Petty was what the moment required. As soon as "Free Falling" started to play, Amber engaged her seatbelt with a loud click and put her truck into reverse.

The white SUV had stopped directly behind her, blocking her in. Amber tapped her brake to let the driver know other people were driving too. It didn't work, so she pressed the horn.

"Hey, could you check your phone somewhere else, please?"

The white truck didn't move. She peered through her rear window, hoping to make eye contact. Maybe it was someone she knew. Or a casino guest who'd found his way into employee parking.

"Too many free drinks?"

Amber was about to lay on the horn when the driver opened their door and the interior light came on, but all she saw was a black coat and beanie. Flat tire or...

"Great," Amber couldn't get the *or* out of her mind after seeing the yellow rope.

Amber grabbed her cell phone to call...well, the woman she was avoiding.

The driver stepped out of the truck. Amber got Britney's voice mail and hung up. She quickly texted *Call me* and threw her phone down on the passenger seat as a roar of thunder echoed outside. She turned down the music and watched in her rearview mirror to see what the person's intentions were. The edge of a black coat was peeking around the back of the truck right when her coworkers burst out of the elevator laughing. The person in black retreated back into the SUV. Right before the door shut, she got a glimpse of a face covered by a full black ski mask and red eyes looking back at her. With a nod and a small wave of a black-gloved hand, the driver was consumed in darkness. The white SUV sped off with a loud squeal and disappeared around the corner.

Amber gulped loudly. She suddenly felt like she couldn't breathe. She forced the air in and out as Iris had always advised. *Think of the ocean gently hitting the shore and then pulling back. In and out*...the rope and the mask, though. She gasped and turned down her heater with a shaking hand. She could rationalize the red eyes being a reflection, but the intent of the person driving the SUV wasn't lost on her. She quickly checked her phone as she cranked up her music again. Finally, the awaited buzz of a reply. They would meet at the club.

CHAPTER 3

*A*mber slowly backed out of her parking spot. She kept glancing in her rearview mirror. As she deliberately drove through the garage, she passed the place where she'd found the feather. The headlights caught a silver object sticking out of the exit sign. A dart? She hit her brakes.

Amber answered herself out loud, "No, it can't be, can it? The police did find drugs I've never heard of in Iris's blood..."

Then she remembered what the police had said.

"Did your sister use any drugs, ma'am?"

"Drugs? Iris? Are you kidding me? She wouldn't even take aspirin! All she took was vitamins. She was a runner and a vegan."

She had noticed the side glance the older officer had given his partner. She then had to answer more questions about the vitamins—what idiots.

That's how the investigation had gone, trying to blame instead of solve. She had lost all patience with that. But that still didn't explain a dart flying over her tonight. Did her sister have a mark on her they had missed? Was this how the drug got into her system? These were questions she was going to get answered.

She took some more calming breaths again. "No, Amber, you're just paranoid. Probably part of a large dart game, but the rope and feather..."

Instead of driving off, she felt weighed down by the rope and the dart. She threw her vehicle into park, got out, and carefully dislodged the long dart from the black-and-white sign. She was mindful not to touch the tip, which was obviously meant to inject something. It definitely wasn't from any game. It reminded her of the darts she'd seen on TV used to catch wild animals and put them to sleep so they could be moved or taken care of. She placed it in an empty shopping bag and added the rope, wishing she could take them to the police, but the look the officer had given her about the vitamins made her reject that idea. No, she'd give it to the private detective she'd saved to hire.

She knew what Iris would say. "Let's talk about this—somewhere else."

And that was still good advice. Even though the masked man could be explained away—he was heading to the Heavenly ski slopes down the street and had on red contacts for a joke—but the rest?

Amber shook her head and then drove to the club. Soon she was in a dark room full of strangers, loud music from the 80s blasting in the background.

A favorite song from the Cars came on, and she allowed herself to be pulled onto the dance floor by Blake from work. She had to regroup before she shared her story.

When the group sat down to eat at the large red booth, amid small talk and laughter, Amber quietly devoured her bacon burger slathered in BBQ sauce. The bacon was crisp, the sauce tangy, and the burger juicy—exactly as she liked it, complete with a side of perfectly seasoned garlic fries, but tonight she could have been eating an unsalted rice cake and not known the difference. Finally, she told her story as she swirled a fry in a small mound of ketchup. Her coworkers all expressed concern, followed by a weak suggestion to report it that included a telling side glance at Britney.

Britney scooted in next to her when the next round of drinks came. "Hun, it's the six-month anniversary. It's only normal you're thinking about Iris. You saw what you wanted to see. You want to solve the murder—I understand—but maybe you should get some therapy. You've been through a lot. You know, the best thing I did after my auntie's murder was talk to a professional. I totally feel for you, Amber, but you're seeing things that aren't there. No one else saw any rope, dart, or masked driver in the garage. If you want, I can give you the name of someone highly recommended. I'll go with you because I don't want you to feel alone."

"Um, I'll call Monday. No need to feel like you have to come with me, but thanks for your offer," Amber muttered through clenched teeth as she took the offered card.

Didn't see the rope or dart? Well, duh. They walked a completely different route than she did. Why did she let Britney keep crossing that line with her? Crossing? No, the line was being run over repeatedly by monster truck Britney, and Amber was allowing it.

"I'll remind you, of course. I don't mind coming—what I wouldn't have done to have someone there for me like I'm here for you. Well, I'm always glad to help, and Kyle doesn't mind my spending time away from him for friends. I think you'd like his brother." Britney smiled so big that her face almost disappeared. It was her classical beauty that concealed her ceaseless insecurities. *Maybe if I could just put some healthy boundaries up,* Amber thought, Britney would back off or calm down enough to be tolerated.

"Yeah, well that's great you get along with his brother." Amber deflected the matchmaking and added, "Thanks again." She forced a smile while stuffing the card into her pocket, knowing it would find its way into the garbage soon. If Amber dared say that she didn't want therapy, it would only make Britney push harder.

"You are *so* welcome. I want you to get on with your life, Amber, and know it will get better. Maybe we can double-date sometime. You know, Kyle and his brother," Britney pressed.

"I'm not ready for that, but thanks."

"Oh, well. Soon, then." Britney's smile veered away from her eyes.

Amber barely held an eyeroll back under a long blink. The only thing she and Britney agreed on was that she felt alone. Amber excused herself to go to the bathroom, hoping Britney wouldn't tag along. She didn't.

Amber felt lighter escaping Britney as she turned the corner heading into the casino-style bathrooms. The hallway was dimly lit, and the facilities were rather plain considering all the gold and glitz in the rest of the club. At least there was no line, and the stalls were clean. Amber studied herself in the mirror as she dried her hands. She pulled her ponytail out and let her hair spread over her shoulders. She ran a brush through it and added some red lipstick. The lighting only accentuated the dark circles under her eyes. Nothing she could do about that.

Stepping into the dim corridor, she immediately bumped into a tall, thin man with glasses who let out a loud grunt. He then swooped out his hand as if to say she should go first, but it didn't feel like a polite gesture to her. She double-checked to make sure his middle finger wasn't extended. No way to tell if he was attractive, but he was certainly arrogant enough, plus he had on a power suit.

"Oh, sorry. I didn't see you. Please, after you." She extended her arm. She couldn't make out his face because it was hidden in the shadows. A chill shot through her body, accenting their aloneness in a crowded building.

He mumbled, "Yeah, thanks."

The man rushed off, managing to stay in the shadows so she couldn't get a good look at him. He held up his hand as he rounded the corner. Some strange people in this world, but not everyone wanted to hurt her. She heaved a sigh and headed back to her friends. The rest of the night flew by: flat beer, bitter coffee, and some dancing to assure Britney she'd forgotten about the parking lot incident.

Britney clinked a spoon against her glass of wine, demanding everyone's attention at the table. "As you all know, it's been six months since Amber's sister was killed. I'm glad everyone could hang out with her tonight. Oh, Kyle wanted me to pass on that he's sorry he couldn't make it and to make sure I said hello for him." Britney paused with a plastic smile that didn't fool Amber. Kyle wasn't the type to send hellos. She continued in her more animated form. "Anyway, I plan on staying with Amber all weekend to make sure she doesn't feel alone, like I did when my auntie died." Britney turned her attention to Amber. "I'm guessing you didn't see my message about that?"

Amber felt her face redden as the looks of sympathy hit her yet again. "Thank you, everyone, for the wonderful evening. I'm very lucky to have you all in my life. And Britney, thank you for your support. I saw your message a little while ago. I was going to talk to you about that." Amber pushed the words out of her mouth, feeling the bile in her throat. "I had planned on spending the weekend writing. My sister had been encouraging me to finish that mystery book I started. I hope you don't mind if I do that. It's such a lovely offer. We can do it another time, right?" Amber finished in a sweet musical tone. Her burger was following the bile as she choked on her words.

She saw a dark shadow pass over the lovely blonde's face, which was quickly hidden under a smile. "Of course. If that's what you need to do, I'm one phone call away. I'm always there for you, and I'll drop whatever I'm doing to help you."

Blake, Amber's dance partner, had his eyes pinned on Britney with a huge grin. He wrote all the sports columns, had the body of an athlete, and would be a catch for the right girl. Quiet Emily was a rather aggressive reporter but was asking no questions now, while Amy, the one in charge of the fluff pieces, was wrapped around her wannabe rock star boyfriend, who was nodding in approval. The one thing they all had in common at that moment was the look of awe they gave assistant editor Britney. Well, what she saw on Blake's face might be more than awe. Maybe there was a love affair blooming, and Britney would stay busy with a love triangle. One could hope, but at least Britney was taken care of for now, until Amber got a handle on those limitations she needed to enact.

Amber took a small sip of her coffee, inhaling its soothing aroma. If she hadn't been driving home, she would have been drinking a lot more to tolerate this evening.

"You wanna hit the floor, Amber?" Blake asked.

"I'm tired. I think I'll head home. Maybe Britney would like to dance."

"Oh, yeah, good idea." Blake's chiseled face reddened. Yup, he had it bad for Britney.

"See you Monday." Amber raised her voice and called out, "Bye, Amy, Emily, and Britney!"

"Drive careful," Blake said as Emily waved. He rushed over to Britney, who held up a finger while Amy and her boyfriend raised their beer bottles in a salute.

Britney pushed her way to Amber's side and put an arm on her shoulder. "Are you sure you don't want me to come with you? I know how bad anniversaries can be."

"It's very sweet of you, honestly. I hope you understand I want to do this for Iris."

"Of course," Britney pulled Amber into an awkward hug and loudly added, "Please drive carefully, and let me know when you arrive home safely. I'll call and check on you later."

"Thanks, I will." Amber pulled away and grabbed her purse.

"Love ya!" Britney called loudly over the music.

Amber pretended she didn't hear those words, the same ones her sister had said to her the last time they talked. The wintry night air woke her up, and she was relieved it wasn't snowing yet. She started down the road that rimmed the lake with the casinos at her back, toward home. Soon she was crossing back into California. For some reason that usually relaxed her, but not tonight. Britney's fake cheerful voice was bouncing around her head like a bad TV show. She could picture it perfectly: *The How Bad People Treat Me Show*, starring Britney Bellflower, whiner extraordinaire! She would be sitting in a comfy paisley chair, perfectly groomed and in a black designer dress:

"Steven was so ungrateful. You people have no idea. My birthday was the day when I found out he was seeing another woman. Right? Then he tells me she didn't mean a thing to him. He was sowing his oats before we got married. He wouldn't do that after, and everything was okay. You know what? It wasn't okay. You see why I left. I couldn't be with a man like that. I mean, I knew my money brought him some comfort for our retirement, but I thought I did too."

A dramatic pause here for full effect.

"You know, he still calls me at work almost every week. He wants me back, of course. Said he's changed, but I know better, don't I, audience? Besides, I've found the perfect man now—Kyle."

Yes, Amber had heard the story too many times. She hated it and felt guilty thinking this about Britney at the same time. She couldn't win. The one thing she had in common with Britney was that they worked in the same place, and she liked that Britney didn't put up with cheaters or freeloaders. She could admire that quality, but the rest of her personality—well, it was a bit over the top. An act to protect the scared person underneath.

Amber turned on her blinker to merge onto the main highway. "Comfortably Numb" by Pink Floyd came on the radio. Britney had made her numb to her worries, anyway. Right now Amber needed to focus on driving, riding the speed limit along the dark and windy road where drunks often made their way home from casinos. Headlights quickly caught up to her, and she pulled over and let them pass. She wasn't into road rage. The only other car she saw stayed way behind her, which was fine with her, until it sped up and started tailing her.

"Hang on!"

Before she could pull over, the driver started to pass her on a curve.

"Excuse me! Sorry I'm in your way."

She squinted into the darkness, trying to see the driver. All she was rewarded with was the outline of a tall, lone silhouette from the dim glow of the car's dash.

"Idiot!"

She turned her attention to the vehicle, slowing down just enough to catch its color and front end.

"Another white SUV?"

She gulped as her pulse quickened. The vehicle continued riding next to her on the two-lane highway. She glanced in her rearview mirror; no one was behind them.

"Just pass already!" Amber shouted at the driver. As she slowed more, the SUV matched her. "Am I imagining this, Britney?"

She glanced ahead and saw a light flash out of the reach of her headlights. In that flash she saw a black bear standing in the middle of the road. She automatically slammed on her brakes at the same time the SUV merged into the space where she would have been.

"What the—?"

The white vehicle sped off. Amber waited for the *thump* when it hit that beautiful bear but heard nothing. She was relieved.

Soon the white SUV disappeared around the curve, leaving Amber sitting alone on the murky road. "What the hell just happened?" she whispered, trying to catch her breath, focusing on the ocean breathing —again.

She scanned the road for the bear she'd just seen. There was no sign of it anywhere. Headlights suddenly reflected in her rearview mirror, so Amber carefully started forward, her entire body shaking. Too many coincidences for her. She grabbed the amethyst-infused water that was supposed to relieve stress and soothed her dry throat, but it did nothing for her raw nerves. Amber glanced in her rearview mirror, grateful for the small car behind her now. Each crossroad or turnout was approached with caution in case that SUV was waiting for her, but it wasn't. The drive seemed to take forever—she was on full alert.

Finally, with a huge sigh of relief, she turned right off the main highway. The little car rushed past her exit. She continued down the dimly lit main road past all the houses glowing with life. A few minutes from an area devoid of humans, she was making the familiar turn onto her street, a single streetlight at its dead end. A lone outdoor light weakly lit her wooden A-frame house. She pulled into her short driveway and stopped within inches of the metal garage door. Although there was a garage door opener in her car, it didn't work. Not that it mattered. She never parked inside because the garage was full of her aunt's—and now her sister's—stuff. She couldn't quite bring herself to get rid of any of it. Besides, the wraparound deck above offered her Blazer protection from the elements. Entering the house from the front or the garage was the same climb, either way.

Amber grabbed the bag containing the dart and rope and stuffed it into her purse. Locking her truck with a beep, she sped up the steep wooden stairs and across the redwood deck through the icy chill. She heard the rumble of a car engine on the small street as she was unlocking her front door.

"Must be visiting that handsome new neighbor I saw unloading his boxes this morning."

A chill shot through her when she saw what type of vehicle it was —a white SUV. It continued past her house, past Mrs. Jones and the new neighbor's house, and parked in the darkness. Its headlights went off, but no one emerged. Her hands shook as she pushed the door open.

"They aren't visiting anyone. It's the same truck."

Gasping, she bolted into the empty house, locking her door firmly behind her and checking it twice. She exhaled loudly and glanced out the blue plaid drapes.

"Not getting out. That must be a good thing," Amber mumbled, moving away from the window.

She flipped on the kitchen lights of the house that she and Iris had once shared with Aunt Kathy. The bag holding the dart and rope felt heavy as she deposited it on top of the fridge.

She peered through the heavy drapery again. Now she could see the dark outline sitting in the driver's seat with the streetlight hitting the inside. At least he—or she—wasn't coming after her...yet. She sank into a kitchen chair as all her fears resurfaced with the force of a tsunami. Her chest felt like it was taking a direct hit. She started to push herself up to call the police but burst into tears and sank back into the chair.

As soon as her tears dried up, her heart skipped a beat. She hadn't checked the house.

"What if they're sitting out there because..."

Her heart pounding now, she made a quick sweep. Checking all her windows, every closet, behind the red shower curtain, and under the beds. Then she headed upstairs to her sister's loft bedroom—or what used to be her room. Tiger, who looked nothing like a tiger, still slept on her sister's pillow. He didn't look worried, and that calmed her. He would be hiding if anyone else was in the house.

"Hi, Tiger."

One green eye peered at her, which was as much of a greeting as she'd get until she filled the little black panther's food bowl. She had hoped they'd bond after, well... So far it hadn't happened. It was like he was still waiting for Iris to walk through the door. Amber understood. There were times she wished the last six months would disappear and Iris would burst through the door in her usual smiling fashion, but that wasn't going to happen, and Tiger was hers now. Someday he'd come to accept that, she hoped.

She glanced out the upper window that had remained uncovered so the loft would have a view of the trees. Her aunt had said at one time you could see a tiny blue glimpse of Lake Tahoe. But over the years, the trees had thickened, and now it was mostly the 160-foot Jeffrey pines, smelling deliciously of vanilla or pineapple, along with lodgepole pines, cedars, and firs. Amber hurried back to the front window and scanned for the SUV. She let out a loud sigh. It was gone.

"Good riddance! But now I can't call the police."

What would she say? Someone was driving erratically and almost hit her on the way home. A truck that looked like it parked on her street, and oh, yeah, a person in a ski mask shot a dart at her in her parking lot with the same type of truck and blocked her in her parking space for a moment. This was a common vehicle in her community. That was what they'd say.

She could imagine the person on the other end of the call listening to her story, knowing who she was, and then, after they hung up with assurances that they'd look into it, they wouldn't. No, they'd tell the rest of the people at the sheriff's office that the poor girl whose sister was killed had completely lost it on the anniversary of her sister's death. Although they might consider a safety check on her to make sure she wasn't...well, losing it. That was the only hope she had of getting help when she needed it. Because why would they believe her if her coworkers didn't? Without an SUV even here now...why did she wait to call? How stupid of her. Or was it? Either way, it wasn't in her head.

A high-pitched meow startled her out of her thoughts. Tiger was waiting patiently at his food bowl. She returned to the kitchen.

"Hungry?" she got no response other than a look at the bowl as if to say, *What do you think, human?*

She opened the can of Fishy Feast that smelled nothing like a feast —more like what was left over the next day in the garbage, but the cat gobbled it down. She peeked out the front window to find her street still clear of unfamiliar SUVs. At least no one was hiding in the shadows of her house, only in her memories. As an afterthought, Amber grabbed the big cleaver with the dry wooden handle out of the butcher block. Tiger strode into the living room and lay by the wood-stove. That was her cue to start a fire.

"Yeah, yeah. I'll get it going for you, Tiger. What do you think about adding a knife to my nightstand? Give the place some class?"

Thankfully, no one was there to hear that joke besides the cat. She placed the cleaver in her bedroom. Heading to the woodstove, she patted Tiger's head, and he didn't try to duck from her touch for once.

She felt her face redden, thinking about needing a knife in her bedroom when she already had a gun in the house. Maybe it was because she had no experience using a gun. She'd always meant to take lessons at the shooting range but never got around to it. She had some idea how to load the bullets, point, and pull the trigger, but that was about it. But from past experience, she'd learned not to argue with her gut feelings. If she ignored them, she usually wished she hadn't. Like when she kept thinking she should get her tires checked and rotated, but she kept putting it off until she had a blowout. Or when she saw something at the grocery store and thought *I should get this*, but it wasn't on her list. Later she'd find out she needed it. So if she thought a knife might come in handy, well, she wasn't going to ignore that idea. Not now.

She added some seasoned oak to the woodstove, which would quickly take the chill off the small house. She knew sleep wouldn't come easily that night. At least not after what had happened over the last few hours. She glanced out her front window, relieved that the SUV hadn't returned. She shook her head.

"Maybe it *is* my imagination working overtime. No one followed me home, Tiger." His eyes opened for a split second, and then he went back to sleep with a huff.

Tiger didn't believe that, nor did she. Amber would certainly sleep better if that were the case.

There was a beep on her cell phone. Oops, she'd forgotten to tell Britney she was home. She scanned the long-winded text about dancing, her drive home, and how Kyle had been worried about her on those dark roads at night. She replied:

Home safe. Thanks for tonight.

Pulling on her blue flannel snowman nightshirt, she headed into the newly painted peach bathroom to brush her teeth. She avoided the guaranteed-to-be-worried expression in the mirror by not turning on the main light. Nighttime routine completed, she checked one more time, thankful to see the SUV wasn't back. Then she sank into her soft, cold, red flannel bedsheets with dancing bears on them, a Christmas gift from Iris last year. Amber had always been fond of anything with a bear on it, and there were plenty of black bears like the one she'd seen earlier living around the lake. She'd never been afraid of them as most people were, including Iris and her aunt. Amber used bears liberally in her home décor. Her theory was if she left them alone, they would leave her alone. So far, it had worked. She'd heard of them breaking into houses, but not her house. Her sister insisted a bear was her spirit guide. She wished it had a message for her now.

She sighed and turned on the small TV she'd bought for when she couldn't sleep. She was getting ready to watch *The Notebook* when she saw that *Arsenic and Old Lace* was playing on the old movie channel. It had been a favorite of hers and Iris's, not a tearjerker like *The Notebook*, but it reminded her of Iris, and that was enough. Plus, it had Cary Grant, one of her favorite actors.

Her eyes and mind were occupied until she got a craving for popcorn. Pausing the movie, she got up and poured white corn kernels into the air popper. She splurged on some melted butter and salt, and the popcorn made her stomach growl. She checked the street again. Clear, but it was beginning to snow hard, blanketing her world. With her bear bowl overflowing with popcorn, she inhaled the scent of melted butter and, comforted, sunk back into bed. The bowl contained nothing but a rime of butter and salt when the movie ended. Those last words about the coffeepot usually had her laughing, but not tonight. Then the screen went dark as the power went out.

"Great." Amber jumped out of bed with her flashlight and added more wood to the woodstove. She warily peeked through the front window and scanned the dark cul-de-sac.

Tiger rubbed against her legs. "At least Mrs. Jones's and the new guy's lights are out, so it doesn't mean someone...well, you know. Shut our power off. Right, Tiger?"

The cat's eyes reflected at her when the light hit his face. He turned and headed to the fire.

"Good idea. Stay warm. I'm going back to where the weapons are. You know, just in case. I'm sure you'll hide if anything happens. You're a survivor." Amber shook her head and muttered, "I need to get out more and stop talking to a cat that doesn't even like me."

Out of the corner of her eye, she saw a flash at the back of her Blazer.

"Huh? What's that?"

She watched, but the flash didn't return. Was a migraine fighting to make an entrance, as she'd thought in the parking lot? That would be the best explanation, but it wasn't the correct one. Across the street, in the darkness, she saw the outline of an SUV. How did she miss that when she first looked out? That familiar chill shot through her again.

"I need to call the police, even if they don't believe me."

She picked up the landline—it was dead. There was no internet with the power out, and her cell phone didn't get a signal at her house. She was completely cut off from civilization, other than her two neighbors. She squinted, trying to make out a license plate but couldn't. She pulled her heavy snowflake robe tightly around her and tied it firmly. She closed the drapes securely and walked quickly down the hall to grab her gun. Reassured by the feel of the cold metal, she gently set it on her nightstand. She slipped the knife under her pillow.

At least she felt a bit safer as she tried to put that truck sitting out front out of her mind. Embracing her fully charged e-reader, she started the new indie murder mystery everyone had been raving about, but she couldn't concentrate. All she could think about was seeing that rope, the dart, the feather, the masked man, and the mysterious SUV. This was a time when real life was scarier than any fictional story.

A slam startled her, and the roar of an engine got her full attention. She tapped the flashlight on her cell phone, slipped into her slippers, and shuffled down the hall. She slowly pulled back the drapes, and to her relief, the SUV was turning the corner of her street. Amber frowned as she squinted, but she still couldn't make out the license plate even with the taillights illuminating it. The end of her Blazer was sticking out from under the deck. Suddenly a bear strolled out from behind her truck. He stopped for a moment and looked up at her before loping off across the street.

"Two bears in one night in the middle of winter? Weird. You watching over me, Iris?"

She rechecked her front door and the door that led to the garage. All safely locked.

"Perhaps they were lost…or…" she lamely tried to reassure herself. Being a Pollyanna didn't suit her. "No, it was for me, and that bear must have scared them off," she whispered as her mouth dried up like mud on a scorching summer day. "As soon as I get the landline back, I'm going to call the police and report this, Tiger."

The cat didn't even lift an eyelid as he stretched out on his back in front of the hearth.

"Well, you stay there. I'll be fine." Amber trembled as she ran down the hall, feeling evil gaining on her.

Pulling back the covers, she hopped into bed and grabbed a picture from her nightstand. It was torn and taped, but it was her favorite of her and Iris, from when they graduated high school. Both faces were bright and full of hope. How she missed her sister's cheerful smile and that one brown curl that was always in her face. How could either of them know that a murder would end both of these smiles in different ways? She gently placed the picture back in the drawer, turned off her cell phone, and took several soothing gulps of water before sinking deep into her soft flannel sheets and letting the tears release some of that loss. After the second good cry of the evening, she fell asleep.

CHAPTER 4

*M*orning arrived with the compact silver alarm clock blinking and the heater humming, thanks to the electricity flowing back into her house. Amber stretched out and ran into a lump by her feet.

"Welcome to my room, Tiger!"

He answered her with a lazy one-eyed glance and then went back to sleep. She stroked his head with no protest. Encouraged, she jumped out of bed. Wrapping a blue fluffy bathrobe around herself, she pushed her woolly-socked feet into blue slippers that, when put together, made a bear exactly like the one who shooed off her stalker last night. She shuffled down the hall, turning off lights as she went. She opened the drapes, cold to her touch. Thankfully, there wasn't a white SUV outside. Although she felt braver in the light of day, she still checked her landline and was met with a heavy silence.

Amber returned the phone receiver to its cradle with a loud *thump*. The sound echoed through the house, reminding her of how alone she was. She couldn't stop herself from peeking out the window again to make sure the SUV hadn't returned. Satisfied she was safe, she got to work on the fire. She could have let the heater do its job, but propane wasn't cheap. Iris had never had an issue paying for propane; she couldn't start a fire no matter what she did. Amber had become an expert at it. Soon the orange flames were shooting up, warming her.

Tiger had followed her out of the bedroom and positioned himself on the rug by the woodstove, ready to absorb the heat. "Look at all that snow. Must be half a foot."

His reply was to start to clean himself.

"Come on, let's eat."

As expected, Tiger got up, stretched, and strolled to his food bowl as she filled it with his favorite smelly fish flakes.

"You're welcome."

No response from the big black cat as he nibbled his breakfast.

Amber ground coffee beans and placed them on the altar of the filter before adding nature's liquid. One stab to the button, and the life-giving aroma guided her morning toward normalcy as the snow continued piling up outside. She generously spread blackberry honey and almond butter on a toasted sourdough English muffin, then poured a cup of the steaming black coffee and sank into her blue L-shaped couch next to a satisfied Tiger.

The large, gentle flakes were mesmerizing to watch as they twirled their way to the ground. She bit into the muffin, which reminded her of her favorite city to visit, San Francisco. A place she and Iris had loved to explore, especially Fisherman's Wharf and Pier 39. They always came home with something tasty—Iris with a loaf of freshly baked sourdough bread and Amber with some of the best chocolate on Earth. She loved to watch, with a grumbling stomach, as the chocolate swirled along a river through its factory process. She always got a sundae slathered in milk chocolate syrup, while Iris, who disliked chocolate, would sip a vanilla shake and people watch. Iris's favorite part of their visits was the man who dressed as a bush and scared people as they walked by. Amber preferred the sea lions. They never had a bad time there, but now she doubted she'd ever go back. Amber sighed and began stroking Tiger's soft fur until he stood up, shaking off her pets, and settled in by the woodstove to soak in the warmth of the fire.

Setting her empty blue plate down, she glanced around the room. Dust draped itself over the room like a jealous lover.

"First, I'll clean this place up, maybe go to the store, and then hire that PI, Tiger."

Satisfied with her plan, she jumped up to put her plate and mug into the dishwasher. A quick check on the landline delivered the familiar dial tone. She quickly called the number she knew by heart.

"I want to report a suspicious vehicle in my neighborhood."

"Do you have a license plate, ma'am?"

"No."

"Are you able to get that?"

"They're gone now."

"Did they get out of their vehicle?"

"Maybe."

"Can you describe the vehicle?"

"It's an older, white SUV that I spotted at my work on Friday when I was leaving. The driver was wearing a ski mask and was blocking me in my parking space. Then he got out and was heading toward me when a group of people came into the garage. He left, which I found odd for many reasons. Then, on my way home later, I saw the very same SUV, and he tried to run me off the road. Later it was parked in front of my house two different times last night. It doesn't belong to either of my neighbors," Amber added firmly.

"So you've had several sightings?"

"Yes."

"If you give me your name and address, we'll get someone out to you as soon as we can. Just be aware it won't be before Monday with this storm, the flu going around, and no crime committed. We are busy and short-staffed."

"I understand." Amber gave her name and address even though she was positive they already had her name on caller ID.

"Thank you, Ms. Dodges. Someone will get to you as soon as they can. If anything changes, don't hesitate to call back. If it's an emergency, dial 911."

"Thank you. I'm sorry, I didn't get your name..."

"Gayle. I believe we've met before regarding your sister, Iris Dodges, about whom we have no added information, sorry." The volume of the woman's voice increased. She was sharing this with others. Great.

"Thank you, Gayle. I was hoping they could drive by and do a check once in a while. I'd feel better."

"I'll see what I can do, Ms. Dodges, but unless it's urgent, it will take a while, as I said. In the meantime it would help if you could provide us with the license plate. Thank you."

Before Amber could say anything else, she heard the dial tone.

"Well, that didn't go well," Amber informed Tiger. "I'm safe now, so." She shrugged.

Tiger was staring at her now, unnerving her. She hopped up when the coffee suddenly charged through her like a real tiger. She let out a long breath and rubbed her hands together. "Let's clean, Tiger." Tiger didn't even glance her way as he walked past her. She watched him slowly climb the stairs to the open loft and settle on Iris's bed.

"I think cleaning would be better than sitting around and waiting," she called upstairs.

Searching for music to motivate her, she found the TV had no signal. Sighing, she pulled on snow boots after a quick glance out the window to make sure there was no white SUV outside.

The frigid air hit her like a wall as she trudged through the snowdrifts to clear the satellite off. Her street looked like a Hallmark movie with the huge snowflakes and the smoke swirling its way out of Mrs. Jones's and her new neighbor's chimneys. She shook her head. Hard to believe that last night it was more like a horror movie. Soon she was listening to her favorite, the Classic Vinyl channel, hoping the music would motivate her. One of her sister's favorites came on —"Listen to the Music" by the Doobie Brothers.

Amber sang along contentedly as she mopped. The song had a lot of good memories, but then the playlist took a strange twist. The next two songs seemed to be sending her a message. Each one had the word danger in the title, and when they sang that word, a chill shot through her and grasped her throat tightly. She took a long, deep breath, pushing the feelings away, and went back to dusting until she found a feather. Was it the same one from the parking lot? She checked her coat pocket. Gone. Tiger was making his way down the stairs slowly.

"A feather, Tiger. Probably fell out, and the fire blew it around." Amber shrugged and changed the music channel. "In the Night (Entering the Danger Zone)" by Sammy Hagar came on. Third song in a row with the word in the title.

"Crap. Three strikes and it's over." That was what she and Iris used to joke after watching the Oakland A's lose. She shut the music off and frowned.

Tiger settled in by the fire again. "I must be losing my mind to think songs are warning me. There must be a theme on the channels today. Or maybe they're all on the letter D. Whatever. I can control what I listen to."

Amber put on Aunt Kathy's Tom Petty album, lit her sister's sage smudging stick, and went back to cleaning. Not that she put much stock in it; she was simply a fan of the scent. It wasn't like she believed smoke from some plant would be able to keep her safe, but it didn't hurt to cover all the bases, either.

No messages of danger now, she thought smugly as she finished dusting. The snowplow rumbled by while she was vacuuming. She watched it push the snow to the side of the road and add a layer of sand, making it drivable again. There was a lull in the snow, her chance to pick up a few items. Then she'd spend the rest of the weekend getting the help she needed to find her sister's killer. She turned off the record player and started to make her list. Bread, lunch meat, pasta, sauce, cheese, spinach, bananas…

The phone rang. Without looking at the number, she quickly picked up.

"Hi, Amber. It's your mother."

Amber rolled her eyes. Like she needed to be told who was on the other end, "Um…hi, Mom."

"I saw on the news this morning that you're getting a lot of snow. I never did like the cold and snow myself, but you girls always did." Her mother rambled on.

Danger songs before her mother called—that would certainly make sense, if she believed in that sort of thing. "Yeah, we have a half a foot so far, with more on the way. They just cleared the roads, and I was leaving to go grocery shopping."

"Oh, well, I won't keep you, then. I wanted to check on you. See how you're doing is all…" Her mother's whine always hit a nerve in Amber that ran through her entire body. What did she want?

"I'm doing as well as can be expected. I'm going to hire a PI to investigate Iris's murder. The police have gotten nowhere."

"Yes, well, I had hoped they'd quickly resolve this. I'm glad you're going to hire a detective. I'll pitch in for that."

"I've got it. Don't worry."

"Well, okay, if you're sure." Her mom paused, but Amber didn't respond, so she continued. "Things are going okay for you, aren't they?"

"Yes, everything is fine. You?"

"I'm okay, I guess. Well, I should let you go. I'll pop a check into the mail Monday to help cover the private investigator. Please drive carefully. I love you, Amber."

"I don't need your money—" Amber started to protest, but her mother had already hung up. "Yep, sure good talking to you, Mother!" she yelled as she slammed the phone down hard enough to make the cat run back upstairs.

The phone rang again. Was her mother calling back? Well, if she were, she'd let her know she wanted nothing from her. She stomped back to the phone. It was a number she didn't recognize. Maybe it was news about her sister.

"Hello?"

"Ms. Dodges?"

"Yes, speaking," Amber replied. So formal. She gulped. Was it bad news? It wasn't the police department's number, maybe a detective?

"This is Senator Stroud, and I just read your article. I wanted to thank you and offer to do an interview later today, if you're available. I hear the weather will be clear until the next storm hits later this evening. They have all the roads plowed in town. You can get out, can't you?"

She felt her face redden. "Senator Stroud. I'm honored you took the time to call and let me know. I'd love to interview you today and have no problem getting out. What time is good for you?"

"Two at Joe's Diner work for you?"

"Yes, that's perfect. Thank you, Senator."

"You're quite welcome. See you then." The phone clicked before she could respond.

She couldn't believe she had finally spoken to the senator. She'd tried to contact him after her sister died, with no response. Amber frowned, remembering Iris commenting on how busy he was but still made sure the employees got a gift on their birthday. So when one of them dies, nothing?

She threw her phone on the couch with a stronger urge to smash it into the wall. She took a few deep breaths and sank into the blue velour chair next to the phone.

"Ahh!" Amber rubbed her face. "No. It wasn't the senator's call, it was my mother's call, Tiger. She has a way of irritating me, ya know?"

Tiger jumped up on the round glass coffee table with a bear-shaped support. Iris had found it at a garage sale. He scattered the newspaper and settled down on the front-page picture of Myles Stroud. The man had movie star looks: tall, dark, and handsome. Coming from a prominent local family with rumors of an impending engagement to a socialite, he was not the usual candidate for president. Finally, she was going to speak with him. A man with this much clout could certainly help her find Iris's killer.

She leaped from the couch to get ready, her eyes drawn back to the front window. No SUV. She caught her reflection in the window. She needed to look her best for this interview and wasn't going to show up in her PJs and slippers.

She set her focus on the meeting as she started the shower. Tiger cautiously approached.

"Sorry for yelling, Tiger, but that woman…well, you know. Do you think I need the staff photographer?"

The cat turned away from her and began cleaning his fur.

"No. I'll just use my phone. No need to bring out someone else in this mess."

Tiger watched the water run down the glass doors like he used to do during Iris's showers.

"Glad you're hanging out with me today."

Soon she was under the soothing warm water. She tried to piece together questions to ask the senator, but the only one she really wanted to ask was about her sister. She needed more than that.

She rinsed off the floral-scented suds and turned off the water, wiping down the old white tile that glowed like the snow. Doing those few simple things almost made her feel normal again, even though nothing was. Having to find her sister's killer wasn't normal. Having someone following her wasn't normal, and feeling like she had to sleep with a knife under her pillow wasn't normal. She sighed loudly and grabbed a towel. She began formulating some political questions to ask as Tiger settled in under the heater at her feet.

"How do you feel about climate change? How will you pay for everyone to have health insurance? What will you do in your first hundred days in office?"

Tiger loudly exhaled and closed his eyes.

"I agree, boring. I'll try to come up with something better."

She slipped into red leggings and a black sweater dress that hugged her curves perfectly. She styled her hair around her face and then added teal eyeshadow, mascara, and eyeliner, with the final addition of red lipstick. She raced through her routine to leave, stubbing out the sage and closing the vents on the fire. She'd try to eat before the meeting. Probably only time for fries, though. She pulled on her snow boots, sure the senator would understand forgoing business footwear. It was like an Olympic event, getting ready to go out into the cold, and the only way onto the podium was trudging through as fast as possible. In record time she was ready to tackle the biggest interview she'd ever had.

Stepping out into the chill, she carefully locked the door behind her, tugging at it when she saw footprints around her front window. A shudder ran through her as she scanned the street. No truck. Her eyes followed the prints, which led straight to her neighbor's house. She hurried down the steps, right as the new neighbor burst out of his house.

"Hi, neighbor!" she called out.

"Hello! I came by earlier to introduce myself." He sauntered up to her through the half-foot of snow with his hand extended. "Elijah Reynolds, but everyone calls me Eli."

"Amber Dodges." Amber smiled brightly as she took his hand.

"Nice to meet you, Amber."

His bare hand felt warm through her glove. "Welcome to the neighborhood." She paused, getting lost in his dark gaze, and clumsily added, "That explains all the footprints in the snow."

"That was me. I didn't knock because it didn't look like you were up yet. Thought maybe you slept in after we lost our lights last night." His charming lopsided grin could melt the snow off her truck window.

"I rarely ever sleep in. I'm surprised I didn't hear you." Amber reluctantly pulled her hand back. "Wait a minute. You aren't Elijah J. Reynolds, the author of the Burt Bloom mystery series, are you?"

"Guilty as charged. I decided to move closer to my sister's family and out of the city. You know, try to be an authentic reclusive writer in a quaint lakeside town like Pine City."

"It's a great place to live and work, and by the way, I love your books."

"Thanks. Always happy to hear that. Anyways, I was wondering about this white SUV I saw lurking around out front after the power went off. I mean, I'm not one of those nosey neighbors if you have guests or anything, but it seemed odd that they just sat there. It would have made sense if it was a couple of teenagers, but it was only one person."

"I wondered the same thing. I called the police about it today, but they didn't seem too interested and can't respond until Monday. You know, the storm, and short of staff. I've read there've been a lot of car break-ins lately."

His brows pressed together, but his smile broke through. "I'll keep my eyes open and call in myself if I see it again. Don't want them breaking into any of our cars here. Oh, and I saw a bear prowling around your driveway. Is that common this time of year?"

"I saw him too. Well, I think most hibernate, but some don't if they have a food supply. I usually don't see them in the winter, but you never know, I suppose."

"Well, I definitely won't be feeding them." Eli held his hands up with a grin.

"Maybe he scared off the guy in the SUV." Amber shrugged.

"Good. Our neighborhood watch bear. One quick question. I was unpacking and found my coffeemaker got broken. I suffered through some instant coffee that was left behind in the pantry this morning, but where can I get a good cup of coffee?" He rubbed his plaid sleeves. His nails showed signs of being bitten. A habit her sister had too.

"I'd have to say Joe's Diner. That's where I'm headed, if you want to follow me. I'd offer you a ride, but I'm not sure how long I'll be there. I'm interviewing Senator Stroud for the local newspaper." Amber blushed. She never rambled on like this.

"Wow, that's quite a feat to interview such a big candidate. I know he's from this area, so that makes sense he'd pick a local girl to do it. Congrats. I'll take you up on following you, if you don't mind. Just need to grab my keys and coat and lock up."

Amber nodded, heading for her truck. A glance at her cell phone showed she still had plenty of time to get there, but not enough time to eat now. A slight smile crossed her face—the new neighbor was even better-looking up close. If her sister were here, she would already have his phone number. Sorry, Iris. She wasn't going to get friendly with the guy, even if he was handsome and a bestselling mystery writer.

Her sister had always been full of advice. "You need to let that past shit go. Start trusting someone besides me. I know the right guy will come along for you. Don't push him away."

No relationship ever got past a few dates, and Amber wasn't going to force it. Besides, she was happy by herself, wasn't she? She had a decent job at a newspaper and…yeah, and what? That was the problem, and now she had a hot next-door neighbor. Nope, she was busy trying to find her sister's killer and write a book. No time.

She used an empty CD case from her purse to push the snow off her truck's windows. The door was slightly open. She was positive she'd shut and locked it last night. That flash of light. Was that what the mysterious driver had been doing, breaking into her vehicle? Her muscles tightened as she frantically searched her truck. Nothing was missing, but her glove compartment was open.

She started her truck and got out to study it. She ran her finger across a long scratch below the driver's-side window. That was new. Why would someone break into her car and then take nothing? He'd even left her twenty and spare change—unless the bear ran him off. She searched again as the heater switched over to warm air.

"Nothing is missing? No, wait. My garage door opener."

No loss since it had fallen in her coffee and stopped working. They weren't getting into her house that way, she thought with a small smile.

But the idea of someone going through her things unnerved her more with what had already happened. She dug through her purse and pulled out a small package of hand wipes. She wiped off the steering wheel and things she'd have to touch while driving. It made her feel better to wipe the criminal away. She could imagine Gayle's nasal response to the car break-in.

"Nothing was stolen but a broken garage door opener. Well, come down and file a report, if you want to, but we're busy right now."

No, why bother calling, knowing their attitude? Besides, she had two neighbors who could be on the lookout now. She would tell Eli and Mrs. Jones later. She glanced back at the berm left from the snowplow. She was glad for her Blazer because it usually rolled right over the berm. She tapped her fingers on the steering wheel. How long did it take to get keys? It was one thirty.

No fries. She had a protein bar in her purse, which she quickly ate and followed with gum. Finally Eli raced out the front door wearing a black ski cap. With his back to her, he reminded her of the person in the ski mask in the parking lot. Amber froze. She almost choked on her peppermint gum, but as soon as he turned around, she saw his face was exposed and relaxed. Her hand reached for the radio but pulled back.

"Nope, not going there."

She didn't want to take the chance of hearing something ominous on the car radio, no matter how dumb that sounded. She took a deep breath and went back to her questions for the senator. "Are you dating anyone?" No, too personal, and she wasn't an entertainment reporter. She watched Eli hop into his red Chevy pickup. He slid onto the street. She led the way to Joe's down the newly sanded road.

Her wheels slipped on the icy corner after making the green signal when she realized Eli wasn't behind her. She pulled over and waited, rubbing her hands together in front of her heater vent. Finally he made an appearance and threw a wave at her.

"Come on." She'd seen her elderly neighbor Mrs. Jones, when she used to drive, navigate the roads faster than this guy. "Must be a rookie snow driver." Amber pulled out and led the way to Main Street.

The diner, with its handmade wooden sign with red-painted letters, was on her left. Out front was a white SUV that contained the waving senator. It was remarkably like the one in the parking lot and in front of her house, but a newer model. She inserted her Blazer into a tight spot at one forty-five. Eli parked two spaces down. He ambled up to her truck while she checked her makeup one more time and fixed her hair. She got out to greet him, grabbing her purse.

"Thank you, Amber. I owe you. I imagine that's the senator over there. I'll find my way in."

"Thanks for understanding," She smoothed her clothes and added, "The lemon pie is excellent here."

"I'll try a piece. Good luck."

"Thanks...um...I need to talk to you later about..." she started, but he was already walking off.

CHAPTER 5

*T*he SUV's door swung open, and a man with an athletic build gracefully leaped out as he scanned the surroundings. His attention passed over Amber and focused on Eli. He snapped a photo of Eli and studied his phone with furrowed brows. As Eli entered the café, the bodyguard turned and gave a thumbs up to the occupants of the SUV.

The senator emerged. He slowly stood and smoothed his gray business suit. The bodyguard nodded in her direction as the senator turned to face her with a quick wave, which she reciprocated. He was even better looking in person. She locked her truck as the senator with perfectly combed brown hair smiled at her.

"Watch your step, Ms. Dodges. The roads are slippery!" the senator called out.

"Thanks," Amber replied with a slight smile. She certainly didn't want to be the reporter who fell during an interview. She waited for a car to pass and slowly started across the street.

A tiny redheaded photographer appeared from behind the senator like a fashion accessory. She was a swirl of fringed leather boots, a tie-dye skirt, and flowy tunic—like someone from the 1960s. She seemed out of place in this well-groomed business crowd, but Amber had a feeling she would be the most interesting one to talk to if she got a chance. The photographer winked at the bodyguard and his blushing reaction said a lot. They were dating.

The senator stepped off the sidewalk, hurrying toward Amber. He was already holding out his hand when they met in the middle of the road.

"Ms. Dodges. I'm so glad you could make it." He smiled toward the camera as they shook hands.

"Thank you for the call and interview." Amber smiled, making sure her best side was facing the insistent clicking.

"Photos are an unfortunate reality for me now, sorry. I hope you don't mind."

"No, I don't mind at all."

"Thank you. Here comes a car. Let's get off the road." He offered her the crook of his elbow, which she took and found an arm that was familiar with the gym.

They were soon safely on the sidewalk as the car slowly drove by, almost stopping. She reluctantly let go of her hold on his arm. He waved at the car, and it sped off.

"Ms. Dodges, this is Marsha, our photographer. She provides all the shots for the campaign."

"Nice to meet you, Marsha," Amber held out her hand, but Marsha kept taking pictures.

She peeked out from behind the camera for a moment. "Yes, it's nice to meet you...Ms. Dodges, correct?"

"I prefer Amber. I love your outfit."

"Everyone loves the classics. I was born too late, I'm afraid."

Senator Stroud grinned, his blue eyes shimmering. "Your talent belongs in this decade, Marsha."

"That's what I'm told," Marsha replied and threw a glance toward the hulking bodyguard.

The senator nodded in the red-faced man's direction. "That's Steve. He keeps me safe."

"Ma'am." Steve pulled his gaze away from Marsha.

He was certainly ex-military. "Nice to meet you," Amber offered her hand again. This time it was taken with a quick, firm squeeze.

A bookish man with black hair peeked out from behind Marsha, "Here's my number one man, Clark. He can get a hold of me any time of the day. Right, Clark?"

Clark seemed familiar to her. His response was to nod without looking in Amber's direction.

"Hi, Clark."

Clark gave a pained smile and a slight shrug. Without a word he got back into the SUV. What was it about him? Maybe it was just his name and glasses. She hoped his last name wasn't Kent. She held back a smile.

"He's a talker when you get to know him. What do you say we get seated? It's not as simple to get a cup of coffee anymore since I decided to run for president. Usually there's press around, but the storm discouraged them today, and well, this was last minute too. Joe has a table for us. After you." He held out his arm, almost bowing.

Amber held her phone up, "Thank you. Do you mind if I take a couple of shots of my own for the article?"

"No, please go ahead. I'll have Marsha send some shots over to you too."

Amber snapped several photos at the same time Marsha did.

"How about a couple together?"

"What? Oh, sure." Amber reluctantly stood by the senator and held out her phone. She had a tough time getting both of them in the shot.

"Here, let me, ma'am." Steve grabbed her cell phone and took the picture.

"Well, let's get out of this cold. Thanks, Steve and Marsha."

Stroud guided Amber into the café, leaving Steve and Marsha outside. Marsha cozied up next to Steve instead of retreating into the warm truck. At least she wouldn't be taking photos during their talk.

Grumpy Joe sat them in a booth next to the door and as far away as possible from Eli. He acted as if he didn't know her, even though she'd been coming in since she was a girl. The man had definitely earned his nickname over the years. But now Grumpy Joe had morphed into Charming Joe with a plastered-on smile and formal manners. He bowed his head after taking their order for coffee and a slice of lemon pie for the senator.

"Sorry, the pie is a weakness of mine. Sure you don't want some?"

"Oh, no, thanks. I just ate," Amber lied as her stomach growled, even after the pecan protein bar.

"Well, if you want a bite. I'm always willing to share." He smiled and then winked at her.

Amber returned the smile. Was he flirting with her or just being a politician? Across the diner the grumpier version of Joe that she recognized was taking Eli's order, his usual scowl in place. Eli glanced over with a raised eyebrow while he ran his fingers through his hat hair. The wavy brown curls quickly bounced back, and he smiled before picking up a discarded newspaper off the white-and-red tablecloth.

Stroud recaptured her attention. "I'm sure you're wondering why I called you today. I apologize for the impromptu meeting on a week-end. I know you left messages for me after your sister's death, but it was hard for me. We were very close." He paused for a moment, studying her.

She felt her face redden, and her jaw dropped. Close?

"By the expression on your face, I can see you had no idea." His tone was hushed as he glanced around the room. Grumpy Joe was with the cook, and Eli was too far away to hear, especially with the radio playing oldies louder than usual.

"You and Iris?"

He nodded to confirm.

"I thought you were dating that woman—um...well, are you saying you and Iris were dating?"

The senator straightened the packages of saltine crackers and sugar with a glance around the diner. "We started as good friends but then went way beyond that quickly. I admit she completely had my heart, but she held back. She didn't want to ruin my presidential run. For her I would have dropped out, but she insisted we keep it quiet. I had finally convinced her it would help me if the world knew of our relationship. We were going to announce our engagement the night she was…" He paused for a moment and closed his eyes. When he opened them, his gaze was pinned on her. He sucked in air and let it out loudly. "Iris was meeting me that night before your movie."

Amber tried taking a deep breath, but her ribcage wasn't cooperating. "You…she…how did I not know? The police know?"

"I told the sheriff, but he kept it quiet. It helps that my father's a district court judge. I thought once I got involved, the killer would be caught, but that hasn't happened. I hope you understand why I wanted to keep this quiet, and I understand the grief you've been dealing with, trust me. The sheriff said you check in every week. Frankly, this has gone on long enough. I think it's time to join forces and find Iris's killer."

Amber couldn't believe what she'd just heard. Her sister had been dating the senator and was going to marry him.

"I, um…I honestly had no idea."

Stroud had moved on with his cleaning to the lazy Susan that contained all the condiments. "We talked about that. She felt guilty not telling you, and I wondered if she finally said something. I hated not reaching out to you after, but I thought to keep the focus on the murder…well, I thought wrong, because the killer hasn't been found." He finished quietly, finally holding her gaze. She recognized the pain rolling off him.

Amber shook her head and held her voice to a whisper. "I don't know what to say. I thought this would be an interview about your political plans. I didn't expect to hear you were planning to marry my sister and…" She fell into an uncomfortable silence as Charming Joe practically pranced to their table to deliver two cups of steaming coffee and one large slice of pie topped with a tower of meringue that concealed the lemon.

"Can I bring you anything else?" he gushed, smoothing his usually wild white hair.

"No, I'm fine, thank you. Amber?"

Amber just shook her head in response as she stirred her coffee.

Joe rushed off to deposit a third cup at Eli's table. She couldn't bring herself to meet the senator's gaze, so she looked around him and caught Eli's eye. He frowned slightly and looked away, stirring his coffee intently. It was as if he had heard their conversation, but that wasn't possible with the Beatles blasting "Can't Buy Me Love" over the speakers. Maybe he was reacting to her stunned expression or wasn't all that interested in her. She was just a neighbor, after all, who must have looked like she had just seen a ghost.

Stroud followed her attention and glanced over his shoulder at Eli, who was still focused on his coffee. He raised his eyebrows at her, expertly maneuvering the subject like any good politician. "Know him?"

"Just met him. He's my new neighbor. He followed me here to get some coffee. You know, still unpacking." Amber wasn't sure why she was giving him so much information. She was the one who usually asked the questions, and she had a lot after what he'd just said.

Joe rushed by them, and Stroud said, loud enough for him to hear, "Yes, that I can understand. This place has the best coffee and pie around." Joe beamed, and he seemed to glide into the kitchen.

"It does." Amber agreed.

The senator leaned forward. "The good coffee cancels out Grumpy Joe. Yes, I know his nickname and thought his niceness was odd too."

"Yeah," Amber mumbled, not wanting to do this small talk.

Stroud glanced back one more time at Eli and formed a practiced smile for her. "I agreed to let Joe serve his customers if he kept them away from us. Steve could monitor them. You know, I've had some standard threats, which are probably harmless, but still, I must take them seriously. Your neighbor's okay because Steve is still outside and not in here with us."

"Look, I'm sorry about the threats, and glad my neighbor checked out, but could we get back to my sister?" Amber's foot tapped impatiently.

He nodded and continued. "Yes, sorry. This is hard for me as well. I guess I thought I was protecting Iris if no one knew, including you. As for the woman you thought I was dating, that was Iris's idea. She leaked a story about Gigi, who I've known since I was a kid—best friends, but that was all it ever was. Iris said the press would leave us alone, and they did. But I wasn't going to let that go on forever. Poor Gigi was followed everywhere with questions that go on even now, but she's a good sport about it. The press is waiting for a wedding announcement that will never come…" He trailed off as a wave of emotions passed over his handsome features.

Amber leaned forward, absorbing the information she had been denied the last six months. "I'm sorry Senator Stroud."

Myles Stroud pulled back and squared his shoulders. "Please call me Myles. You should know Iris insisted you be the first to know. And I believe the public would have loved her as much as I did."

"I agree with you there. Iris was the best." Amber felt her throat tighten as it all hit her at once like a solid punch in her heart.

Myles lowered his voice. "I loved Iris. It feels good to be able to say that out loud finally. I've kept it all bottled up inside since that night. I honestly don't think I could have said that before now without breaking down. You understand?"

Amber crossed her arms. "Yes. I wish—"

Myles cut in. "I know, and I'm sorry. I mean, we would have been family, and I want us to be friends. Your sister thought the world of you, and I feel like I let her down by not contacting you before. Do you understand? Because I'm not so sure I do." He set his fork down and took a long gulp of his coffee, emptying the white mug. The half-eaten pie was pushed away.

He didn't look like the man who had posed for pictures outside. He reminded her of a small, confused child lost in a store. "I'm not sure what to say."

"I get that. I would understand if you hated me, but I hope you won't." He held her gaze with tear-filled eyes.

She swallowed her shock. "I've had support from people I work with—you haven't. I certainly don't hate you, but I wish I'd known sooner. But it is what it is. We go from here. Do you know why she was behind that casino the night she died? No one's ever been able to answer that for me."

He rubbed his hands over his face and shook his head as if to wake up. His public facade was firmly in place when Joe appeared at the table to refill their coffee mugs.

"Thanks, Joe. Although this is by far the best coffee I've ever had, I'd better make it my last cup. Or I might regret it later." The senator beamed his best smile.

"Oh, thank you, sir. Need anything else?" Joe glanced quizzically at Amber, who successfully held back a large eyeroll.

"No, thank you, Joe. We're all set."

Joe grinned and hurried back to the kitchen.

Myles's smile fell off his face as he rubbed his temples. "To answer your question, I honestly don't know why she was in that alley so far away from the store. I was running late, as usual, and she offered to pick up her engagement ring. If I had gone and picked it up like I said I would—well, things would have turned out so differently."

"You can't blame yourself for someone else's actions." Amber reached out, but Myles grabbed his coffee cup with both hands and ignored her gesture with a slight nod to Eli. "Oh, yeah, okay, sorry."

"Don't be. You aren't used to this type of life—I am. As for blaming myself, it's hard not to. It should have been me there picking it up, and then it wouldn't have happened. What if it was connected to me?" He sighed loudly.

"You think someone wanted you dead and killed her instead? Why? She was picking up the ring for Gigi would have been the assumption, unless it was someone who did know. Could anyone have known the truth?"

Myles shook his head. "Only me and Iris. Even Steve didn't know. It wasn't unusual to spend a lot of time with an employee working on the campaign. We kept it a tight secret."

Amber frowned as goosebumps covered her arms. "So killing her to hurt you wouldn't make sense, but robbery does. I'm sure the ring was worth a lot."

He closed his eyes and sucked in air before responding. "It was, but that wasn't the reason. At first the police didn't find the ring with her, but later they found it in the trash bin next to her. It wasn't a robbery. I'm sorry this information has been kept from you, but I hoped that once they figured it out, I could come to you. Never happened." A frown crossed his face right before he finished his second coffee in a single gulp.

Amber hugged herself and then set her hands in front of her, twisting them together like she was trying to piece it all together. She was good at puzzles, but this was like the jigsaw Iris bought her one Christmas that was all one color. She only got halfway through that, but this she couldn't walk away from. "She wasn't near her car or the jewelry store. So finding out why she was in that alley behind the casino seems like the right approach."

Myles nodded as he studied a sugar package like it would supply them with all the answers. "Yes, and what I've been focused on, with no answers. It makes no sense."

Amber grasped her cup like it was a life preserver. "It makes no sense to us, but it does to the killer. The ring and store are new additions to me. Do the police have the ring?"

Myles pushed the condiments aside and frowned. "They do. Like I said, only the sheriff knows it was for Iris and not Gigi. This has been hard to contain." He looked out the window.

Amber picked up the discarded sugar packet and clasped it tightly. "I wish I had known sooner, but I suppose I understand your reasoning, or lack of it." She added the sugar to her coffee, which was already heavily laden with cream. She ended up with an undrinkable cup of coffee that she focused on stirring. She felt his eyes on her and met his anguish. "Nothing's been right since she died."

Myles gently wiped the table in front of him, and with a smile and deliberate sigh, he bent in closer. "Yes, that sums this nightmare up perfectly. I want to talk about this more in depth, but I can't right now."

Amber put her spoon down and pushed the cup away. "I'm not stopping until I know the truth."

His face transformed right before her eyes as his public mask clamped down, concealing the emotions as Joe walked to Eli's table. It was successful except for his eyes. "Good, we agree on that. I have a proposition for you, if you're interested."

"A proposition?"

He nodded, glancing at the kitchen after Joe entered it. "I've already spoken to your boss. He's agreed to have you follow the campaign exclusively for the next few weeks while I'm here before I head on the campaign trail. Then we can work on this more with no interruptions, and of course, you'd get stories for your paper on my bid for the presidency. We can decide if my relationship with Iris goes public or not. I can keep it quiet if you so choose. So what do you say?"

Amber ran her fingers through her hair and felt an urge to braid it like Iris used to do. She resisted that unprofessional move. "I would like us to work together to find my sister's killer, and I can write the articles, but you'll need to let me process this for a bit after what you've just told me."

"I understand. Know you aren't alone in dealing with a broken heart." He glanced back at Eli, who was reading the newspaper. He grabbed her hand and gave it a quick squeeze before releasing it. "Can you keep this between the two of us until we can talk again? If we want others to know, it has to be done right with the press."

"Yes, I can agree to that."

"Good. Let's meet Monday morning at my office. Say around eight? Then we can talk more. Compare notes and resolve this." He smiled and gave a curt nod when Steve peeked in the door.

"There have been some strange—"

Myles interrupted. "Sorry, I have to go. I have another meeting."

He shoved one more bite of pie into his mouth and stood up. The photographer rushed in to snap some more shots as he walked out the door in a quick, rehearsed exit. He was gone before she could react. She had been about to tell him about the parking lot and the car that had tried to hit her and her car break-in. Well, maybe it was for the better. He'd probably think she'd lost it, like all her coworkers.

Amber watched Clark get out of the truck and wait for Myles to enter. He glanced her way before standing back to allow Myles entry. Then, like a Victorian gentleman, he swooped down and flung out his arm toward Myles. Myles seemed unaware of the gesture, but Clark's face broke out in a smile that he quickly contained. When everyone was in the vehicle, the smile became a frown. The man was awkward, bordering on strange, and she couldn't shake the feeling that he looked familiar. He cast one more look in her direction and held up a hand. Then he slumped into the vehicle and shut the door. What was it about him? Had he been photographed with the senator? No, wait. He was the guy she'd bumped into at the bar. That gesture. It was the same, as was the build and the power suit. Did he recognize her? It had been dark and all, but what was he doing there? Well, she guessed senators' assistants got time off to have fun.

Amber had considered ordering a burger, but her appetite had disappeared. Eli tossed down some money. He threw a grin at Amber on his way out the door and added a small wink.

Amber felt disappointed that both men had left her alone as she watched the SUV pull away. Part of her had hoped that Eli would wait for her in his car, but he disappeared too. She never got a chance to tell him about the break-in. No matter, she had a lot to take in after that conversation. Was Myles authentic, like she thought, or was he not what he seemed? And as for his assistant, why was he at the club last night? Was Iris killed because of Myles or for another reason that included her now? Questions swirled like a blizzard, preventing her from seeing any answers. She'd figure it all out when this storm of information cleared.

She slid across the cold red vinyl seat and exited the booth, feeling very alone suddenly. She could feel Grumpy Joe's eyes on her as she left. She turned to wave at the door, but he looked away. He was back to his old self. At least something was normal.

CHAPTER 6

Soon Amber was pulling into an almost empty parking lot. Her cell phone beeped, and she thrust it into her purse without bothering to read the message. Shaking her head, she grabbed a cold shopping basket from outside the brightly lit store. She loaded the cart with her comfort foods first. A gallon of rocky road ice cream, some chocolate chip cookies, and three bottles of chardonnay. She had a feeling ice cream would be her main course tonight, along with wine. She grabbed a premade turkey sandwich on sourdough— her favorite.

As she nibbled on the sandwich, she went into automatic shopping mode, pushing the cart down every aisle whether she needed anything there or not. As she marched down the final aisle, she stopped to check her list. Pasta was the only thing she'd missed. Her phone beeped again. Sighing, she grabbed her phone as she maneuvered her cart back to the noodles, running it straight into another shopper's basket. Her phone went flying.

"Clark?" Amber said, stunned. He looked like a deer in headlights and tried to go around her, but not before he managed to kick her phone down the aisle. He followed it and swooped to pick it up like he was Harry Potter as a Seeker.

"I'm so sorry. Did you have this off?" He held her phone up. "The screen is black. If there's any damage, I will fix or replace it. Please check it out."

He was sweating as he fumbled at his collar, looking more like he wanted to push past her rather than help.

"I was going to reply to a coworker. It's not off. See?" She held up the undamaged phone.

"Oh, yes, I see. I'm glad."

"No worries."

"I was focused on getting some supplies before the big storm."

"Me too. Didn't Myles have another meeting, or did it get canceled?" Amber shoved the phone back into her purse.

Clark smiled broadly, balancing out his nerdy exterior. "Not canceled, but the senator didn't need me there. Well, he really didn't need me for your meeting, either, Ms. Dodges, but I worked on a project while I was there. The senator insisted he didn't want me driving and told me to go home. So he dropped me off at my car, and here I am."

Clark extended his arms, one hand facing upward in another formal gesture. Amber held back a giggle. She put her half-eaten sandwich into her cart. "Please call me Amber. Running into another person when I thought I had the store to myself startled me. Then the questions seem to come out before I can think sometimes."

"I get that. We all have our nervous habits. I was thinking the same thing, that I had the store to myself. Guess everyone got their shopping done."

"True. Yes, I think everyone else is home already."

He pushed back his glasses and pasted what looked like a pained smile on his face. "That poor cashier probably wants us out of here so she can close."

Amber glanced at the green-haired young woman all alone up front. She was typing away on her phone. "I think you're right. I should finish up."

"Me too. Oh, and Amber? Since we're working together now, I don't mind questions."

"Oh, good, thank you. I don't mind them either."

"Great. Now can you point me to the pasta?"

Amber pointed. "It's the next aisle over."

"Thanks, I might stock up. Good in these types of storms, right?" Clark laughed.

Amber forced a small chuckle. "Yes."

"I will keep my eyes ahead so we don't collide again."

Amber's laughter flowed naturally this time. "Me too. I think this is the second time we've done this. That was you at the club last night? I ran right into you walking out of the bathroom."

His face took on the color of marinara sauce. It wasn't a good look for his pale skin. "I was at the Moby Blue Club with some friends last night. I don't recall running into you, but that doesn't mean anything. Sometimes I'm lost in my thoughts. I'm sorry—you must think I'm completely clumsy."

Amber shook her head. "No, not at all. I was the other half of those collisions."

Clark leaned forward and spoke gently. "Well, thank you. I think a part of it is having just started working with the senator six months ago. I'm always on the job, if you know what I mean. I want to leave a good impression."

"I understand completely. No problem. You looked familiar at the café, but it didn't hit me until you gestured the way you did at the club. It's a fun place to go with friends. I do enjoy getting out to dance. Do you dance?"

Clark pulled back and raised his eyebrows. "Dance? Me? No."

"They had some good 80s music last night."

"I prefer country, but yes, I remember that."

"My sister loved country music." Amber watched his face closely for any expression indicating he knew about Myles and Iris. Nothing.

Clark shifted his feet and glanced up at the cashier waiting for them to leave. "Who doesn't? It's what the senator listens to—well, part of the time, and then he changes over to the classic rock."

"I listen to many types of music, but we all have our favorites. You met my sister, Iris? She was killed." Amber pressed.

53

"I had just met her. She was nice. I'm very sorry about what happened to her." He frowned and gave his collar a final tug before grasping his cart tightly.

"Yes, thank you. She was the best." Amber felt the familiar tightening in her throat.

"Everyone that knew her always has good things to say about her. Well, I think we better finish up. Or the employee might go home and leave us stuck in here."

"I agree. Have a great weekend, and see you Monday."

"Thank you, Amber. If you could point me to the wine aisle too, I have a guest coming for dinner," Clark added with a shy grin.

"One over from the pasta."

"Thanks. It was good to run into you."

Amber called out to his retreating figure. "The deli here has some great turkey if you like that and don't want to cook."

"I do like turkey, thank you. I will keep that in mind. See you soon."

"Yes, bye!"

Clark disappeared around the corner with his little red basket that had only contained a bag of chips, beef jerky, protein bars, and water. It didn't look like he had a guest coming with that load, but maybe all he needed was the wine and pasta, she supposed. She walked slowly and grabbed some Parmesan cheese. He glanced back at her one more time before he turned the corner, holding up a box of pasta. Then he waved and headed to the wine section. That was her cue to get her own pasta.

He seemed nice enough, just a bit odd and shy. To avoid more chatting at the register, she grabbed another bottle of wine and made one more round of the store in case she had forgotten something. When she noted Clark was bagging the last of his order, she headed up front. He had added a wine box and three jars of pasta sauce to his order, along with several candy bars. He loaded his cart and, with a wave in her direction, was out the door before she got to the register.

She had bought more things than she had planned, as usual. Well, if she got snowed in, she'd be set, she assured herself as the young cashier bagged it all up.

"Drive safe, ma'am."

"Thank you. Are you closing up?"

"Yes, soon. Wanna beat the snow."

Amber nodded. She saw the woman lock the door as soon as she was at her truck. The parking lot was empty except for her truck and a white Honda. She threw the bags in the back as a chilly unease shot through her. She felt like she was being watched. She scanned the parking lot and street but didn't see a white SUV lurking.

"Thank God." She climbed into her truck and locked the doors.

She couldn't shake the feeling that the masked man was some-where nearby waiting for her, but the roads were empty. Amber navi-gated the icy roads while finishing her sandwich. As soon as she turned onto her street, it started snowing again. She saw Mrs. Jones, who was like a surrogate grandma, a bundle of bright red in what she liked to call her sleeping bag jacket. It covered everything but her feet, hands, and face. She carried a handful of mail as she trudged through the snow, reminding Amber of Winnie-the-Pooh. Mrs. Jones waved as soon as she got to her door, her good-natured face reddened from the cold. Amber honked and rolled down her window.

"Mrs. Jones! I wanted to let you know about a break-in," she yelled, but the old woman, hard of hearing, disappeared inside without responding.

Amber hesitated for a moment and considered going over to her neighbor's but grabbed her groceries instead. She'd call later. She threw a glance at Eli's dark house. She felt some disappointment that his truck wasn't there.

Amber put her food away while nibbling on a soft chocolate cookie that she'd spread with a thick layer of peanut butter. No need for a big dinner now, after the sandwich. She peeked through the front window again, looking not for the SUV but Eli's Chevy. She was beginning to feel like a teenager waiting for the cute neighbor boy to come home. Would Eli be safe driving in the snow? Maybe he wasn't coming home tonight.

Her head still spinning from the talk with Myles, she decided a nap or a book would give her some perspective. She would put the detective on hold for today. She pulled off her boots, climbed under her comforter, and dialed Mrs. Jones's number. She got the answering machine and carefully explained the break-in. "Call me if you need anything." She hung up, hoping Mrs. Jones would remember to check her messages soon. Sometimes she forgot, so Amber would try again tomorrow.

Her cell phone beeped She plucked it out her purse to charge it and found three messages from Britney.

3:00 p.m. *Is everything okay? I'm just checking in with you. Let me know if you're okay, please. Love ya, B*

3:30 p.m. *I haven't heard back from you. I'm worried. I've tried calling your cell and house phone. Please respond, B*

4:25 p.m. *It's really snowing now. I hope you aren't out driving in this. I know this weekend is hard for you, but I'm here. I should have come home with you. Maybe I should send someone to check on you or get a ride to you. B*

Amber sighed and typed out a response.

Sorry, Britney. Thank you for checking in on me. I've been busy, though. I had a meeting with Senator Stroud and then did some grocery shopping. I forgot to check my phone until now. I'm fine. No need to check on me. Oh, I won't be in the office for a few weeks, I'm assigned to work with the senator for a story. I will keep you posted. Stay warm and safe.

"There, that should do it," Amber murmured, picking up her e-reader.

She heard her phone beep again with what she was sure was Britney's reply and a lot of questions. Britney wouldn't be pleased to have been out of the loop with the senator's story. Amber tried to read, but the words passed before her eyes like a roaring river. Her mind was spinning with questions, and the only answer she had for them was sleep. It overtook her quickly.

CHAPTER 7

$\mathcal{N}$ester frowned deeply. The evildwel inside the host would push for the kill, and the host was more than ready to oblige. Time was short for Amber. Nester wanted to help her, but he had no idea how, so he tried to communicate with the winged one again.

"I wish I could warn Amber that the killer is watching her sleep through her bedroom window. Can you hear me, or am I just talking to myself?"

Nester could have sworn that she responded with a sigh and a nod in his direction. Encouraged, he continued. "Was that a sign you can hear me? I'll continue to try to educate you on my dilemma just in case. I've become fond of this place called Earth, which is something evildwels aren't known for. I want to stay here if possible. I'm... hopeful—that's a word I've never used to describe myself—that evildwels won't completely destroy this world while you winged ones do your part to prevent that. Yes, I know I said you aren't making much of a large-scale difference, but I think it might be enough with the small things you do. Anyways, I'm conflicted with these new feelings and have developed this thing humans call 'empathy.' I feel the pain. It's almost like I understand it.

"The first time I felt this was when a raging alcoholic host strangled his wife to death in front of their kids. I found myself hoping she'd escape him, but she didn't. He left her lifeless body on the cold hardwood floor while her children crouched behind an old sofa. He walked out and never came back. Although he was caught three days later and eventually sent to prison, I left him at that point. It was an unusual thing for an evildwel to do since he was going to pay for his murder in jail. I just couldn't stay after that. It made me feel...I'm not sure how to explain...but, uncomfortable. It was similar to being too close to a winged one, which I wasn't. Those children's cries vibrated through my body, almost like I was starving. That episode haunted me, and I did the only thing I could think of, keep feeding on the fear and pain to push away the strange feelings. It worked at first, but later I came to realize that it wasn't hunger causing the problem—it was my food. It was like I'd developed an allergy to fear and anger, but at the same time my body needed it to survive.

"So, conflicted, I hid my affliction well for the last several years, but now it's beginning to emerge. My black mist is lighter, my red eyes are developing this odd muddy color, and sometimes I lose control. I'm not sure how much longer I can keep my secret. Since that night I've only fed on the fear and misery from natural disasters or deaths that I'm not responsible for. It feels better not being the cause of the anguish I feed on, but that doesn't make it any easier to digest. I'm not sure how these humans tolerate feeling these emotions. I despise them—I've considered just letting myself fade away. Yet I want to live, even with this horrible condition."

Nester almost started speaking out loud to the winged one in desperation but stopped himself. He knew the other evildwel would hear him.

"Even as I speak, I feel hunger. Do you understand that? Because I certainly don't! I feel crazy sitting here talking to myself. It isn't something evildwels do. We're a proud race, and I'm acting, well, like my food. Lately I've been wondering if I got this sickness from winged ones. Can your goodness be contagious?"

A strange jolt shot through Nester, causing his mist to swirl erratically outward. It terrified him to lose control. He quickly glanced at the other evildwel, hoping he didn't witness this display. Thankfully, he hadn't. The evildwel was completely focused on the girl and the winged one. Nester forced the mist back into himself and felt the usual evildwel calm take over.

It was normal for the mist to flow in a slow, controlled state, much like Earth traveling around the sun. Slow and easy, repeating the process over and over—not out of control like a comet streaking across the sky, begging to be seen. Nester sighed with more than a bit of relief that his lack of composure hadn't been observed. He had no idea where those chaotic moments came from, but they were happening more often. Soon he wouldn't be able to hide them, and that worry pressed him to continue.

"We've been enemies for so long, and I know you have no reason to trust anything I'm saying. Still, I'm hoping you might know if my requirement to feed off fear negates the desire to do...good? I can only justify what I do by accepting the fact that humans don't need help with creating pain and evil in their world."

Nester withdrew back into silence while watching the winged one intently. He was hoping for something, anything. He felt strangely comfortable in her presence.

"Do I cause you any discomfort? Since I can be around you now without all the pain I used to feel, I've developed a theory—it's why I'm talking to you—that without that pain barrier, you could read me like you winged ones do with each other. I know you're in tune to what the humans think as well. I'm sure the other evildwel is causing you some discomfort, but my I worry that the day is almost here when my kind does that to me. Can you imagine that? What a mess. It was certainly easier to be Nester, the second-oldest evildwel next to Aten, with no feelings. In the far simpler days. I wonder if there is a way to become like the humans that are vegetarians and not feed on them at all? But I haven't figured that part out yet."

The winged one wrapped her wings around Amber and cast another stern glance at the window, where the host was. Nester could feel the host was ready to act on its desire to inflict cruel torture.

"I've tried to stop feeding, but hunger is so painful, and death comes so slowly. I watched this happen to an older evildwel like me, Arius. He said he couldn't do it anymore only two decades ago. He avoided us from then on because we caused him pain. He withered away for months until a group of evildwels hunted him down and helped his death along. Then they fed on him."

A grimace crossed the winged one's face but was gone as quickly as it came.

"I don't mean to offend, but it is our way. We can feed on our kind and use their energy to make us stronger. It's not common, though. It usually only happens when the older ones feed on the young ones who aren't strong enough. With Arius, he was removed for being sick or weak. When he was put out of his misery, I watched. I let the others think I was letting them have some fun, but I couldn't do it. It didn't seem right. Because I'm an elder, I can get away with that, because I'm respected. Although there will come that day when the thin veil of respect will be gone, and then I'll be the next Arius. Since his death I've been wondering whether he faded away or became something else, like humans do. He's the first one I've wondered about because he was different from the rest of us.

"Do you have any insights or answers? Do you think I've been on Earth too long? Is empathy contagious—from humans or from you? Or is this a process of evolving or devolving? I've considered communicating with you more directly. I almost did a little while ago, but that evildwel would hear and then, of course—you know."

Nester didn't need to keep reminding the winged one of his difficulty with other evildwels. That part was his problem, not hers. Watching Zelina's glow increase mesmerized him as the woman slept soundly, unaware of what surrounded her. Zelina gently straightened the comforter around her. Nester suddenly wished he could feel that peaceful slumber with wings wrapped around him. His kind didn't sleep, though. A familiar ache gnawed him. He needed to feed soon, but he was going to keep trying a little longer.

"You are so intent, Zelina, on protecting this female. You might pull it off. That feather in the parking lot was a nice touch. It saved her life. You had Thomas—nice to see you working together again—encourage that coworker of Amber's, Britney, to rush the other coworkers out of the building to look for her. And getting Amber to slam on her brakes driving home last night with a reflection of a bear was quick thinking. The light in her parked car forced that host to abandon its search—well, along with the huge bear showing up. But I think I most appreciated your inspired warnings through the music she was listening to, with the word 'danger' so obvious, even to her. I have no idea how you do it. Maybe someday you'll teach me, huh?"

Nester paused. He tried his best smile on the winged one. He didn't think she noticed, so he kept rambling on.

"Besides, my hope is that you can save my life, which I'm sure is low on your list of things to do. I've also been wondering about the feelings I'm picking up. I feel like you'll need all the help you can gather. Amber's death could trigger some horrific events that involve someone else, but I'm not sure how I know that or what the events are. Hey, Zelina, am I getting this from you?"

Nester had hoped that would get a response from her. Nothing. She just glanced at the window again and sighed loudly. The host was bold coming here, but trying to take her in the parking lot, trying to run her off the road, and breaking into her car were bold moves too. Nester's mist began to swirl in confusion again. He quickly got it back under control without the other evildwel noticing. How long was his luck going to hold?

"Evildwels have to speak to each other. We can't read each other's thoughts, and the privacy is what's keeping me alive right now. That isolation was something I treasured, but now I would give it all up if you could just hear me. Why do I want to call that happening a 'blessing'? That is not a word that means anything to me.

"No matter. I think I'm beginning to understand you winged ones. I've watched you interact with the humans and Thomas. I liked that time when you helped that Lynn Hill girl survive that host and the evildwel, Dian. Lynn bravely rescued her best friend, Staci, and had to figure out a murder that would have been pinned on her. I was cheering you on as you helped her—inside. I had to avoid Dian—she was too perceptive—but I was there through the whole thing. Lynn had a lot of spunk—and a strange obsession with buttons."

The host in the black ski mask tugged on the side of the double-paned window, but it didn't budge. It was locked, with the extra protection of a round piece of wood wedged behind the bottom lock. The host's breath fogged up the glass as it struggled to open it. Finally, the host stopped and shrugged. There was a smile peeking through the mouth of the mask that showed in the evildwel's red eyes.

"The host wants to break the glass but is afraid of the noise. Snow is always so quiet—it magnifies any sounds. I'm really focusing on the human's motives and trying to figure out a plan to help. Not a very evildwel-like thing to do. My kind are single-minded. We are either hunting or feeding. Once a century, we procreate, but only a few of those new evildwels will be allowed to grow up. I have three that survived. Only the strongest I've heard more than once. All the small evildwel sparks that have been extinguished for minor infractions or not being evil enough—I feel a bit of 'guilt,' I think it's called, when I think about them, so I don't. Of my three procreations, one left the planet and two are around…somewhere."

The host wiped away the fog and began clicking pictures of Amber sleeping. It was an expensive camera, and the host seemed to know what it was doing. It held the camera up against the glass and adjusted its stance by spreading its legs wide to hold still. With the lack of natural lighting, Nester knew the lens would stay open longer, and that required stillness on the photographer's part. Photography had always held Nester's interest. Capturing what they saw was a huge step in human evolution, in his opinion.

"I guess that means the host is giving up tonight since it's putting the lens cap back on the camera. I'll follow when it leaves. I know the host and the evildwel need the kill, and I need to feed. I hope you understand. I'll be back, and hopefully, the host won't."

Nester drank in Zelina's swirling silver gown and her peacock-green wings with her black hair cascading down between them. She was a thing of beauty. She looked up at Nester with a small smile.

"Can you hear me?"

Her grin was gone as quickly as it appeared, and she was back to watching Amber sleep, her wings still wrapped around her.

"Okay. I have to go."

No response as Nester left the house. He saw the bear standing by Amber's bedroom window. Was that to shoo off the host again? He followed close behind the host and the evildwel. It was time to acknowledge the youngling.

"How did a strong host get such a weakling evildwel such as yourself?" Nester asked.

The evildwel smiled proudly. "I'm Geo, and I'm honored you are here with me, Nester."

"Focus on your host," Nester reprimanded.

"I am giving it all my focus, which is why I left now to avoid any injury to my host from that bear. Those winged ones never give up."

"I saw the bear. Wise choice." Nester sided him.

"Thank you. I don't want to lose this host yet, since I was very lucky to obtain it."

"Hard to believe that an elder didn't desire such a purely evil host. You did get lucky with this one, I agree. I'm not in the habit of talking to other evildwels, especially ones of your age, so don't think we're buddies and you can chat with me whenever you choose. I do need to feed, though, so you'd better make sure that happens. I'd hate to have to end your unimportant life." Nester really wouldn't have killed him, but Geo didn't know that.

"Yes. I promise not to let you down."

Nester watched his mist darken and his eyes glow. Geo would show off for Nester now. Prove his worth. Evildwels were prideful above all. None of that mattered to Nester if he didn't have to kill to feed. He followed Geo and his host into a dark alley behind the grocery store where Amber had stopped earlier. It didn't take long to find a man sleeping behind the garbage bins under a tower of cardboard and plastic shaped into a makeshift tent.

After they fed on what was now a lump in the snow, the sun started to rise. This homeless man, whose name was Fred, had taken his last jagged breath. His time on Earth had been limited—he was already close to death. His body was filled with cancer. Probably wouldn't have made it too many more nights, but this host didn't let him die easily. Geo and his host enjoyed watching the life drain out of the terrified man's eyes. The snow soaked up the blood, a red stain of cruelty. Nester didn't like it, but he had to eat. At least this host fed on a man so sick and full of drugs that his heart barely beat. Now Fred was at peace. A winged one he'd never seen before took him away. Geo smiled at Nester right before he departed. Nester knew he'd see Geo and his host later. Feeling strong and at the same time pained from the man's death, he headed back to the A-frame house where a winged one protected a human.

Zelina was where he'd left her, seated by Amber. She didn't acknowledge his return, but that was no surprise. A small part of him had hoped. Stupid feeling, hope was. At least he knew Zelina wouldn't give up on Amber, and that gave him some comfort. Well-fed now and the pain from the kill subsiding, Nester decided to reach out a final time.

"I'm fed now and feel stronger, and at the same time, I hurt. I was happy to see a winged one there waiting for the poor human's soul. He seemed so peaceful then. I'm sure you don't want to hear about the brutal details, so I'll talk about something else, like the bear that chased off the host again."

He waited for a response to that. Nothing.

"Well, um…I've seen you train other winged ones. They've saved so many humans and ruined my feedings more than once. I admit that I hated you and all the winged ones, but now you have my full admiration. That's strange for me to say, even in my thoughts. Anyways, I have that feeling that this is coming to a head now. Again, how do I know this? Don't know."

Nester grunted, feeling stronger but no less conflicted. No, he was more confused and pained by his new thoughts and feelings.

"I've been there watching when you've helped. Ed was a favorite of mine. He had an evildwel inside whose name I forget. Of course, you know what happened, but it's such an exceptional story, I hope you don't mind me repeating what I saw. Ed had a horrible childhood and became an abusive drunk. He was encouraged by his evildwel to get behind the wheel when he'd been drinking heavily. I was there when his car crashed, you know. His life ebbed away with you by his side. It's what you did next that completely threw me. After he watched his life over and over—I heard you talking about that once—his punishment became his redemption instead. You knew what he was capable of when you insisted that he work with you. I forgot the term you used, but he was a test subject. You have a good judge of character because he saved his family. He understood how he had been wrong and wanted his ex-wife to be happy.

"After what happened in the mountains when Ed heaved the oldest evildwel out of his host, I had to endure the complaints by Aten. He was not happy about being extracted from his host. He took his soul collection with him. You know that's not a customary practice. We usually move on when their souls do. But Aten likes to hang on to those souls. Says it makes him stronger, and he enjoys playing with them after. It reminds me of the birds eating and then throwing it up to feed their babies. Who wants thrown-up food? That's what those souls are to me. This has all led me to become a traitor to my kind, and there's nothing I can do to prevent this new side of me. It's here to stay.

"I've developed empathy even for my own kind. I can imagine the pain Aten and other evildwels must have felt when they were ejected from their hosts before they were done with them. Aten had to feel humiliation—no, we don't feel that, but maybe anger or rage. That separation could be lethal to the younger of our kind, but not for the stronger ones like Aten—and me, of course.

"Right now, I can't worry about other evildwels' displeasure, including this young Geo. They would feel no remorse removing me from existence, and I'm sure they're starting to wonder why I haven't taken a host in so long. I can't keep following them around feeding, at least not the more mature evildwels. This one here doesn't seem too smart, but it could be an act. After his last kill, I'm leaning toward the latter, which means I need to be even more careful.

"I have a lot going against me, don't I? I wonder if the smart evildwels left this planet before they got my illness, or whatever this is. I'm having a tough time figuring this out. I wish you could hear me, but you can't. So I guess it's up to me."

Nester sighed and watched Zelina leave Amber's side. She looked out the window for several seconds. She slowly circled the room, filling it with her goodness like the rising sun, but ignoring Nester. Finally, she settled down next to her again as the morning arrived. She nodded with a slightly sad smile and then pinned her gaze on Nester while holding a finger to her lips.

Zelina spoke out loud. "I hear you, Nester, but do not communicate anymore until we can be alone. It is not safe. Stay near."

CHAPTER 8

*a*mber was falling in slow motion. A red-eyed black mist consumed her with an eerie smile. She threw her arms out, trying to grasp anything to prevent her descent, but her hands clutched at nothing. She fell for what seemed like an eternity until she snapped back into reality. Sitting up in bed, shivering and hugging her legs, she filled her lungs, trying to slow her racing heart.

"It's been so long," she mumbled to herself.

A dark hole with red eyes—she hadn't had that nightmare since leaving her mom's house. But it had never smiled at her before, which made it even more terrifying. She'd wake up drenched in sweat and unable to sleep the rest of the night. Now was no different, but luckily it was eight o'clock. She'd slept for over fifteen hours, something she hadn't done since she'd been sick with the flu years ago. She felt her forehead. No fever. Maybe the last few months had caught up with her all at once. Whatever the reason for the sleepathon, she felt heavy and tired.

She stretched her legs and arms as her heart rate returned to normal. Glancing out the uncovered window as she gulped down some water, she noted it was still snowing. She settled back into the warm flannel, but her stomach demanded attention. She shivered as she tied her bathrobe around her.

"Better make breakfast," she announced to Tiger, who continued sleeping serenely at the foot of her bed.

She shuffled past him, pulling on her bear slippers, to turn on the heater. The rumble of the heater was soothing to her, blowing warm air from the hidden vent at her feet by the kitchen sink. She stood there for a moment, letting the warmth fill her.

Feeling a more positive tug from her past that overrode her nightmare, she embraced it as she rummaged through the cabinets and fridge to find everything she needed. Then, making her usual mess, she started the breakfast that she and Iris used to help their dad make as kids. It had been a Sunday tradition for the sisters. Banana pancakes with a dash of cinnamon, oven-baked bacon, and cheesy scrambled eggs. She didn't have any oranges to squeeze for juice, but she preferred coffee now.

Amber swirled the pancake batter with a whisk. She'd never used all the fancy tools her sister and father did. No food processors for her—nope, she'd stir or chop it herself, thanks. She still longed for those mornings when they'd come home from church and gather in the kitchen to cook—well, everyone but her mother. Amber shook her head as the memories continued to roar through her mind.

"Your mother is tired, girls, and needs to catch up on her sleep." That was her father's standard line on weekends. Even as a young girl, she hadn't believed it.

That last Sunday, when she and Iris were just eleven years old, breakfast didn't happen. Amber and Iris were ready for church and about to join their dad when they overheard their parents' loud conversation from the shadows of the hallway.

"I've given you too many chances, Eve. You always have an excuse for why you can't quit drinking. Why you can't go to meetings or rehab. I don't trust you to take care of our girls anymore. You drove them to school *drunk* on Friday. The girls' teacher called me right after you dropped them off. She was concerned you were sick or something. Didn't you wonder why I took off work early to pick them up? I'm not taking any more chances with you. I'm taking the girls and going to live with my sister. I have a couple more things to tie up, then I can start a leave of absence and give our daughters my full attention."

"No, Don, you're wrong. You can't leave with them. I *will* follow through this time, I promise. I won't drive drunk anymore. Give our family another chance."

"You've made that promise before. I don't even care about that man, Jeb Cadwell. Don't look so surprised. After that call I had you followed, for their sake. The very next day, it paid off when you went to your so-called yoga class with an accountant. Guess he needed some extra money if he was giving private yoga classes!"

"It's not true! It wasn't me."

"It was. According to the motel manager, you've been doing this for the last few months. It only took a hundred dollars to jog his memory. Apparently, you always showed up with a brown paper bag that you'd drink from. Everything you've said has been a lie. This marriage is over. I honestly hope you get some help for the girls' sake, but they aren't staying another night in this house with you. We'll live with Kathy until I can get my own place. Pack up their stuff, or I will. I've contacted a lawyer. Don't make me have you declared unfit."

"He means nothing to me. It was stupid, I know. I have no excuse, but you are my everything, and I love you. I'm a drunk, like you said. I need help."

"You do. I hope you get it."

The door slammed, and then a glass shattered loudly. Iris had squeezed Amber's hand tightly as they heard their mother's voice.

"He knows. He's taking the girls from me when he gets back Yes, that's what he said. He said the girl's teacher called him, asking if I was sick. No, I wasn't driving them drunk, I swear. I was just tired and distracted. We need to talk. Yes, I understand you are busy today. I will. Yes, thank you. I love you too."

The girls silently retreated into their room, where they survived the day on leftover Halloween candy. Iris peeked out and saw their mother openly drinking in the kitchen. She continued until the police showed up at the door. Listening from the hallway, they learned they no longer had a father. Killed in a car accident by what the police believed, ironically enough, was a drunk driver, who left the scene and was never found. They looked around the corner to see their mom's shocked expression, but it was the sympathetic look on the cop's red, round face that made it real. That was the only adult compassion the girls saw that night. While the woman who had never really been a mother resumed drinking, Iris and Amber tried to comfort each other. When their mother fell into a drunken slumber on the couch, Iris snuck into the kitchen to retrieve some food. Dinner consisted of cheese puffs, lunch meat, and root beer.

Aunt Kathy showed up the next day. Iris and Amber heard muffled arguing in the kitchen, where they pieced together words like lawyer, child protection, and rehab. The meaning was clear. Their mother called them into the kitchen and quickly smothered them in a sloppy hug reeking of alcohol.

"You girls are going with your aunt today. You need to pack your suitcases. It might be a couple of weeks because I need some time to recover from losing your dad. You understand, right?"

"Yes, Mother, we understand," Amber replied, noting her aunt's deep frown and narrowed eyes directed at their mother.

"Good. I expect you both to be good for your aunt. We'll be together soon. I love you." She finished with a big wet kiss on the top of their heads.

Aunt Kathy spoke for the first time. "Do you want some help packing, girls?"

"We got it, Aunt Kathy. Thanks," Iris replied.

"Okay, I'm going to move some stuff around in my car. Make sure you grab all of your favorite things, okay?" Aunt Kathy's face was tight with a forced smile.

That was the last time Amber or Iris set foot in that house. Their mother put it on the market the following week. What they had left behind they never saw again. She moved in with her lover from the motel, whom she quickly married. Amber and Iris visited them for holidays and summers only because she had a good lawyer. But their mother couldn't hide her drinking or how overbearing her new husband was. They avoided going anywhere with them as much as possible.

This went on for five years, until they were ripped away from a happy life with Aunt Kathy and all their friends. Amber could still feel the pain of that day.

"Have them pack their stuff, Kathy. They're coming home, where they belong." Amber heard her mother's voice boom through the cabin.

Their mother had thrown enough money at this new custody battle and finally won. They were ripped away from the one woman who'd showed them love and forced to live with a mother incapable of any loving emotions. Those were two of the longest years of their lives.

Dinners had always been prepared by the cook, the only person in that house who cared for them. It wasn't the obvious lack of interest from their mother that was the worst part of living in that house. It was dealing with their stepfather, Jeb, who took a more hands-on approach. He made the tight curfew rules, controlled the noise level to zero, and held back the money budgeted for their care.

Finally, their time there was at an end. "We are done serving our prison sentence. Tomorrow is our release day," Iris joked, but there was more truth than humor in her statement.

Amber trembled when she recalled that horrible night before her eighteenth birthday. She checked the bacon cooking in the oven. It was still pink. She wished she could push all those bad memories away, but like that dream, they kept coming back. She cracked the eggs into a bowl and beat them furiously before pouring them into a pan. These were the moments when losing Iris hurt the most. She was the only person Amber could talk to about what happened that night.

Amber's stepfather had staggered into her room, squinting at her packed suitcases with bloodshot eyes. She pulled her pink comforter high up to her neck and tightly closed her eyes, hoping he'd leave. She only had a few hours until it was time to board a plane and never have to see him again. Then she and Iris would land in Reno, where Aunt

Kathy would be waiting to take them back to Lake Tahoe. They'd finally be home in Pine City, where they belonged. Morning couldn't come fast enough, especially now that her stepfather was trespassing in her room. Fear gripped her chest, making it hard to breathe as he sat on the bed next to her. He started rubbing her back, and alarms went off in her head. The man was about rules and control—not comfort or kindness.

"I thought I heard you cry out like you had a bad dream, Amber. You don't have to be brave and pretend to be asleep. I saw your eyes open when I came in, and you have no idea how much I love you girls. Your mom is everything to me, and you especially remind me of her."

"I...um didn't cry out, but yeah, thanks." Amber's body was tense and on high alert.

She could still remember how strong the alcohol was on his breath as he scooted closer to her.

"Everything has been for you girls and your mother. I would never hurt any of you. You believe that, right?"

"Yeah, sure," Amber replied through a clenched jaw, thinking now would be an appropriate time to cry out. But her mother was dead to the world, and she didn't want Iris involved in whatever this was.

"Of course you do. I was the one who pushed for you girls to move in with us. You know, to be a family, like we always should have been."

"Well, yes, we all live together," Amber choked out.

"You want to know a little secret?" He moved in closer and leaned over Amber so he could see her face. Amber pushed herself away against the green padded headboard as the covers fell off. "I've noticed how you look at me. Ever since you were a young teen."

Amber couldn't believe what she was hearing. Her fear was pushed aside as anger coursed through her body, and she sat up with him leaning over her, "How I look at you? What the hell are you talking about?"

"It's okay to admit it. I forgive your poor choice of words because I've waited so patiently for your eighteenth birthday tomorrow. You'll be an adult and ready for that next step. I think we both know that you're leaving because of how you feel about me."

"What?" Amber could barely get any words out as her mouth dried up. The creep thought she was in love with him.

He cupped her chin in one hand tightly while his other hand rubbed her shoulder. "You know what I mean. No need to pretend anymore." He smiled and then winked at her.

Amber's heart was pounding. "No, I don't know what you mean. Please stop touching me."

"You're shy. That's sweet. I'm flattered. Of course, I'd never act on it, but I can't control you acting on your feelings. You've made it so obvious I'm surprised your mother hasn't noticed." He smiled at her as he released her chin and started massaging her other shoulder.

"I'm not attracted to you." A shudder ran through Amber's body.

"Well, your words say one thing and your body another. That's okay. I'm here to help."

Was he going to try to rape her? "I do not want you. I am not attracted to you. I hate you! Get the hell away from me!" Amber demanded, trying to pull away, but his grip was firm on her shoulders, his fingers digging painfully into her bare skin.

A scowl passed over his face, and he shook her slightly in his iron grip. The look was replaced by a forced smile as he released her, but his hands caressed her arms and stopped at her hips, which he briefly squeezed. Then he moved away from her, standing up. "You don't really mean that, and I will ignore your trashy, unladylike language again. I know you're scared that your mother will find out, but—"

"I do mean it!"

Jeb smiled and ran his fingers through his hair. "Your eyes are telling me something completely different, but no matter. There might be another solution for you. Did you know I have a son, Dean?"

"You? What does—Yes." Amber pulled the covers over her again. He had gone from thinking he was going to rape her to talking about his son. He was drunk, but he was also acting crazy.

"I know you've never met him. I don't keep pictures of him because it reminds your mother of my past marriage. She's the jealous type. I talk to my son all the time, though. He's graduating from college this year. I'm so proud of him."

"Okay."

"Deanie has seen pictures of you and Iris. He's taken with you. I'd like for you two to meet, but we couldn't tell your mom."

"I'm not comfortable with that."

"That's too bad. I did say I'd try, but I know when a young girl gets a crush on a handsome man like myself, it's hard to change her feelings."

"I'm not in love with anyone—including you." Amber insisted.

Jeb's mouth turned up into what should have been a grin, but it was more like the Joker from Batman. "It's okay. I won't tell anyone that you're in love with me, I promise." He staggered back toward the door, to Amber's relief, and added, "I'm sorry your dream confused you so much. If you change your mind about my son, just let me know. Sleep well."

As soon as he shut the door, Amber burst into action, racing across the room and locking her door. What had just happened? He was delusional and drunk. Was he trying to sleep with her or set her up with his son—or both? Why was he talking about a dream? She'd never told him or her mother about her dreams. Did he watch her sleep?

She shook her head and got dressed. Grabbing her suitcase, she hurried into Iris's room, locking the door behind her. Still dressed, she climbed into her sister's bed without waking her up. That would be the last night she would ever spend under the same roof as her clueless mother and delusional Jeb.

She barely slept that night, and when morning came, she had some explaining to do.

"Oh, Amber, I'm so sorry." Iris had comforted her after she told her what happened.

Her mother's response was quite the opposite. "Amber, you misunderstood. Jeb loves you girls so much. He heard you cry out. You were having a nightmare, and he was trying to comfort you is all."

Someday her mother would find out what a nightmare she was married to, but Amber wasn't so sure she'd ever be able to forgive her when that day came. The morning was capped off by the expected scene of her mother fake crying and Jeb fake comforting her, along with their audience of Jeb's constant visitor and best friend, Bo Wright, appearing almost amused. Those three were suited to each other. Now Bo was running for president against Senator Stroud.

Their mother had carefully wiped a tear away. "Your ride will be here in a half hour, girls. The cook has prepared you a birthday break-fast before you leave. We'll be right back to see you off. First, we have to check on some urgent paperwork. Make yourself at home, Bo." Amber's mother glanced at Jeb with a quivering lip.

Iris and Amber gobbled down their Belgian waffles topped with whipped cream and a single lit candle. No song or birthday wishes. Bo awkwardly came into the kitchen for coffee. While he waited, he smiled at the girls.

"I'm going to wait in Jeb's office. Have a safe trip, and happy birth-day, girls."

"Thanks," Amber mumbled as he left the kitchen.

"He makes me nervous," Iris had whispered.

"Me too," Amber whispered back.

She could have sworn Doris, the cook who barely spoke any English, nodded in agreement.

"I left my purse upstairs. Come with me."

They overheard an argument coming from their mother and Jeb's room.

"I want you to change your will. Those girls don't care about you like I do. They're abandoning you, honey. I'm the only one who's been here for you. I love you. It's only fair I get what we've created together, not them."

Amber had never heard her mother stand up to him before. "I need to make sure they're taken care of. Don't worry, I'll take care of you too. I promise."

Jeb stormed out of the bedroom without a glance at them and thundered downstairs to his office, where Bo waited, slamming the door behind him.

"Let's get out of here." Iris nudged Amber and nodded toward her room. Amber quickly grabbed her purse and closed the door on this chapter of her life. It would be great to walk out of that house and back into sanity.

Their mother emerged from her bedroom with a huge smile plastered on her face before they could escape. "Ready? Got all your stuff, girls?"

"Yes, we're ready to leave," Iris curtly replied.

"Too bad you aren't staying for lunch. Dean is coming for a visit."

"What? Jeb's son? He's never come here before." Amber felt goosebumps forming on her cold skin.

"Yes. It's way overdue—my idea. Sweet Jeb thought seeing him would upset me. Can you imagine that? Me? Sweet man that he is." Her mother managed to say all of that without making any eye contact. It was as if the previous conversation hadn't happened.

"Well, that's great for all of you," Amber's words were woven with sarcasm.

"It is. You girls better get going. Here's a check for your birthday. Split it, of course. Love you both. Come visit." A quick kiss on their cheeks, and she retreated into her bedroom and shut the door.

Amber held the check up to Iris and then headed down the stairs.

"Someone feeling guilty?" Iris asked.

"Big time. I almost don't want it, but I feel like we've earned it," Amber held the $20,000 check away from her like it might explode in her face.

"No time to go to the bank now. Have to deposit it when we get to Lake Tahoe."

Amber smiled for the first time on her birthday. "Yes, I can't wait."

"Let's get out of here."

As Amber took her last step out of the house where she'd endured two years of hell, she made the mistake of glancing back from the driveway. Her stepfather was standing at his office window watching. He was bold enough to wink at her and blow her a quick kiss. Amber rolled her eyes and shook her head in disgust. She was going to stand in the shower for a long time when she got to Aunt Kathy's and rinse that look out of her mind forever. Relief shot through her when the taxi pulled up.

Iris and Amber took their packed bags and their birthday money and caught the flight Aunt Kathy had arranged for them. Their mother didn't talk to them for two years after that. They didn't miss her or the possessions she'd provided, including their cars. Finally, they were back where they belonged, at the lake with Aunt Kathy. Now Amber stood alone in that place where she had always felt safe and loved.

She rubbed her arms. It was so unfair that her father, aunt, and sister were all dead while her mother still stumbled around, very much alive. But the biggest travesty was that her stepfather, who only cared about money and young women, was still breathing. Amber sighed, watching the large flakes cover the previous snowfall completely. Layer after layer, like her memories. You couldn't see them, but they were there always...underneath.

"You let your food get cold, girls," her aunt would scold them when they didn't show up at the dinner table promptly. Amber had done just that—let her food get cold. Kathy would always chastise them about wasting good food. She forced herself to eat the cold, dry eggs, and crispy bacon. The waffle was dry even under the syrup. It was like a mouthful of dirt, not that she'd ever eaten dirt before, but it had no flavor other than the syrup. Did she forget to add something to it, like sugar? She got the first bite down, followed by half a cup of coffee. The second bite she spit out.

Picking up her plate, she slammed her way through the breakfast dishes. She'd made enough for a family she didn't have anymore, so she had dinner already, minus the waffles. Anyway, she had more important things to do than reliving the past.

She sunk into her chair in front of her computer. "Sorry, Myles. I can't wait any longer to find out who killed her."

CHAPTER 9

*A*mber sipped her bitter coffee and started searching. The snowflakes were enormous now. She had always loved to watch them float delicately from the sky, but today they reminded her of frozen tears. It was as if sorrow had permanently taken up residence in her life. She straightened up in her chair as she scrolled through the first site. Not anymore.

Amber sighed loudly. She kind of wished now that she'd saved the extra money her mother had sent for her sister's funeral when she saw the first set of prices. But she had always found it hard to accept anything from that woman, and the unwanted money had gone to her sister's favorite wildlife rescue.

"Not like you worked for your money, Mother, like I do," Amber grumbled as she exited the site that wanted a deposit bigger than the amount she had saved.

Besides the insurance money her mother had collected, she had an inheritance from grandparents she'd never met. Amber wondered how much of that money Jeb had already spent and if he would disappear if it ran out. Not that she really cared, one way or another. She glanced out the window. The snow had turned into blizzard conditions, and the roads weren't cleared. No one was coming to her house, and she had the whole day stretched out in front of her.

She heard a beep and checked her phone.

I haven't heard back from you. Surprised about your meeting, but maybe it will be good for you to work with him for the next couple of weeks. I will miss you, of course. I just got a message that tomorrow is a snow day, which I knew includes you. I'm coming over to keep you company. Don't worry, I'm positive I can get there safely in the morning, or I wouldn't do it. I'd better pack. Love ya, B

Amber rubbed her temples.

I was surprised too. I appreciate you wanting to keep me company, but I insist you don't go out in this weather. I know Kyle's brother runs a snowplow business, but PLEASE stay home and enjoy your new guy. Thank you, Britney. I probably won't see you for a few weeks, but I'll be back at the office before you know it. Stay warm.

Amber hit send. She couldn't bring herself to tell Britney she'd miss her. *Leave me alone* would have been a more accurate message. She didn't bother reading the previous texts from Britney. She checked her emails. All junk except for the one from her boss confirming she'd be working with the senator with a fresh start date of Tuesday. She responded with a quick thanks.

She settled back into her search for a PI. After the first overpriced one, she quickly found two that suited her budget and needs. Very modern, and nothing like she'd imagined from watching old movies. No good-looking man with a cigarette hanging out of his mouth and a trench coat would show up at her door. No, they probably did most of their work on computers unless they needed to follow someone, like the guy her dad had hired for her mother. Amber chose the detective who seemed to fit her needs the best.

"A former FBI agent and works with the police. Do I need a fresh perspective? Yeah, I sure do." She quickly typed out an email about her sister's murder with a bit of guilt tugging at her. Should she wait to talk to Myles first? No, she didn't need to mention her relationship with Myles, even though it was important. Just the basic facts first, and then she added the parking lot, drive home, truck out front, and break-in. Whether it sounded crazy or not, at least it could be investigated. Get the dart tested and see if there were any prints on that rope. Too bad she had wiped her car down. She felt hopeful for the first time in six months.

Her cell phone beeped again. Probably Britney. Amber worried that if she didn't respond right away, Britney would show up riding on the back of a snowplow, leading the charge to save Amber. But before she could hit send or check her message, the power went out. Along with the internet and all communication with the outside world.

"Damn it! I'll have to send it later, Tiger."

The cat was sprawled in the front window, sleeping. His only response was a slight twitch of his tail.

The landline startled her with a shrill ring, and she dropped her phone as she raced over to answer.

"Hi, Amber, it's Myles. I'm declaring a snow day tomorrow—I've already talked to your boss. So we start working together Tuesday at eight. Does that work for you?"

"Yes. They say it's supposed to continue through the night, but if the roads are cleared, I don't mind coming in."

"No, I'd rather my staff—and you too, Amber—stay off the icy roads. I hear the temperatures are going to drop into the low teens Monday morning." His voice lowered. "I could come to you, and we could talk some more today."

"What about the roads?"

"I'm skilled at driving in the snow and have a truck with a plow on it. I thought the privacy might be nice. No one is going to follow me around today, including the press. No extra ears."

"I would like to talk more, but I have no electricity right now."

"I don't mind that. I have a generator I could bring if you want some lights or your fridge to run."

"I have one in the garage. I'm too lazy to go drag it out and start it up. My aunt had it wired for our fridge, well, microwave, and the downstairs bedroom. You know, the basics. I doubt I have much gas for it. I have wood heat, a propane stove, and some saved water in the bathtub."

"Okay. I can help you with that, and I'll bring some gas."

"Thanks. We usually don't need it cause the power never stays out long—except for that one time it was out for a week. That was a pain with no water." Amber hesitated. "And...I, um...well, I was about to leave a message with a PI when I lost power. I want to get a new pair of eyes to look at this case."

"I bet going without running water was challenging for a week. I completely agree with you that hiring a PI is the next step. I have someone in mind, unless you know this person?"

"No, just from their website. Ex-FBI, works with the police. Sounded like a good fit."

"Yes, that certainly does. We can talk about this when I see you. The company I had in mind is run by a good friend I went to school with. He's an ex-marine and started his own PI firm. He's worked for me in the past, and I've always been satisfied with his work. Besides, I know I can trust him to be discreet. You know, with my position, I must be careful who I trust. You understand, right? I don't want to swoop in and take over, so speak up if anything bothers you, please. You haven't mentioned my connection, have you?"

Amber frowned. Was he really leaving it up to her whether the public knew about her sister or not? "No, I didn't mention you in the email. I wanted to talk to you about it first. All I was going to say, before I lost power, was I wanted to find my sister's killer and check into what's been happening to me. I honestly have no preference in PI, besides the fact that I want one, that is."

There was a long silence, and Amber thought she'd lost him. "What's been happening to you?"

Amber plunged forward with her explanation, hoping he believed her.

His voice boomed through the phone. "A person in a ski mask? Are you kidding me? On the six-month anniversary of Iris? This doesn't sound right. Did you tell the police?"

"I told them that a white SUV was following me, but not about the dart or anything. I did tell my friends, though, and they thought it was just an overactive imagination."

"Well, despite the very short time I've known you, I believe you. You were wise not to touch the end of that dart, and I'm so glad you saved it. Maybe this will lead us to your sister's killer, but if they're coming after you...can you think of any reason for that?"

Amber shook her head. "No, none at all."

"I remember Iris talking about your mom remarrying. She's well off—do you think it could be about that?"

"My mom's money? I barely speak to my mother. Although years ago, I heard her arguing with my stepdad about a will. He wanted her to leave everything to him. Not sure if she made any changes. I would imagine by now she would have. It's not like we're close or anything."

"Well, we can't speculate on that, but I want it looked into now that I've heard this. Iris didn't like to talk about her past, but she did share with me some things about your mother and stepfather. This concerns me."

"It concerns me too, but I can't see it having anything to do with my mom. I don't want anything from her, including an inheritance."

She heard what sounded like a chair tipping over and then shuffling paper.

"Hello? Myles? Are you okay?"

"I'm sorry. I spilled my coffee. With someone coming after you, I have to consider that it might be the same person who killed Iris. If it isn't your family, and I'm not taking that off the table yet, another possibility is one of those crazy threats I get. No one claimed responsibility for Iris which I am sure they would if it was related to me. Only Clark and my bodyguard, who I completely trust, knew I wanted to speak with you, and why. If someone else found out about Iris and my intended meeting, it *might* explain why you are a target now."

Amber frowned. "Well, I could be completely wrong about what happened in the parking garage, as my friends suggested. It could just be a strange coincidence that—"

He quickly cut her off. "I don't think you're wrong. I've learned that when there are too many coincidences, it's time to investigate. I'm going to call my PI buddy right after I hang up and get him working on this and then get you some full-time security until we figure this out. Don't even think of arguing with me on this point. It's for Iris."

"I wasn't going to argue, but I feel safe here with all the snow. I don't think anyone will be prowling around my house. I think this can wait."

"No. If something happened to you too, I'm not sure I could live with myself. I couldn't save the woman I loved, but I can sure save the person she loved. You will let me do that, won't you?"

"Well, yeah, I guess."

"Good. Then I'll call you back in a while and let you know what's going on. Keep that dart and rope in a safe place. They might be important. In the meantime, make sure you don't let in anyone that you don't know."

"I won't. Oh, good."

"What?"

"The power just came back on." Amber watched the computer start up.

"I don't like the idea of you without power. Let's hope it stays on."

"That's my hope. Don't worry. I'll be fine."

"I can't help but worry. Please keep your doors and windows locked. I'll call you right before I come over. Unless your line is down, then I'll show up. Bye."

"Wait—" Amber sighed loudly, hearing the click.

Myles said he wanted to keep her safe, but now, instead of feeling relief, she felt on edge. What if she had misjudged him and trusted the wrong person?

She gulped as the power went out again. She wasn't so sure she'd answer the phone or trust his PI. She wished she hadn't told him about the dart and the rope. If he were the killer, he would want them back. Maybe she should hide them for now. No, she was being ridiculous. Wasn't she? How could a public figure get away with murder?

She shivered and started a fire with ease. She suddenly felt a pres-

83

ence next to her, and a whiff of gardenia startled her. She snapped her head around, but there was no one there. Yet the smell lingered. Her sister's favorite perfume. She felt disappointed not to see a ghostly outline but relieved at the same time. The fire crackled, triggering a memory.

"You know I'd freeze to death if I had to depend on starting a fire, sis," Iris had joked.

"Lucky for you, I know what I'm doing. Here, watch me."

Iris shook her head. "We're very lucky to have each other to depend on. You stick to the fires, and I'll do the baking. I think it's an even trade."

"It is." Amber laughed. Her sister joined in. What she wouldn't do to hear that high chirrup of a laugh again.

Amber would have done anything for her sister, and now she was going to find her killer, even if it was the man she had loved and trusted. *Especially* if it was the man she had fallen in love with.

With the power out, there was nothing else she could do. She grabbed her e-reader and settled in by the fire. Her attention wasn't on the story, though, as she watched the large flakes continue to weigh down the landscape. It was hypnotic, and at least it didn't remind her of tears now. Soon the white spectacle lured her into sleep.

Amber was in midair, like in her old nightmares, but this time she wasn't falling into the black thing with red eyes. The thing was plunging with her, and she felt no fear. Its smile didn't alarm her this time. Then its red mouth began moving, but she couldn't hear what it was saying.

"What are you trying to tell me?"

She heard it speak. "Be careful, Amber. Evil lies."

A loud bang tore her out of the dream, or had that been a part of it? She rubbed her eyes and stretched, thinking about the message.

"Evil lies? What does that mean?"

Another bang forced her into action. It was a loud knock at the front door. What if the dream had been warning her about who was behind the door? Shaking her head to clear it, she glanced out the front window and didn't see a white SUV. The roads weren't plowed yet, so it probably wasn't Myles. She reached for the doorknob and then hesitated. Did she believe the dream meant something?

She closed her eyes and sent up a quick prayer of protection from evil she'd learned from her aunt. She smoothed down her hair and, out of habit, glanced around the house, making sure it was presentable. Then a small frown crossed her face. She didn't believe evil would come to her front door and knock, or did she? No, more likely it was Mrs. Jones. She peered through the peephole.

It wasn't Mrs. Jones, but it was her handsome new neighbor, Eli. He was moving side to side like he was cold, but it reminded her of a little kid who had to use the bathroom. In ungloved hands that were red from the chill was a pie. It was Mrs. Jones's famous Dutch apple pie in her recognizable blue-flowered pie dish. Could she trust her new neighbor, the famous author? A lot of her issues had started when he moved in, but he hadn't been here when her sister was killed. That was the deciding factor for opening the door.

"Why are you walking around in a snowstorm with a pie?" Amber asked with a small smile.

"I don't mean to intrude, but I'm freezing with my power out. I used up what little wood that had been left behind, including two bundles I bought at the store for an exorbitant price yesterday. I thought I'd be okay until next week when I get some delivered. Guess not. I was going to ask to borrow some wood, but wood isn't like a cup of sugar. My only hope was I could share some pie with you, and you could share some heat with me. Mrs. Jones brought it over this morning to welcome me. Sweet lady, and I let her know about the unwanted SUV in our neighborhood. She's keeping an eye out for it too. Yes, I know I could have gone over to her house, but truthfully..." Eli took a deep breath and continued. "I wanted to talk to you again." He let out a loud exhale and smiled. A slight blush crossed his face as he held her gaze.

Amber laughed, returning the blush, and waved him in. "You aren't intruding at all. Sorry it took me so long to get to the door. I'm glad you let Mrs. Jones know, thanks. I tried to call her last night, but she doesn't always answer her phone or check her messages."

"You're welcome." Eli stood awkwardly in the entrance after she shut the door.

"Go get warm by the fire. You're in for a treat—Mrs. Jones makes the best pies, especially her apple. You want a piece now?"

"I meant it for a gift."

"I'm not going to eat the entire pie by myself. I insist you help me." She held out her hands.

He quickly handed it over and offered her that sweet, crooked grin again, "Okay, you talked me into a piece. Oh, I saw that bear prowling around your house again last night." He rubbed his hands together while he blew on them.

"Again? You know, most people are afraid of them, but I would love to have one, you know, live with me. So I don't mind one hanging around."

Eli grinned. "A pet bear? I can see that. I'm sure he's found a snack and is heading back to sleep."

"Yes, a nice garbage can to feast on."

"Or a picnic basket."

Amber laughed. "Yup."

She watched Eli settle on the floor by the fire with his back against the side of the couch, just as she liked to do, as she sliced through the crumbly top into the juicy apple filling. Tiger jumped down from the windowsill. He slowly circled Eli before going in for an investigative sniff.

"Hey, kitty."

The cat settled in, allowing Eli to pet him. Tiger's stamp of approval was a good sign. Amber carefully put a huge slice of pie on her best china for Eli and cut a smaller one for herself. Stupid to bring out the good plates, but how often did she have company? Good-looking company at that. She admired the way his jeans fit him. She pasted on a huge smile and was handing him the plate when she tripped over Tiger, who had moved to the other side of him. She landed right in Eli's lap with an *oomph*.

"Oh! I didn't—" she choked out, turning red.

"No, you didn't. Nice landing—and great service, ma'am." His brown eyes twinkled.

"Sorry, I misjudged where Tiger was. He does blend into the shadows. Not sure how I managed not to drop the pie everywhere."

"It's my catching skills. I take full credit for that." He grinned and then burst out laughing.

She joined in the laughter without getting up, and he found her gaze. His eyes wouldn't let go of hers. She felt her pulse quicken and held her breath. Was he going to kiss her? He gave her a lopsided grin and brushed her hair off her face. He smelled of cedar and sandalwood. It was intoxicating.

She felt her cheeks redden more as he leaned toward her. She turned away and blurted out the first thing that came to mind. "I give you full credit. Writer's hands, I suppose?"

"Yes, all that typing makes me respond to falling women with lightning speed. No, truthfully, I'm equally as clumsy."

Amber set the plates down on the coffee table and scooted off his lap onto the floor next to him. "Well, um, thanks for the catch." She glared at the offending cat, who didn't even have the good grace to look ashamed.

They enjoyed the pie quietly next to each other. She'd always loved how tart the apples were against the sweet topping with the addition of cinnamon and a flaky, buttery crust. It really did melt in her mouth. Every time her arm bumped his, she felt a bolt of electricity run through her. She hoped he felt it too because she never did things like this. She could see herself coming home to him every night and cuddling next to the fire. That was something her sister always did, jump right into a relationship, but not her. Amber had been avoiding relationships her entire life after being disappointed so many times. She pulled back until they weren't touching. He looked up at her inquiringly, but she ignored it. The comfortable moment was gone.

"What do you think? Good, huh?"

"Best apple pie I've ever had. You were right."

"Told you. Are you working on anything special?" She put her empty plate down and made sure her teeth were crumb free.

He pushed the last bite off his plate into his mouth and set his plate on top of hers. How could he make that look so sexy?

"I'm working on two things, actually, fiction and nonfiction. My usual mystery, but I want to write about the senator too. He's the most interesting candidate we've had in a very long time, don't you think?"

Uh oh. Was this what all this was about? Her meeting with Myles and a book? She moved away from him, picking up the plates.

"Yes, very interesting." She deposited them in the sink, feeling like she was going to throw up. She'd almost thrown herself at him, and he was here to get information.

"Did I say something wrong?" His dark eyes followed her.

"What? No. I just...I have a lot on my mind." She added the dishes to the dishwasher even though she couldn't run it.

"I'm sorry. Is there something I can do?"

Amber shook her head in response.

He twisted around more, studying her. She did her best to ignore him—and those bulging arm muscles that weren't from typing. He worked out, but she knew that from his bio, also that his older sister had raised him after their parents had died in a plane that his father had built. It ran out of gas and crashed into the Pacific Ocean on its maiden voyage. He had been born and raised in the Bay Area and never married. Oh, and he liked animals, or at least he put them in his books. That was all she knew about him, really—what he wanted his readers to know.

Amber used a towel to wipe off the counters as Eli began talking again. "Mrs. Jones is very talkative. She, um...told me about what happened, you know, with your sister. I'm sorry. I know it's tough to lose loved ones."

Amber couldn't answer. Her eyes overflowed with tears as she dropped the towel on the floor. Eli jumped up and grabbed it. She turned away from him, but he pulled her into a comforting hug. That was all it took for the tears to overwhelm her. He held her tightly as her trust flowed back. She breathed in his comforting aroma, now mixed with apple pie. It was a soothing combination. She hadn't felt this comfortable in a simple hug since her aunt had died. At that moment she felt like she had known him her whole life, which sounded exactly like her sister's romantic outlook, not her own realistic one.

She pulled away and immediately regretted losing his heat as she wiped away the tears. His eyes held the warmth that was lacking in her life. She was falling for him fast. She hoped she wouldn't regret it as she turned up her face to his. He held back, studying her quietly, until she began to feel like an awkward teen. She was about to pull away when he leaned in and gently kissed her. His soft lips encompassed hers like they belonged together. Later she would figure it out. Right now, she needed this, even if it was just for a night. Instead of the kiss intensifying, as she'd hoped, he pulled away from her with a smile and wrapped his arms around her. Then he guided her back to the fire, where they sank back down together.

She leaned into him, completely content, but felt him studying her.

Finally he spoke. "I hadn't planned on doing that yet. I got lost in those eyes of yours—they're the same color as Lake Tahoe."

"My aunt used to tell me that. The deepest blue she'd ever seen." Amber blushed.

Eli pushed a lock of blond hair behind her ear and then ran his finger down her cheek, sending a shiver through her body, "They are. And I only meant to comfort you, but I'm glad it happened."

"I'm not complaining, and it was very comforting," Amber replied, not recognizing the flirtatious tone in her voice.

"I was hoping it would trigger more than comfort." Eli tilted her chin up toward him.

"It did," she murmured and reluctantly tore her gaze away from his.

"Good. I'm sorry I brought up your sister and upset you." He stroked her arm and stretched his legs out straight in front of him. The moment, again, was gone.

"I don't mind talking about Iris. It keeps her memory alive, and besides, I need to know…" A slight frown crossed her face before she could prevent it.

Eli's eyebrows wove together. "What do you need to know?"

Amber told him everything. Well, everything except her sister dating Myles. She didn't want that in his book. But she did tell him Iris worked for Myles and he was going to help find her killer.

"Well, I'm glad the senator is helping, but I don't like the sound of any of this." His face took on deep worry lines as he ran his fingers through his hair.

"Yeah, well, about the senator…" She started to tell him her concerns about Myles's motives, but she wasn't sure how she could without mentioning her sister. She wanted to trust Eli completely, but at that moment, she didn't completely trust anyone.

"What?" Eli asked. "If you're worried about saying anything about the senator to me because I'm writing a book, I'll keep anything you tell me out of it, if that's what you want. I'm here for you, not a book."

Amber nodded, relieved. "Yeah, well, this is personal. Let me talk to him. Yes, I'd appreciate some things not coming out. You'll understand more when I can explain it to you."

Eli took her hand. "You're making me even more concerned, but I'm glad I'm here. You shouldn't be alone. As for the senator, I promise you I won't print anything that will hurt you. I'm not even sure I want to write a book like this. It was just an idea since I was living in his hometown and my sister does nothing but talk about how wonderful he is."

"Well, I don't want to stop you from writing a book. I promise we'll talk more about this later. You should know, though, that—" She was about to tell him Myles might be on his way when the doorbell rang. Too late—he would find out now.

Eli jumped up. "Who could that be? Do you think Mrs. Jones is checking up on us?"

She shrugged as he pulled her standing. "Maybe."

"Well, with what's going on, let me get it." He pushed past her and threw the door open.

CHAPTER 10

$\mathcal{N}$ester had barely been able to repress swirling out of control after Zelina confirmed she'd heard him. He had to immediately acknowledge the new arrivals with a privileged smirk, to which they returned a respectful nod. They were wiser than youthful Geo, who hadn't the sense to greet an elder with respect. Too bad Nester had been so involved with the winged one that he'd let that snub pass unchallenged, but he had established his rank during the hunt.

Wise or foolish, evildwels would be the end of him, not the winged ones. He knew his time was extremely limited. The most important thing was to remain calm so his mist swirled slowly in the ordinary evildwel fashion. It took all his focus to keep it flowing, to appear normal. He followed Amber and Zelina around, wishing he could do more for the human. It was hard not to talk to Zelina.

The two evildwels left, most likely to feed, and the host was engaged elsewhere. He heard Zelina's voice in his mind.

"It will be soon, Nester. This may be our only chance to talk. Follow me."

He glanced at Eli at the door. "What if Amber needs us?"

"She will be okay for now. Come on."

Zelina's wings opened, and he followed behind her the best he could. He could tell he was slowing her down, but at least they got out of there without being seen. He knew those two evildwels would return, and more would follow. His kind couldn't help but be there for large-scale pain and suffering.

Zelina landed on a snowdrift by the lake and put a finger to her lips. The pristine snow had covered the landscape, making it glow almost as bright as the winged one. Nester had a flash of that newly fallen snow being covered in the blood of the innocent, like the poor homeless man Geo killed with such glee. What if Zelina couldn't stop what was coming? How could she help that girl? What could he do? He was bursting with questions but remained quiet. He followed Zelina's gaze, but all he saw were clouds.

Zelina turned to him and nodded. "It is safe here. I will do whatever I can. So will you. I did not want to take any extra chances, especially when those evildwels arrived. I was worried you would grow frustrated and try to communicate. Thank you for being so patient. Do you mind if we hold off the rest of this conversation until Ed and Thomas arrive? That way, we are all, as the humans call it, on the same page."

Nester inched closer to her to see if the expected pain would hit. It didn't, and she showed no signs of it either. "Yes, of course. I want to be on the same page. I'm so glad you heard what I was saying. I was worried you wouldn't have listened if I'd just approached you and spoken out loud like this."

"Yes, I am not sure how I would have received that. I admit it startled me when I heard your first thoughts. I almost blocked them, but then I understood you meant no harm. After you tried to warn Amber in her dream, I knew you were different. I have learned a lot from you —thank you. And Nester, I am sorry you have gone through this alone, but you are not alone anymore."

"Thank you. I got the idea from you to enter the dream. And it feels very strange to say this, but I feel like you're a friend, not my enemy."

Zelina reached out and touched his darkness. The dark mist

responded with a flash of bright light that pleasantly coursed through him. Nester had no idea what to make of it, but it brought a smile to Zelina's face, "It is never strange to embrace a friend. Good will always win over evil. I believe that is what is happening to you."

"Good wins over evil?" Nester studied the white sparkle floating around his dark mist.

"Exactly."

Zelina pulled away, and the lightness was gone as the black closed over it. She studied her hand for a moment and brought it back to her side, returning her gaze to the heavy clouds. All he saw was a dark gray sky ready to dump more whiteness. Zelina's touch soothed him. He wanted to figure out how to keep that packed tightly inside.

She smiled at Nester and pushed her long black hair off her brow. "Friends need to trust each other, Nester. It is the only way this will work. Just know that I will do all I can for you. If this works out, then we may have a choice in dealing with your kind—I mean other evildwels."

A bright flash of light lit up the sky, and then Ed appeared.

"I was beginning to worry that you would not be able to make it. I want you to meet Nester."

"I got here as soon as I could after your summons." Ed's eyes widened when he took in Nester. "What the...when did we start hanging out with misty monsters?"

"Right now is when." Zelina raised her eyebrows and pursed her lips together.

"Okay, well...great," Ed replied with a smirk. Nester recognized he was being sarcastic. Evildwels had that emotion.

Nester gave him his best smile. "I admire what you've done, Ed. I'm pleased to meet you."

"You admire...what is going on, Zelina?" Ed asked, the smirk disappearing under his confusion.

Zelina shook her head. "Hang on, Ed. I will explain it all when Thomas gets here. Let me go check if he can attend this." Zelina was suddenly gone, leaving Ed and Nester alone.

"I can't wait to hear the explanation," Ed mumbled, squinting at

Nester.

Nester's mist took off in all directions. He had to pull it all back in, but he saw it was even lighter this time. Soon he wouldn't have a bit of darkness left, and any evildwel would know there was something wrong with him. He knew Ed was observing his issue with a suppressed smile as he folded his arms and leaned against a tree. Nester hoped they would be—well, friends.

As soon as Nester got his mist under control, he tried talking to Ed. "I know we've been your enemy. You have no good reason to trust me."

"No, you're right. I don't. Zelina seems to. If she vouches for you, well, I guess I'll try to understand what's going on."

"Thank you," Nester felt some encouragement. "You should know I've changed enough to where I'm comfortable around winged ones as much as they're comfortable around me."

"Yeah, I noticed she seemed okay around you. I've never seen an evildwel's mist swirl like that before."

"I doubt we have time for the explanation, but something is wrong with me. I feel empathy, and, well...I did tell Zelina everything I could."

Ed stood up and uncrossed his arms. "Well, misty-man, it sounds like you might be different. I guess we'll see what she has in mind."

A flash lit up the sky like lightning, and soon the light was next to them. Zelina and the winged one named Thomas came out of it. Thomas was frowning at Nester.

"This is Nester. We do not have time for the complete story right now. All you need to know is he wants to help us," Zelina said.

"What?" Thomas burst out laughing and hit his thigh. "Since when do you joke around?"

Ed held his hands up. "She's not joking. I can feel something is wrong with this one. Misty-man here isn't like the others."

Zelina put her hands on her hips and planted her sandaled feet in the snow. "Ed is right, and I am not joking. Nester has developed compassion and came to me for help. We will give him help, but we cannot let the other evildwels know."

"You sure this is not a trick?" Thomas frowned deeply at Nester.

Zelina took Thomas's hand and placed it on Nester. "As sure as I can be."

"Huh?" was all Thomas could get out as his mouth swung open. His green eyes were pinned on the blackness swirled around his hand. He watched it lighten. As soon as Zelina released him, he pulled away, studying his hand.

Nester was eager to impress after the dose of whatever he was getting from the winged ones coursed through him. "I am very glad to meet you, Thomas. I wish we didn't have to sneak off and have this rushed conversation with Amber in danger."

Thomas rubbed his hands together and gave Ed a discreet eyeroll out of Zelina's sight. Ed's smile turned back into a smirk. Nester knew he had his work cut out to earn their trust. Thomas raised his eyebrows at Nester and shook his head. "That was…bizarre, and yes, Nester, you do have your work cut out for you, I agree."

Nester offered a small smile. He needed to remember to control his thoughts around these winged ones. "I accept that."

Zelina clapped her hands together like she was teaching a classroom of children. Thomas jumped a little. "We do not have time for any of this. You will have to trust me. We have to focus on keeping Amber safe, and that includes Nester now, all right?" She sent a scathing look toward Thomas and Ed.

"Yes," they both mumbled like young schoolboys.

"Thank you." Nester held back a smile.

Zelina stood tall and expanded her green wings. They reflected against the falling snow, making it look like green glitter. "Do not thank me yet, Nester. I can read you, and you are fighting yourself. That battle will have to wait, and I will try to help you. I need you to play your part in this. Try always to follow my lead."

Zelina paused as her eyes seemed to bore inside Nester like that tick that had found its way into one of his hosts. It was a bit unnerving. He mumbled, "I will."

Zelina seemed satisfied and then turned her attention to the others. "Understood, everyone?"

Thomas nodded while Ed responded. "Understood. If you say he's good, well, then he's good."

Zelina smoothed her flowing gown while she gave the area a quick scan. "Ed, I need you to keep an eye on the evildwel who killed Iris. Maybe you can do what you do best when we are all there, but something is different about that one. Not an elder but…stronger somehow. So be careful."

"Got it."

"Thomas, you will be helping me with the other area of this issue, which I will explain in a moment." Zelina held his gaze until he nodded back to her. Nester was disappointed he couldn't hear them and felt left out. Zelina spoke again, with the confidence of a five-star general. "Ed, one more thing. Even if you can evict this evildwel, the human must be stopped too."

"I will do my best with the misty monster and horrible human."

"I know you will. Nester, you will stick close by me. Later I will update everyone on the full story you told me, and maybe we can find a solution for you."

"I thank you for that. I wish…well, that I knew what I was looking for."

"So do I. I am not even sure who I would trust in the angel world right now regarding you besides Thomas or Ed, but I might have to go on faith."

"Thanks. Just give me some time to get used to this situation," Thomas added.

Ed nodded. "Ditto."

"Thank you. That is all I ask from you right now. Thomas, you can communicate with Nester like another angel, but use that only in an emergency until we figure this all out."

"He can—okay, I understand. Can the other evildwels hear us now too?" Thomas studied Nester with an intensity that was making it difficult to keep his mist intact.

"No. He is not like them anymore."

Thomas nodded and then frowned, watching Nester's mist lighten and then swirl outward.

Zelina reached out, and a calm white glow infused him, slowing it all down. "Hang on. You need to be careful around all those evildwels when we get back. I cannot do this for you then. Try centering yourself, and repeat, 'I am not alone anymore.' We are here for you. If it ever gets to that point, well, come to me. I will repel them for you, but I would rather not do that."

Nester's swirls went back to the normal flow. "I understand and will do my best. Thank you."

"You are welcome."

Thomas blurted out, "I wish Olive was here. She can be trusted and would want to help."

Zelina smiled. "I agree with you. She is another angel I can add to my list of trust. She is an extraordinarily strong and capable angel. I am glad you two are together. She is good for you."

"Thanks." Thomas blushed and looked away. "She is with a child who needed her to cross over. It is her time. Of course, you know that."

"I don't. What's going on, dude?" Ed asked.

Zelina shrugged, so Thomas continued. "Olive has to help a little girl, Carrie or she would be with us. She is such a beautiful young soul, but her time is ending. The cancer is spreading."

"Bummer." Ed shook his head.

"Yes, it is a bummer, Ed. Olive then might have another soul to help cross and then help us before she can go back to that family. Everything is tied into this situation, unfortunately. Olive will have to keep an eye on Carrie's brother. Robert is headed in a bad direction by hanging around the wrong crowd. Unless this works out—then there might be hope."

Thomas's eyebrows went up. "Poor kid. You are saying that the little girl and Olive's next crossover are all linked to Amber somehow?"

"Yes. You will understand soon. If Amber writes her article, it will be an inspiration to Robert and might encourage better choices. Of course, that is completely his decision, but no family should lose both their children if we can help it. Right now, we have a chance to make this a better world for all children to exist in by keeping Amber alive —if we can."

Ed kicked the snow, with no effect. "Well, what do you want us to do? I assume you have something in mind."

Zelina scanned the landscape again and replied in a hushed tone. "It is complicated, and we each have our part to play. You must understand, if Senator Stroud loses the election, we will be left with a man who will push that destructive war button based on pride. So many will die on both sides, and society will go backward then. I am talking about World War III in the worst way. A dictator will rise from these ashes, or the man who pushed the button and those who survive will have to battle illness. Well, I would rather not focus on that outcome." Zelina shuddered.

"You're saying Amber prevents a world war?" Ed asked, rubbing his face.

"Yes. A single human can affect so many. That is why each individual is so important. I wished they realized that." Zelina sighed.

"Wow." Ed shook his head and looked away.

Thomas was scanning the tree line. "Wow is right. I knew this was important, but not that important. Maybe having an evildwel on our side is just what we need."

"I was thinking the very same thing. Ed, would you mind keeping an eye on Nester? Thomas and I will be right back. We are going to check on Amber and see what we are up against."

"Shouldn't we go back with you?" Nester's mist began to swirl out of control again.

Zelina reached out, calming him. "I hate to say this, but you might need to feed to get through. Remember to keep that calm. Ed?" Zelina nodded at him.

"Gotcha." Ed nodded back.

Zelina and Thomas fully extended their wings. Nester took in their beauty like a feeding. Maybe he wouldn't have to feed on the dying anymore, but the good feeling left with the winged ones, and then he was filled with doubt. Whatever was happening to him was coming on quicker now, and he hoped he would be able to help his new friends.

"Dude. You're a mess."

"Yes, I am," Nester admitted, finally reining his energy back in.

Ed laughed and shrugged. Although he was in jeans and a red plaid shirt and looked human, he was a spirit. He kept his humanness even in death. What was Nester becoming? He was already like a spirit in some ways. What would happen if he died?

Ed grimaced as Nester felt his swirl going out of control again. "No idea, dude. Kind of creepy to think about, but so you know, I don't eat. You need to eat bad feelings. So you aren't one of us, dead or alive."

Nester's red mouth flew open as he forced his swirl under control.

"Yeah, I can read minds like the angels now, misty-man. Sorry I didn't mention that sooner, but I wanted to see what you were about. It's a recent upgrade. Maybe I should stop calling you misty-man now that you're hanging out with us?"

Nester reminded himself that he wasn't alone, and his swirl returned to normal. "I don't mind being called misty man. It's rather funny if you think about it."

"Yeah, I'm hilarious. Even get Zelina to smile here and there."

"I've seen that. I watched you help your family. I figured if you could change, why couldn't I?"

"You've been hanging around us? Surprised I didn't notice."

"I was careful."

"Yeah, well, cool, but you still feed on fear and anger."

"I do, Ed. But I don't cause the pain or fear."

"Have you tried feeding on love?"

"Feed on love? No, it used to repel me, although Zelina's touch helps my swirl, so maybe I can. The worst it can do to me is give me a good sting, like insects do humans."

Ed frowned. "Yeah, give it a try sometime, misty-man—just not right now. You know Zelina is putting a lot of trust in you."

"I understand, and I'm glad Zelina has such loyalty around her."

"She's one of the best angels there is. I'm not sure this is the time to help a stray evildwel, but as long as you realize Amber is much more important than you, I'm cool with it."

"Well, I don't want to die, but I'm willing to do what I can to help all of you. The other evildwels would kill me if they knew."

"That doesn't surprise me. I've had one and been inside them. It's horrible."

"It's normal for an evildwel. Or it was—now I don't know."

"You stay loyal to Zelina, you hear, and we're good. If not, I'll let your evildwel buddies know you've been helping us. Got it?" Ed grinned.

"I got it. Thank you."

Ed chuckled and smoothed his hair back. "You're welcome, misty-man."

Zelina and Thomas were suddenly in front of them in a bright flash.

"The host is making a move soon. The evildwels are gathering. They know what these next few hours mean. The difference between millions of people dying or not."

"It is going to be a long shot, but that has never stopped us before." Thomas's gaze was behind them, searching.

Nester looked behind him but didn't see anything. "Never under-estimate an evildwel, even a young one like Geo. Sometimes they can fool you."

"Well, if you offered yourself to your buddies as a traitor, I could get that dark cloud from its host." Ed added a wink.

"No, Ed, that is *not* the plan." Zelina arched her brow.

"I know, I was just kidding with our new evildwel buddy, right, Nester?"

"Right. I understood, but I will do what is best, I promise." Nester's mist started swirling out of control again.

Zelina reached out and soothed him again. "We are not asking that you sacrifice yourself. You do need to go back and be around your kind. Can you do that?"

Nester hesitated. "I will do what I need to."

Zelina looked away. "Good. Try to keep your thoughts to a minimum. Do your best to distract Geo if you can."

"Geo is pretty full of himself. I could play on that."

"Any help is always welcome, misty-man."

Thomas tugged at his gown. "Olive needs me before she goes to her next human."

Zelina nodded grimly. "She does. It is time. Then I need you right back here. Your talent for herding humans might be useful."

"This is all very cryptic, as always. I'm sure getting Britney and the work buddies to the garage to save Amber is what she's referring to." Ed rolled his eyes at Thomas.

"Yes, that is one thing I'm implying, and it worked. Thank you for clarifying for me."

Thomas started to smile, but then it faded away when Zelina glowered. He turned his attention to Nester. "You do the right thing, and we do the same for you, understand?"

He would have sounded like Ed if he had added a "dude" at the end, "I do, thank—"

Zelina held her hand up. "Go, Thomas. We have this under control."

Thomas frowned as he opened his navy wings and disappeared in a bright flash.

"Who will Thomas be herding this time?" Ed asked.

Zelina shook her head. "It pertains to the young girl and her brother, keeping them together at the end, but it will play out as it does, of course. I sense something. Let us go back to communicating with thoughts."

Ed glanced around. "Sure, Zelina. And as for it playing out, I'm sure it will. It always does, but I wish...Well, never mind."

"Did you wish for a direct answer, Ed?"

"Well, one can hope."

"Yes, one can and should, but that information is not necessary now."

Nester felt calm for the first time as his mist slowed down to normal motion. He was on the right side finally. "I think I'm beginning to understand."

Zelina looked at him, pursing her lips together. "Good, because evildwels have almost tipped the scales in their favor here on this planet. There was already evil here that we were busy fighting, and evildwels just added to it. If we do not win this battle, I am afraid it will take decades for humans to recover—if they do. Humans are now fighting each other without even knowing the real enemy."

"Yes, I understand."

She smiled, and it calmed Nester.

Ed sighed as the snow continued to fall around them without landing on them. "So weird to have misty-man in my thoughts. It will take some getting used to. If Amber dies, then all hope is gone, and there's no one else?"

Zelina's smile turned into a deep grimace. "Hope is never completely gone. But her death will trigger events that we may not be able to counter."

Ed held out his hand, palm up, and raised his eyebrows in a way that would be disrespectful coming from anyone else. "You aren't sure what will happen if she dies or aren't going to say anymore?"

"I cannot say anymore. It is too fluid. We all must remember that love is stronger than hate. That is our best weapon here. Nester, it would do you some good to reflect on what love is. You have seen it enough and felt it from us. Use that. You have acted on it before—I have seen you."

"I have?"

"You have."

"Um, misty-man shouldn't show up with us, should he?"

Nester spoke up. "No. I will come after I've fed."

"Hopefully, you won't need to feed on fear anymore after this. Right now, I think you should do what you need to so you are at your best." Zelina scanned the blue lake and tree line.

"I don't want to, but I feel weak," Nester admitted.

"I know. If I could change that, I would. But I have been able to help you too. You are feeding on both sides right now."

"This gets weirder and weirder." Ed shook his head.

"Yes, it does. Thank you for trusting me, Zelina."

"I have faith in you."

Zelina and Ed disappeared in a flash of light, leaving Nester standing alone in the snow. He jumped into action, quickly finding a man beating his wife two blocks away, just as he had done many times before. This time was fatal. The man had a weak evildwel that Nestor didn't recognize. The young one bowed to him. They finished feeding together as a winged one guided the woman away. He made sure not to acknowledge its presence.

The young evildwel finally spoke. "I thought you would be there with the rest of them. I'd be there now, but I had to finish this."

"I have been. I needed to feed, and you provided me with that. That was a weak death. Barely a meal for us. I suggest you hurry here."

"Thank you, Nester. I will."

Nester wondered if it would help to kill this evildwel, but he couldn't do it. He didn't want to kill anything anymore. The fear strengthened him yet made him feel sick, which was tearing him apart.

"Let the man kill himself."

The younger evildwel smiled. "I will. Then we can go."

Nester concentrated on keeping control. "We can."

Although Nester felt some guilt, after what the man had done to his wife, he was either going to jail or dying. He might get more sympathy on Earth than from the winged ones, though. Nester turned away when the man put his gun to his forehead. The death wouldn't be immediate. The metallic smell of the blood made him feel sick. His mist threatened to whirl out of control, so he rushed out of the room, with the young evildwel following. He focused on Zelina's face and her words. He was able to pull his swirl back in. He felt an infusion of calm course through him as he stood by a group of young evildwels. They were all intently watching what was going on in the house. Nester could feel the excitement coming from this pack, so much like the one he had been a part of for so long. He quivered, feeling sick again. He hoped he could help the winged ones, but he couldn't feel that hope at the moment.

CHAPTER 11

*A*mber leaped up to follow Eli to the door, fully expecting it to be Myles.

"Can I help you?" Amber heard Eli ask in a loud businesslike tone that indicated it wasn't someone he recognized.

A muffled voice replied, "Perhaps I am at the wrong house? I'm looking for Amber Dodges."

The voice didn't trigger who it might be. Amber peeked around Eli's wide shoulders and trim, muscular body, but all she could see was a puffy black coat with the hood pulled up, a scarf wrapped around the lower face, and oddly large white sunglasses. Eli glanced over his shoulder with a reassuring smile and wink to Amber, then turned back to the man at the door.

"You have the right place. With the storm and power out, I offered to answer her door."

"Oh, well, yes. Can't be too careful of people you don't know." The man at the door mumbled. Amber felt a chill shoot through her, and it wasn't from the door being open. The statement sounded like a threat or warning to her. Who should she be afraid of?

Eli nodded, and his body tensed like he was ready to defend her. That felt nice. He emphasized each word. "No…you…can't." The man at her door pulled off his sunglasses, and she realized who it was. Before she could speak, Eli asked, "Hey, didn't I see you with Senator Stroud?"

He pushed down his hood and unwound his scarf. "Yes, sorry. I should have introduced myself at once. I'm Clark Mason, his assistant. I do remember seeing you at the café. Can't stand the cold, even though I grew up in Minnesota. And the snow glare is the worst part of it." He offered a weak smile. His clear gray eyes met Amber's.

Eli held his hand out with a lopsided grin. "You do look warm. I'm Eli Reynolds, Amber's new next-door neighbor. I lack wood, and Amber graciously allowed me to stay warm in her home."

Amber watched the men shake hands as her muscles relaxed. Myles probably sent him or was meeting him here. Maybe Clark could help.

"Please come in out of the cold," Amber called as Eli stepped back.

Clark stomped his snowy boots before stepping inside. He quickly removed them and set them neatly by the door as Eli closed it. "The senator sent me ahead. I tried to call, but your phone line is dead." Red-faced, he rubbed his hands together. "I'm sorry to intrude. I should have waited in my truck for the senator—if he can even make it. I could still do that. My truck has heated seats." How could she ever have been afraid of Clark "Kent"? She suppressed a grin as he tried to fix his hat hair.

"You aren't intruding, Clark. Don't be silly. You aren't going to wait in your truck. Come in by the fire and warm up."

"Let me take your coat, and it can dry out by the fire." Eli advanced on the man with his hand extended.

Clark took a step back, holding his hand up while shaking his head. His red cheeks burned brightly against his dark hair. "No, thank you. I can hang up my coat. Please don't go to any trouble for me."

Eli retracted his hand and smiled. "No trouble on my part. Maybe you could use one of these kitchen chairs to hang your coat and scarf. Would you mind, Amber?"

"No, I don't mind at all. Great suggestion."

She could easily see Eli answering her door every day, and he was certainly a better host than she was. She grabbed a wooden chair and placed it by the stove. "Here you go. That will dry it fast."

"Yes, thank you." Clark sat down on the offered kitchen chair and pulled off an extra pair of socks. He looked different out of his suit and in green Dockers topped off with an awful lime-colored sweater. She caught Eli's gaze, and he raised an eyebrow at her in response.

"Do you mind if I use your restroom? It was a long drive in this weather," Clark asked. Although he had big shoulders, and was the same height as Eli, Clark seemed oddly frail to her. He was almost cute, but his personality—or lack thereof—made him the type that would end up in the friend zone.

"Sure, it's right down the hall on your left."

Clark met Eli's gaze. Neither looked away. Maybe she was wrong about the man. He didn't seem weak at that moment. They seemed like two dogs meeting for the first time trying to see who was the alpha. Too much testosterone for her taste, but it passed quickly, like it had never happened, as Clark padded down the hall.

"Clark?" she called. "We were enjoying some apple pie. Would you like a piece?"

"I would enjoy that very much, thank you," Clark replied and disappeared into the bathroom.

Eli shrugged at her and mouthed the word *unusual*. She agreed with that assessment of him, but she wrinkled her nose in return. Was Eli feeling a bit jealous already?

"I'll get him a piece of the pie."

"Thanks. How do you feel about hot chocolate?"

"That sounds good to me right now."

"Deal, and Eli? I'm not interested," she whispered.

"In whom?"

"Not sure yet," she continued in a low voice, adding a small shrug while raising her eyebrows.

"We'll see about that later." He winked and moved in front of her.

"I hope so." She was acting so un-Amber, hoping he'd kiss her again even with company in the bathroom. What was she thinking?

He smiled down at her and gently stroked her cheek before stepping back.

"I'd like to take you out on a—" Eli started as the bathroom door swung open.

Clark popped out of the bathroom. Her face reddened, hoping that he hadn't overheard them. Clark seemed—well, she wasn't sure what he seemed.

"I'm going to put a pot of water on the woodstove to make some hot chocolate. Would you like some? Or I have coffee and tea too." Amber jumped into action.

"Hot chocolate sounds perfect today, thanks." Clark ran his fingers through his freshly wetted hair.

"Great! I have some marshmallows if anyone is interested." Amber poured bottled water into a large saucepan. That was the biggest downside of the power outage—limited water. Good thing she'd filled the bathtub with water for other things, including her company's haircare.

"I haven't had that in years. I'd like some marshmallows, please," Clark replied.

"Me too!" Eli added, cutting a large piece of apple pie for Clark. Amber returned to the kitchen and handed him one of her good plates.

Eli smiled at her and added a fork. He presented it to Clark by the fire.

Clark smiled. "Thank you, Eli. Did you bake it?"

Eli grinned. "No. Our neighbor brought it over as a housewarming gift. I'm sure you'll enjoy it much better than if I had baked it." There was that tone that sounded like a challenge again.

Amber cut through their male conversation. "Please sit down and enjoy the pie. The water will be ready soon."

Clark sank onto the couch in front of the fire while Eli quietly picked up the phone and shook his head. No dial tone. He stayed right by her side protectively as she grabbed three cups and poured chocolate mix into them. A matching set with small blue flowers Iris had found at a garage sale. She frowned for a moment. When would it stop hurting?

She heard the woodstove open. Clark was adding wood.

"Thanks, Clark!"

"It's the least I can do for your hospitality, Amber. Beautiful home, by the way. So peaceful. You must love living here. I know I would." He smiled at her.

"Yes, I do love it here, thanks."

"Indeed. It fits you perfectly. A beauty living in beauty." He turned and smiled broadly.

Eli frowned at her, and she almost burst out laughing. No one had been interested in her in months, and now suddenly two men seemed determined to get her attention. Her ego was certainly enjoying all that stroking.

Soon the three of them, Amber in the middle, were sitting on the couch quietly, drinking hot chocolate.

Clark set his cup down and glanced out the window. "I was hoping we could go over a few things on your computer, but that's not going to happen with the power out. Well, I hear the snowplow, so that's my cue to head home."

Amber glanced at Eli, who was frowning. "It's up to you, but I do have extra beds here if you want to wait out the storm."

Clark blushed fiercely like she'd just asked him to sleep with her. "I'm a good driver. Don't worry. You have someone here to keep you company, so I'll thank you for the drink and pie and be on my way."

Clark stood up and pulled on his coat, socks, scarf, and boots. He stuffed his hat into his coat pocket. The fact that he wasn't wearing a full-face mask like the man in the parking garage sent a surge of relief through her body.

Amber jumped up. "Well, yes, I'm sure growing up in Minnesota, you know how to drive in this mess. Thank you for coming by. I look forward to working with you."

Clark nodded. "Yes, we'll be working closely together. I enjoyed meeting you, Eli."

"The same, Clark," Eli replied, picking up the empty mugs.

Amber locked the door behind him. Before she even got into the kitchen, there was another knock.

"He must have forgotten something." Amber reluctantly turned toward the door.

Eli held up his hand. "Wait, I'll answer it."

"It's okay. We know who it is." Amber threw the door open. It wasn't Clark. "Britney?"

There was her worst nightmare, holding a large, sparkly, pink backpack.

"I knew you were just being nice. Kyle's brother drove me right to your front door in his snowplow."

"You...oh, um...come in."

"Thank you. It's *so* cold out!"

Britney marched in as the snowplow honked and drove off. Amber glanced out her front door before closing it and saw Clark watching the snowplow turn onto the main road. Then he waved at her in Clark fashion before climbing into his SUV. She wondered if he used the same wave with his date last night. She wanted to ask how it went but didn't want to embarrass him. She held her hand up before closing the door again. Clark's truck looked much like the one she'd seen at the parking lot, an older version of the senator's but with a ski rack on top. Myles probably had a fleet of them. She turned just in time to see Britney stopped in her tracks.

"You have company. I'm so sorry, but my ride just left, and I thought..." It was the first time Amber had ever seen Britney speechless. She looked like she was about to cry.

Amber smiled brightly. "This is my new neighbor, Eli, who ran out of firewood and is keeping warm here during the outage."

Britney quickly recovered and plastered a fake smile on her face, but it couldn't hide the pain-filled eyes. "Oh, yes, well, that makes sense. I'm Britney, Amber's best friend. I'm here to make sure the six-month anniversary of her sister's murder isn't too hard for her with the upcoming snow day. I simply couldn't leave her alone for three days."

Britney held her hand out, and Eli's smile increased as he took it.

His expression bordered on fake, but she didn't think Britney would notice since she was doing the same thing.

"It's very nice to meet you, Britney. I'm so glad Amber has caring friends."

Amber shook her head behind Britney, and he responded with a raised eyebrow. He got it.

"You just missed Clark, Senator Stroud's assistant."

Britney threw her fluffy pink coat over the chair still by the fire. "No, I saw him. He reminds me of someone."

"Clark Kent?" Eli suggested with a real grin.

Amber chuckled. "I believe his last name is Mason, but he reminded me of Clark Kent too. Although I don't see him turning into Superman, do you?"

Eli shook his head. "No, but he isn't as fragile as he portrays himself, trust me. He had a strong grip when we shook hands."

Britney pulled off her sparkly pink boots and set them next to her matching hat and gloves as she frowned. "No, it wasn't Clark Kent… never seen a Superman movie. I know—he was at the club Friday night."

Amber nodded. "He was. You're right, Britney."

"Never seen a Superman movie, really?" Eli asked.

"No. I haven't. I really don't watch many movies. I'm always so busy, you know. Besides, I prefer books."

"Yes, well…then I'm sure you'd know Eli's work, the Burt Bloom series."

"What? Really? I love those books! You're Elijah J. Reynolds? Oh, I'm surprised I didn't recognize you," Britney gushed. Her fake charm disappeared into sincere fandom.

Eli shrugged. "Yes, that's me. I always wear a hat in my photos. For some reason people don't recognize me without it."

"Well, I'm a huge fan, and to think you moved next to my best friend's house! Wow. I think you'd find our stories interesting enough to use in a book. I wouldn't mind sharing mine with you sometime."

"I don't base my stories on real life, but thank you for offering. If I do, you'll be the first person I call to talk to."

"Thank you. And I don't mean like a date. I have a boyfriend." Britney stopped. Her eyes filled with tears for a moment before her fake smile returned, surprising Amber.

Eli's attention was directly on Amber, "Oh, well, that's a shame for the rest of us. You tell him I said he's a lucky man. I did understand what you meant, though," he responded with obvious practiced charm.

Britney frowned deeply but looked away. "We are technically together, although after what his brother told me, I'm not sure. But thank you."

"His brother?" Amber found herself asking.

"Yes. He said I was different than the other girls his brother has been with, and he couldn't stay silent. He claims Kyle has been cheating on me, and he enjoys trying to date several women at once. Same old thing. I wanted to give Kyle the chance to explain, but the more I think about it, the more I don't think I want to hear it. Nothing new for me," Britney finished quietly.

Her statement hung in the room. Amber wasn't sure what to say. This was a side of Britney she hadn't seen. An honest and hurt one. A real one. She could admire that in her.

"I'm sorry."

"Yeah, me too. But I didn't come over for you to feel sorry for me."

"Then, I won't. Good riddance, Kyle," Amber replied.

"Yes, definitely his loss," Eli added with another one of his bright smiles.

It was like the air had been sucked out of the room. Amber didn't want to spend the rest of the evening trying to cheer Britney up. She wasn't completely unsympathetic to Britney's pain, even though the woman drove her completely nuts, but the thought of spending the night with Britney and Eli made her head hurt. An idea hit her.

She glanced out the front window and saw Clark was still here. A bit of luck. She rushed out the front door in her slippers into the snow. Her feet sank in, but that didn't stop her mission to get her friend a ride home. Britney's love life and issues weren't her concern.

Amber knew Britney would tell this guy all about it. This was the exact reason Amber avoided relationships in the first place.

"Clark!" she yelled out to the street. "You haven't left. I was wondering if I could ask you a favor." She turned back and shut the door behind her while Britney was engaged in a conversation with Eli about his books.

Clark waved up at her. "A favor? Sure, what can I do for you?"

Amber trudged through the snow and down the steps. "I was hoping my friend could hitch a ride with you—if you live in South Lake Tahoe, that is."

Clark popped his hood. "Well, that is where I have an apartment, and I would love to help, but I've run into a problem here. My truck died."

"It did?" Amber felt her world caving in around her. She didn't look forward to spending the rest of the weekend with Britney or Clark.

He lifted the hood and peered inside.

"Car troubles?" Amber jumped. Eli's voice cut through the conversation from the doorway. She saw he had pulled on his boots and coat.

"Clark said his truck died." Amber came back up the stairs, her slippers and socks now soaked.

"I wondered why you ran out into the snow like that." Eli frowned at her feet.

Amber glanced inside and saw Britney warming herself by the fire, looking completely dejected. Eli quickly shut the door.

"I was going to ask him if he'd give Britney a ride back since I'm not alone or anything," she whispered.

Eli nodded and responded in a muffled voice close to her ear. "Oh, well, um…she seems very nice. That was unfortunate about her boyfriend. I'm not a fan of men like that, so you know."

She looked up at him, feeling like they could melt the snow around them. "She's a bit overbearing and a few other things, but yes, I agree that sucked. I'm glad to hear you don't approve of that behavior. As for Britney, I'll explain later."

"Got it. But you might want to cut her some slack here. I think she's all show, and the real person isn't so bad, just hidden under a super-insecure facade. She's a reader, so that goes a long way with me." He continued in a normal voice. "I'll see if I can help Clark. Could be a dead battery. I've got jumper cables in my truck, and I know Auto 101—how to jump a battery, change a tire, add fluids. I even learned how to put on chains if I needed them on top of my four-wheel drive. So go back inside. I got this. You'll freeze out here in your slippers." Eli squeezed her icy hand.

Amber absorbed his warmth and felt the cold more intently when he let go of her. She whispered, "Well, you might change your mind about her, but I'll keep that open mind for your reader." She resumed her normal conversational volume. "By the way, if it needs a jump, my truck is right there."

"If we need it, I'll come get the keys, and I have no doubts about your survival skills or judgment of others. Hey, Clark, need a hand?" Eli rushed down the stairs.

"I might. It started fine and went a few feet and then just died." Clark jumped back into his truck. Amber could hear the ignition clicking. No lights or anything, and his truck was now blocking her truck in the driveway. She watched the two men talk and look under the hood. Eli pointed to his truck, and Amber headed back into the warmth.

"Clark is having car troubles," Amber announced as she stripped off her wet socks and stood by the fire to warm up.

Britney nodded, staring at the crackling fire like she was in a trance. Then she began to braid her long, red hair.

"Britney?"

"What, huh? Sorry, I was lost in my thoughts. You know, thinking about Kyle. What did you say?"

"I was just saying that Clark was having car problems."

"Yes. That's what Eli thought. His truck was running when I got here."

"Weird. Well, I should probably go back out and try to give him a jump with my truck since it's right there."

"I'm sure Eli would do that for you." Britney smiled sadly at Amber as she finished a perfect French braid.

"Well, he can't use my truck for the jump without the keys."

"True." What, no matchmaking? "Do you mind if I wait here? It's so cold outside, and I want to send a text to Kyle. I decided I don't want to hear what he says. I'm better off without that crap."

"Yeah, you are. But you know I don't have Wi-Fi without power, and we don't get a cell signal here. It'll have to be sent later."

"Sure, I know. But once the power comes on, it will send, and I will be through with him. Don't worry. I'm not going to cry and pull out my hair. I've been hurt worse in the past. This is nothing. We haven't been together all that long and...well, you know. I'm here for you."

There was the old Britney. "Well, you don't have to be. I prefer this new, softer side of you I'm seeing."

"Softer? Oh, well, yeah, I do come on a bit strong, but it's how I survive," she admitted.

Amber held back a smile. "Around me it's okay not to be that, um...strong, Britney. Cool?"

"Yeah, I guess. I'll try, but I do want to help you in any way I can, and if you don't go for Eli, you're crazy."

"I'm, uh...well, not big into relationships at this point, but I'll keep that in mind."

"Okay. Well, I'm going to sit by the fire and send the best breakup text ever. To think I told him about how much my last cheating boyfriend hurt me." Britney shook her head as her tears threatened to spill over.

"Sorry."

"Don't be—he's a loser, and I don't need that. It's time I took over worrying about myself more. I've been avoiding that for too long. Or at least that's what my therapist keeps telling me." Britney gave a weak smile, wiped her eyes, and began a second braid on the other side.

"Good idea. Make yourself at home. I have hair ties in the bathroom, and there's apple pie in the kitchen."

"Thanks, maybe later. I always have a hair tie on me, see?" Britney pulled a pink scrunchy out of her pocket. She was always prepared—Amber gave her that.

"Yup, I should know that." Amber chuckled. "There's bottled water in the kitchen. We just had some hot chocolate, if you're interested."

Britney's smile looked more like a grimace. "I'll make some tea later, but I'm fine now. Or plan to be."

"Yeah. I know you. You got this." Amber realized this was the first time she was the one giving advice. Britney was staring at her phone. Then she started typing. Amber wouldn't want to be Kyle right now.

She bundled into her coat, gloves, and boots. She grabbed her keys and scarf off the hanger and pushed back out into the icy air. Britney might have a point about Eli. Amber did want him in that way, but she had to get to know him better. But first things first—she had to find a way to get rid of all her unwanted guests, and the one still coming.

CHAPTER 12

*A*mber wound the plaid woolen scarf around her neck and lower face as she carefully descended the snow-shrouded steps. She had always loved these big storms. Reading by the fire or watching movies, knowing visitors wouldn't disturb her peace, was her idea of heaven on Earth. Well, until this storm. Now she had three uninvited guests, only one of which she wouldn't mind hanging out with. She sighed, missed the last step, and landed in the snow with an *oomph*.

"You okay?" Clark called out from his truck.

"Yeah. Fine. Thanks." Amber stood up quickly and brushed the snow off.

"Good. Well, no luck here." Clark bent back over the engine.

"Battery?"

He shrugged. "Maybe. Eli went to get his truck."

"Mine is right here. It will do."

Clark looked up and smiled. Amber jumped into her Blazer and turned over the key. Nothing. Had she left a car light on? Creepy didn't begin to cover the situation.

She saw Eli race out of his house to his truck as she got out of her vehicle and punctuated their current circumstance with a door slam.

All she heard was a click coming from Clark's truck. She set her jaw and met Clark's gaze. He shook his head and wiped his hands on his pants.

Eli shouted, "My truck won't start!"

"Neither will mine!" she shouted back, adding unconvincingly, "Although I might have left a light on."

Eli shook his head and tried one more time. Nothing but that familiar click. He tried to run back through the snow, which any other time would have made her laugh. As he sank deeper with each step, so did her mood.

"None of your vehicles will start?" Clark was suddenly next to her.

Amber jumped. "Oh, you startled me. No. This isn't right."

Clark's gray eyes held hers. "No, it isn't. I'm concerned. The senator told me about what's been going on, which is why I came over. To make sure you were okay until he arrived, but you had company, so I thought you'd be fine. Where can I get a cell signal so I can call a tow truck?"

Amber laced her eyebrows together and frowned. "Sometimes we get a slight signal on the deck on a cloudless day, but that isn't today. You might get one down the road...maybe."

"Well, that's not good. What about your neighbor?"

"No, Mrs. Jones has the same issues on her side of the street. We are cut off from the world right now."

Clark slipped his gloves back on. "That's an eerie thought."

"Yeah, well, at least we have shelter and heat," Amber's voice sounded more confident than she felt.

"True," Clark's tone didn't sound convinced, and his focus was on Eli.

Eli breathlessly removed the distance between them. He bent over, taking a deep breath. "I tried my cell phone, and my house phone is dead too. I don't like this. I know it sounds like an overused book plot, but it feels like someone wants us all here."

"I was thinking the same thing," Clark said.

Chills ran down Amber's body, and they weren't from the weather. "Who would want all of us together? It makes no sense, but nothing that's happened does. Well, I'm gonna go check on Mrs. Jones and make sure she's okay. You guys keep trying to get one of these cars running." Amber threw her keys to Eli. He deftly caught them in midair.

"I don't like you leaving now." Eli crossed his arms.

Clark didn't look at her. He seemed to be studying Eli a little too intently. "I have to agree. Besides, if she's older, don't they usually go to bed early?"

"I don't know about all older people, but she usually stays up and reads. I'm going over. You can plainly see me. I'll be right back."

Eli grunted and walked to her truck, but she felt Clark's eyes on her as she crossed the street.

Amber used her cell phone's flashlight and hurried across the icy plowed road that was being buried under more snow. She glanced back and saw the men at their respective trucks with the gentle glow of headlamps lighting the engines. The only logical explanation scared her. Up until this weekend, she'd always loved that there were only three houses on their small dead-end road. The main development was over two miles away—not walking distance in this weather. For the first time, she felt the loneliness of their small neighborhood.

The snow crunched under her boots on her way to the heavy wooden door with a bear carved on it. Mr. Jones had done that years ago, right after they got married. He died two years ago after a massive stroke. It had been like losing a grandpa—he always had peppermint taffy in his pocket for her and Iris. Amber lifted the brass pinecone knocker and let it fall. She expected to hear Mrs. Jones call out that she was coming. Nothing. Amber glanced at her phone. It was only five fifteen—had she already gone to bed, like Clark suggested? She took off her glove and knocked harder and tried the doorbell. No reply. Worried, she tried the door, but it was locked. She peered into the front window and didn't see any flicker of candles. It was dark except for the glow from the wooden stove. She put her ear to the door but only heard the crackling of the fire. No cries for help, at least. Amber reluctantly walked away, weighed down with an unease she couldn't explain. It seemed darker when she crossed back to her side of the road as the night blanketed the storm's rage.

"Mrs. Jones okay?" Eli shut her hood with a bang.

"I think she went to bed. She's not answering, but her woodstove is being used, so I'm sure she's fine. Plus, she's a bit deaf," Amber added with a slight shrug.

Eli nodded. "With the power out, there's not much to do. I just saw her this morning. She told me she was going to get some knitting done and then read. She had plenty of wood in the house and lots of food. She was more concerned about me. We'll check on her again in the morning."

"Yeah, that sounds like her."

Eli rubbed his hands together. "I have some sleeping bags you can use, since it looks like you're having a sleepover tonight."

Amber nodded. "Yeah. Good idea. Maybe we can invite Mrs. Jones over tomorrow if the power is still out."

Eli grinned. "Yes, she can join us for breakfast."

Clark closed the hood on his truck with a loud thud. "I'm sorry to be a burden. My truck has a brand-new battery, so I'm not convinced it's that. Not sure what the problem is with all three of our trucks down."

Amber shook her head. "You are no burden, and I know nothing about engines. It does seem to be quite a coincidence, unless it's from the cold." Her tone indicated she didn't think it was from the weather.

Eli caught her eye. "Well, as I said, it's really weird that all our vehicles won't start. But then I'm the type who gets in and hopes the magic key works." His attempt at humor fell flat. He kicked some snow and then stuffed his hands into his pockets.

"Yeah, it's the weird part that tells me we should be careful tonight," Clark said in a thin voice.

"No one is going to get hurt with all of us here, that's for sure. Right, Clark?" Eli threw him a look.

"Of course. What could happen with all three—no, four of us here together?" Clark tugged at his collar like it was too tight. His groomed hair was hidden under snow.

119

"I have extra beanies, Clark, if you're going to keep working on your truck."

"I'm fine, thanks. My hood got in the way, and my spare hat got soaked from my half-frozen water bottle. Besides, the beanie would mess up my hair, and we wouldn't want that." He smiled broadly at his own joke. He was cute when he smiled.

Eli chuckled. "Why don't you go inside and keep Britney company, Amber? We'll fiddle around with his truck a bit longer."

"I thought neither of you were mechanically inclined?" Amber smirked.

"I can turn over an engine, no problem." Eli kept up his attempt to lighten the mood.

Clark wiped off his glasses and then pushed them back on his face. "I know a few basics from my dad, but not much more than doing a tune-up or checking the brakes."

Amber licked her dry lips. "I'll go check the landline. Maybe we'll get lucky and get a tow truck up here—if they aren't too busy pulling cars out of the snow, that is."

Clark frowned briefly and turned his attention to the road. She followed his gaze and saw something moving. She squinted as she studied it. Was it a bear or—no, it was a person. Yes, a person carrying something and heading toward them.

She pointed. "Do you see that?"

Clark responded softly. "I do."

"Hey!" Eli called out. "You okay?"

The figure waved to them and said something they couldn't hear.

"What if he did this to our cars?" Amber asked.

"Well, there are three of us."

Amber felt her heart racing, and she was sweating under her coat. "What if he has a gun?"

Eli's smile fell off his face. "Oh, yeah, well...I grabbed this." He pulled a small gun out of his coat pocket and moved in front of her protectively.

Clark's eyes were on Eli's gun as the figure grew closer. He headed away from the figure and climbed into his truck. Was he abandoning them? Then she saw him reach into the glove compartment. Light flashed, and she saw he had pulled out a gun. She didn't know if she was relieved or alarmed that everyone was armed. Too bad hers was in the house. Clark thrust the gun into his pocket right when the man called out.

"What?" Eli yelled.

They finally heard him. "Hey, it's me. Myles."

"Senator?" Clark replied. He ran toward him.

Now there are five, she thought. Would she be safe with this group or in danger? She wished she knew. Britney was watching from the window. Amber waved up at her, but she turned away. Fine.

"I shouldn't have sent you out in this, Clark, and should have heeded your warnings to stay off the road. Never drove into a bank of snow before. Luckily a snowplow driver found me and brought me to the end of the road. Said he was just here a while ago. Oh, I brought you the promised gas." Myles held up the red can and then set it down.

"You okay?" Amber studied him as Eli moved closer to her.

"Fine. The truck took the brunt of it, not me."

Amber was satisfied; he looked okay. "Good, but you didn't need to lug gas here."

Myles gave her his politician smile. "No problem at all."

Clark quickly informed him of the situation.

Myles shook his head. "I don't like any of this. Can you get a signal, Clark?"

Clark held up his phone. "No, Senator."

"No, I don't like this at all. I wish I had a gun on me. You still have yours in the glove compartment, Clark?" Myles rubbed his gloved hands together.

"I have it right here." Clark patted his pocket.

Myles stuffed his hands into his black ski jacket. He was wearing jeans that she hoped were flannel lined, but at least he had on a good pair of snow boots. Top of the line—that brand cost well over $1,000. Out of her price range. "Good. Let me look at the engine. Elijah, is it?"

"Eli."

Myles's face took on a more relaxed expression. "I saw you at the diner. Well, why don't you take Amber back inside where it's warm and safe?"

Eli frowned. "Yes, that's a good idea, Senator."

"Please call me Myles."

"I will. Let me take the gas in too."

"Sure, thank you."

"Come on." Eli grasped Amber's arm firmly.

They walked quietly up the stairs. The warmth hit them like an oven as they entered. Britney had added some wood to the fire and was stirring it with the poker. Amber knew it was time to offer her a real explanation since they were all stuck together.

"Britney, you know about my sister being murdered—" Amber started.

"Of course I do. That's why I found a way here, even at my peril, to make sure you were going to be okay." There was the old Britney. She closed the woodstove and sank back onto the couch.

Amber clenched her jaw, causing a cramp. She saw Eli roll his eyes behind Britney. That helped her continue as she loosened her jaw. "I know, and thank you. I'm sorry about Kyle, but you need to listen to what I have to say. Some things have been going on, and we could all be in danger."

"What! What are you talking about?" Britney stood up, her mouth hanging open.

"It might be best if you sit down and let her tell the story, Britney," Eli suggested.

"Yes, of course. I was just surprised is all." Britney sat back down, finally quiet.

"Remember what I told you happened in the parking lot?" Britney nodded. "Well, a similar truck tried to run me off the road on the way home. Then I saw this same truck parked out front, and someone had broken into my Blazer. The worst part of all of this is all three of our vehicles won't start. We're worried the killer isn't done. I might be next, for reasons we don't understand, maybe because of my sister. And you are here now right in the middle of this. But Myles—Senator

Stroud—knows and agrees with me that we need to bring in help and security." Amber left out the small detail of her sister dating Myles, but otherwise, she felt Britney knew what she had gotten into.

Britney chewed her fingernails. "Are you sure? I mean, you are stressed by your sister's death. Why would the senator want to help you, anyway?"

"My sister worked for him, and they were friends."

"I didn't know that. I mean, I knew she was an employee, but not that they were friends. Well, then there must be more to this if he's involved." Britney frowned and stood up again.

"We won't go into all the details, and one more thing—the senator is here." Amber's tone was quiet, and Eli frowned at her.

Britney looked down at her hands and then put them in her lap. "He's here? Oh…that—well, I guess if you're in danger, the more of us here, the better. And Amber…I'm sorry if that all came out wrong. I wasn't suggesting anything."

"No problem, Britney."

"The more of us, the better." Eli repeated, standing at the front window with his attention on Myles and Clark.

Amber rolled her shoulders, trying to release the tightness. "Yes. I'm sure we'll all be fine."

Britney stood up. "You have any guns here? My aunt taught me to shoot before—well, you know. Too bad that skill didn't help save her life. But this is different, of course."

"Yes, I have a gun here. It seems like everyone does." Who did she trust with a gun was the real question.

"Good, show me later. We got this." Britney smiled brightly at Eli.

"Yes, we do," he replied.

"Well, I'm going to use the ladies' room. I know you're on a well— what should I flush with?"

"Here, I'll show you."

After Amber showed Britney the tub full of water and the bucket, Britney spoke quietly. "You know, Amber. I'm fully aware people don't like me. I'm, well—I always want to help, and perhaps I'm a bit pushy and try too hard. I feel like you wish I weren't around, but honestly, I want to be your friend. I don't have many friends, in fact none here. I picked you because I admire your strength. I feel like we have that in common. We could spend some time talking about what I learned in therapy and why I don't apply what I've learned yet, but you know… um…well…I guess I'm always trying to be the hero, even when one isn't needed."

"You know what I like in people?"

Britney shook her head.

"Honesty. I think this is the first time you've shown me that since I've known you. Thanks for that." Amber smiled and shut the door behind her. Maybe there was some hope for that woman yet.

Eli took Amber's hand when she slid next to him by the fire. It was probably the last moment they would have alone for the rest of the night. "I heard what you said to her. I think you might have gotten through, but if not, I like the woman I heard talking to her—a lot. But that situation aside, I'm worried. How well do you know Myles, Britney, or Clark?"

"I don't, but then I barely know you, either."

He raised his eyebrows and shrugged. "True. I know I'm not a killer. I write about them. That doesn't help you. Just be careful. I'd like you to keep your gun near you from now on."

Amber soaked in his heat. "I will. I bought one because…well, you know." She turned away. She felt his arms go around her, and she leaned into him. It felt right even though she had no clue if she could trust him.

"I'm sorry," he whispered to her. Being wrapped up in him made her feel safe for the first time since Iris had been killed. She didn't want it to end, but she had guests. "Do you have a lock on your bedroom door?"

"Yes, why?"

"Lock it tonight. Someone has made sure you're trapped here with guests during a major snowstorm. Don't trust anyone. Promise me?"

"I will, but shouldn't everyone be concerned?"

"Yes, we all should, I agree." His voice deepened. "My attraction to you is off the charts, and I'd like to investigate it when this is over." Eli placed a small kiss on her waiting lips. She reached up and caressed his face. He moved to kiss her finger, and she felt it throughout her entire body like an electrical shock. Then he pulled back, studying her.

Amber let out a small sigh. "I'd like to investigate that too. But I can't promise you anything. I'm not big on relationships."

Eli smiled gently and stroked her cheek once more. "I'm open to whatever is comfortable for you. Right now, I'd rather you stay alert and trust no one." She stiffened and disengaged from his embrace. Why did he keep warning her about everyone, including himself? Shouldn't he want her to trust him? His smile evaporated, and he rubbed his arms.

Doubt crept back in, crushing her euphoria. "You're doing a book on Myles, aren't you?"

"Right, but like I said, that's not important."

"You've done some research?"

"Yes. He is a public figure, and rumors have surfaced. He was seeing someone, and it wasn't the socialite that was in the papers, either. I've just gotten started, so I've drawn no conclusions. His side-kick gives me the creeps. I think he has a crush on you."

"So, you are researching his relationships?" Amber carefully asked.

"Yes, but I'm not interested in gossip. Nothing unusual has shown up, if that's what you're asking. I do wonder—" Eli stopped when they heard the toilet flush and the bathroom door open.

At the same time, both men burst through the door. Eli stepped back from Amber as they pulled off their snow gear.

"No luck. Clark's truck isn't going to start—it's completely dead. It could be as simple as a bad sensor, but we won't know until later. I didn't check the other trucks, though, but if they won't start either, then it appears we are all intentionally trapped," Myles said as his eyes found Britney.

Amber emptied her lungs. "Well, that's just awesome. Oh, this is Britney, and Britney, this is Senator Stroud."

Myles held his hand out. "Please call me Myles, Britney."

Britney was furiously blushing as she shook his hand. "Nice to meet you, Myles. I'm happy to hear you're working with Amber to find Iris's killer."

Myles glanced over at Amber. She gently shook her hand and mouthed the word *no*.

Relief crossed Myles's face. "Yes, well, Iris was a wonderful person who I was lucky to have work for me. It's the least I can do."

"Wonderful enough for you to come over in a huge storm bringing gas." Britney blushed again. "That didn't come out right. I didn't mean you had any other intentions. Well, I didn't know her sister, but if she was anything like Amber, she had to be great."

"No worries," Myles responded with his patented smile. "You're staying here, Eli?"

"I, well, yes, I had planned on it. I have no wood at my house. Just moved in next door, and I'm new to this area."

"Aw, well, welcome! So you don't mind if I borrow Amber for a moment, do you? I believe Clark was going out for another load of firewood. There's a healthy stack out front."

"I'll give him a hand. Why don't you come with us, Britney? I have a couple of sleeping bags at my house to bring over and could use the extra hands to carry them. Then you can see how a famous author lives and carries wood."

Britney glanced over at Myles. "Sure. I'd be happy to help." She grabbed her coat.

Amber watched Eli, Britney, and Clark head out into the storm before she turned to face Myles. His good looks were hidden behind a deep frown. Light from the woodstove caught the feather sitting on the table. She glanced over at the fridge, happy to see the bag was still there. Maybe she should hide it. She patiently waited for Myles to begin.

"I didn't want to say anything in front of Eli or Britney. I mean, I know hardly anything about them. Do you?"

"Well, he just moved in next door, but he's a famous author, so he's not an unknown. I've worked with Britney for the last six months. She can be a bit annoying at times but wants to help."

"She does appear to be harmless, but right now, we can't take any chances. As for Eli, I heard he was writing a book about me."

Amber's mouth opened, and then she quickly shut it.

"I said I was keeping an eye on everything. It's safer that way, but not what it sounds like. Honestly, I was worried about you. I was going to find a way to keep you safe no matter what it took after what you told me. The security I ordered doesn't start until tomorrow. I sent Clark ahead to be sure you weren't alone, which you weren't. My usual security, Steve, is holed up with Marsha in a cabin, or he'd be here too. So it seems Clark and I are your best defense until tomorrow. Also, I think we might want to consider Eli might have something to do with this. I mean, it all started up when he got here, although he did check out when Steve looked into him, but that was only superficial. And as for Britney, well, you never know. It could all be an act with her. Do you have a gun?" Myles looked around the room.

Again? "Yes, I do."

His face tightened. "Well, keep it near you. And lock your door tonight. If you don't have a lock, push something against your door. I'll keep an eye on Eli and Britney for you."

Amber folded her arms tightly in front of her. "I know my sister trusted you, but right now, I trust no one, and that includes Clark."

Myles nodded slightly and put a hand on her tense shoulder. "That may be the smartest thing you've said since I met you. Be careful."

Amber sighed. She was getting tired of hearing that. "I plan to, but I am going to figure this out."

Myles took a step back and held her gaze. "Sounds like a plan. You know it could be someone who isn't here too?"

The fire crackled loudly as one of the logs moved. "I know. Did you hire the detective?"

He glanced at the door. "Yes. Tonight he's researching. If he finds something, he'll call. Of course, I may not get that call."

Amber nodded her head and looked at the feather, which seemed to be glowing. Must be catching light off the stove, she thought.

"Do you mind if I use your restroom?"

Amber pointed him in the right direction and gave him instructions on how to flush. Tiger peeked from the top of the stairs right as Eli burst through the door with an armful of wood, Clark following behind with an equal load. Britney proudly carried in three sleeping bags. Tiger retreated into the bedroom. Four people snowbound at her house, and one of them could be the killer—or the killer was nearby. It was going to be a long night.

CHAPTER 13

*A*s Nester crept through the throng of evildwels, small shocks of pain surged through his mist. He tried to focus on Zelina's gentle, loving touch, but he couldn't hang on to that as the darkness consumed those feelings. All he could do was control his swirl as he entered the house where the two evildwels he recognized from earlier at the window were waiting.

"Welcome back, Nester. I'm Xene, and this is Nyx. We are very excited you're here."

Nester needed to give most of his energy to his appearance, making it hard to push the words out. "Yes, I'm here."

Xene nodded. "There's that winged one, with her pet Ed thing."

"That Ed thing can remove an evildwel from its host," Nester quietly reminded them.

Nyx smirked. "I've heard rumors of that. Must have been weak evildwels, right?"

Nester frowned but didn't respond, which only encouraged Nyx. "With all of us here together, those winged ones and their pet don't stand a chance. I mean, Geo is young like us, but I'm sure he won't let that Ed thing bother him and his host, right, Nester?"

Nester held the foolish one's gaze. Being near Zelina made him feel stronger again. "Geo is young, but I believe he's stronger than the two of you put together. But strength aside, I'm unsure how us being here could stop him being ripped from the host by that Ed thing. Not that I think it will matter either way, because I think the host will provide a great show for all of us."

Nyx glanced at Xene with a frown. Xene smiled with evildwel pride. "We have a theory that we can protect Geo in his host and not let that Ed thing get past us."

Nester felt his swirl misfiring. No, not now. He felt Zelina's concerned gaze on him as he pulled his mist back in and carefully replied, "We only repel winged ones, not the Ed thing."

"Be patient, Nester, and calm. Go along with them for now." Zelina's warning broke through his thoughts.

He felt his swirling go back to normal and the calm return.

Nyx's mist darkened as she smirked. "Come on, Nester. I know I can take the pain of being around a winged one for a while, can't you?"

Nester moved in front of the insolent evildwel, feeling the discomfort intensely. He pulled that feeling in and used it against the young evildwels. "I would take care of the tone you use with me. I don't allow ungrateful evildwels to exist."

Her mist lightened in the same fashion as Geo's did. So far, the evildwels were backing down from his challenges.

Nyx's smile was gone. "I meant no disrespect. My only thought is to help Geo so that Ed thing doesn't get to him."

Nester slowly moved back, and the pain he felt disappeared. "Evildwels don't help each other. That is not our way. If that changes, I'll let you know."

"Yes, of course," Nyx mumbled, and Xene nodded.

"Besides, I'm here to feed on this outcome, however it plays out. Is that the reason you're here?"

"Yes," they mumbled together.

Nester smiled. "Good. It seems calm right now. I recommend you both feed like I just did. You'll need your full strength to be around these winged ones."

"We fed a little while ago," Xene declared.

Nester wanted them to leave so he could figure out what to do next. "I don't sense the strength in you that I'd expect from evildwels your age. I imagine you didn't get a very strong meal before. Am I correct?"

Xene nodded. "You might be right. We shared another's kill. Come, Nyx."

"Good. Hurry back. I'll be waiting for you."

He felt relief when they left. The other evildwels kept their distance by staying outside, at least for now. He hoped to have at least ten minutes of peace. He held back a laugh, knowing Nyx and Xene were at full strength but too dumb to know it.

Nester watched with great interest as Amber interacted with the other humans. It would be so simple if she could be told who the host was. Then she could protect herself and get the others to safety. But he knew that wasn't how things worked with the whole free will thing. Pain shot through Nester again. The two evildwels were already back. Nester smirked at them.

Xene's mist had darkened, and her eyes were a deeper red. "We got lucky with a death so close. The human died rather quickly after we arrived, but her terror gave us the boost we needed. If we see a way to help Geo and the host, you won't deny us that, will you?"

Nyx had her red eyes intently pinned on her new prey.

Nester had to defuse this situation for as long as he could. "No, I won't deny you that, but only if your help is needed."

"Okay." Nyx smirked again.

The three watched the humans and winged ones, along with the growing crowd of evildwels outside. Geo's red mouth formed into a huge sardonic smile. None of the humans had a clue there was a killer so close to them. Silence fell over the misty crowd as Ed approached the host.

"We must help now," Nyx's red eyes were glowing brightly as she pushed her way in front of Nester.

"Do nothing now. We must let Geo try to handle this first, or you might have to answer to him."

"Yeah, sure." Nyx threw a look at Xene.

Nester knew he had to act the part better. "Let's get closer, but I warn you, it will be painful."

"Sure."

Nester hoped the pain would be too much for them, but it wasn't. Meanwhile, the humans functioned as if nothing was happening as they drew warmth from the fire.

Ed dove into the host, and they could see his outline. The three evildwels tightened their circle.

Xene's red eyes glowed. "I wish I could reach in and pull that Ed thing out."

Nyx smiled. "We could try."

"You will wait. You don't want Geo to die—or yourselves. A host can't support two evildwels," Nester firmly told the younglings with an added frown.

"Only a rumor." Nyx rolled her eyes.

Nester pushed himself directly in front of her, "You're not very smart. I'm surprised you've lived all these years, Nyx. Go ahead and do it, and see how long you live. Then there will be more for Xene and me to feed on later."

Xene smiled at Nester, and Nyx frowned deeply. Her dark mist lightened for a moment. "I am smart. But my instinct is telling me we can take him down, and my instinct is never wrong."

"What if this is the time it *is* wrong?"

"I…well, doubtful." Nyx frowned.

Xene smiled. "We could send him some of our strength without entering him."

Nester laughed. "Send him our strength? What are you, a winged one? If he's weak, then he should die. Do you disagree that only the strongest of evildwels survive?"

"I…um. Well, of course, we only want the strongest. I thought this was important to all of us, and we should help out." Xene pulled back slightly from Nester.

Nester inched closer to the young evildwels. "I'm glad you understand who survives. I will give you the importance of this, though. It could either make you a hero or very dead. Up to you, I suppose. Go ahead and try to help Geo." Nester's red eyes flashed at them.

"I will try. I *am* a hero." Nyx closed her red eyes, and her black mist tightened around her. Xene watched carefully. Everything grew dark around them for a moment, and then it returned to normal. What had just happened?

"I think—" Nyx began to move closer right as the figure of Ed screamed and then was thrust out of the host's body past them onto the dark carpet. Nester gulped. Evildwels helping each other would be unbelievably bad for the winged ones, and their mist had combined somehow to help Geo. This was going to be a battle.

"It worked. I helped," Nyx said smugly.

Nester shook his head. "You think it worked. I know it was Geo. Don't get too prideful, Nyx."

Xene's eyes reddened. "You had to feel that, Nester. Everything went dark."

"I felt nothing but us and then that Ed thing being thrown out," Nester tried.

"Maybe you need to go feed so you can feel what we do. You aren't as dark as us. And your eyes are a weird color." Nyx directed her smirk at Xene.

Nester slowly backed away into a corner, hoping they'd follow, while not breaking eye contact with Nyx. Luckily, they did, and Nester tired again. "You are both getting on my nerves. I'm this color because I'm older and much wiser than you. Don't push your luck anymore, or you'll see how fast I can end your inconsequential lives."

Xene's mist lightened, but Nyx quietly turned her darkened attention back to Geo and Ed. The situation was spinning out of control, much like himself.

"I apologize. No disrespect, but I felt that power too. I'm sure it helped Geo. If we can work together like this against those pesky winged ones and that Ed thing, we can dominate this world and not have to leave." Xene's darkness was increasing.

"Xene and I travel together now for strength. It may not be a popular idea, but you can see it worked. We won't give up on it, but I do offer my apology for how we're acting toward you if you feel it's disrespectful."

"No, it's not a popular idea for a good reason. We do not work together because we are singularly strong on our own. We have never mixed our flows. It might weaken us; then where would we be?" They would be invincible is what they would be. Nester started to feel the familiar hopelessness creep back in.

Nyx's red mouth pursed. "I don't feel weaker."

Nester shook his head. "You are weaker—I can feel it. We only blocked the winged one; we didn't combine our mist."

"What if Nyx is right?" Xene frowned.

"She isn't. We are all weaker now."

"I feel strong," Xene muttered.

Nyx shook her head. Her mouth was a closed line. "We should try it again, to be sure."

"Yes, if that will convince you of my wisdom," Nester reluctantly agreed.

What choice did he have? He put his trust in Ed and moved around the host. Nester saw the worry etched on Zelina's face as she spoke quickly to Ed. The three evildwels squeezed even tighter, leaving no space between them. Nester wondered if the two evildwels felt the sparks of pain from him. Would they figure out it was from him or believe it was the winged one? Ed walked into Nester and he was pushed back. It caused the other two evildwels to cry out in pain. Nester added a fake cry to theirs. The unfortunate part was that Nyx's and Xene's mists were mixing again and getting stronger. Evildwels were changing, but not like him, and they were getting stronger together. The mist mixing caused Nester to darken. He felt shades of his old self, but he didn't want to go back to that way of living again.

Geo smiled brightly at Nester. He couldn't feel Zelina anymore, just all the evil. Nester felt like he was being squeezed into a tight ball, while Xene and Nyx were darker and expanding. Then sudden pain surged through him like hunger, but he knew the other evildwels felt elated and sated. He remembered feeling like that once, back when things were normal and the sun wasn't trying to rise inside of him.

Did Ed feel the same pain? Ed's face was red, and his palms were clenched. His nonexistent muscles were tight, which was hard for Nester to think about, but that was what he saw. It was going to be a lengthy battle. He had no idea who would win. The host continued as if nothing was happening because it had no idea.

He hoped Zelina would endure the pain and come closer to them. Ed let out a piercing scream and fell at Zelina's feet. Geo laughed and shot a grin at Nester.

Then Thomas and Olive appeared next to Zelina. That gave him a sliver of hope as Thomas helped Ed up. Zelina nodded, and they all joined hands and moved forward, stopping just short of the pain zone. He saw another evildwel at the window, watching. Soon they would understand and join the fight inside.

CHAPTER 14

*A*mber studied the four people in her home. She wouldn't have believed it last week if someone had told her she'd have a senator, his assistant, a best-selling author, and Britney staying with her during a snowstorm. Oh, and a killer could be among them or nearby. But here she was, and she had better make the best of it —for now.

"Is anyone hungry? I have some pasta I can make for dinner."

Clark's face lit up. "Let me help you. Cooking is my specialty."

"I've had his meals. They are a treat," Myles added. "I'm better with cleanup. How about you, Eli—you cook?"

"My last girlfriend didn't cook, and we needed to eat, so I learned. But she wasn't fond of my cooking or the author lifestyle, so she started dating a professional football player. Of course, before we broke up." He glanced at Britney, who nodded at him solemnly. "You didn't need my life story—all I was trying to say was I can cook." Eli caught Amber's eyes and gave her a quick wink.

Britney stood up. "Thank you, Eli. I know I'm not the only one who goes through that. Anyways, tonight I can cook. You relax, Clark. Us gals have this one. You can take breakfast since I'm not a morning person, deal?"

"Well, if that's what you want." Clark raised an eyebrow at her.

Amber held her hands up. "Sounds like a plan. Girls do the cooking tonight, and the guys have breakfast...if we're still snowed in," she added, hoping they could all go home soon.

"I don't mind at all—just an offer. Let me know if you want help, and I'll step in gladly." Clark's voice sounded pleasant enough, but his tone didn't match his slight frown.

Eli nodded. "Yes, us guys will take cleanup and breakfast, no problem."

"Now, if it was just this easy to make reasonable decisions in the senate." Myles grinned.

Britney burst into unusually loud laughter. Eli joined her with a small chuckle. Clark had a forced smile. Maybe he would have been the better choice to cook with, and Britney could do—well, what was she doing? Flirting with the senator after just breaking up with Kyle? Why not? He didn't deserve any woman grieving over him. Britney sashayed past the men into the kitchen with Myles's eyes following her. But it did bother her.

Clark turned toward the woodstove, rubbing his hands together. There seemed to be a more confident side to him coming out that Amber liked. Myles and Eli were very formal with each other, like diplomats at a summit from countries who didn't like each other. She found herself attracted to all these men, but she wasn't like some woman on a reality TV show who dates a bunch of guys and then picks one to marry. She didn't even want to date one guy, much less three. She wasn't husband-hunting, but her heart was still leaning toward one of those men. She hoped her heart knew what it was doing.

At least dinner was pleasant enough. It was filled with small talk, spaghetti, salad, two bottles of wine, and the bakery French bread she had in the freezer. Everyone avoided the obvious topic, and she was relieved and worried at the same time. Like going to the doctor for a shot you hoped they'd forget, but you needed it not to get sick.

"That was a wonderful meal, Amber and Britney. Thank you." Myles picked up his plate.

"No problem." Amber began collecting the plates.

"No, I have this. Sit down." Myles waved his free hand.

"Thanks." The candlelight accented a slight blush that flowed over Britney's face as she handed Myles her plate.

Myles's smile was directed at Britney as he emptied his wineglass in one gulp. "You are very welcome. First I think I'll get the generator going. Get us some water."

Amber spoke up. "I'm okay with candles and dirty dishes."

"I don't mind at all. If you'll just show me where it is."

"I'll go too," Britney chimed in, bouncing to her feet. She smiled brightly at Amber and then turned her attention back to Myles.

Eli shrugged. "I'll man the fire. Maybe get more wood."

"I'll stay here too. Unless you need my help, Senator?" Clark added with a small sigh, sipping from his almost full glass of chardonnay.

"I've got this. Thanks."

Amber automatically tried to switch on the light at the top of the stairs that led to the garage. Myles led the way using a flashlight, which made the narrow wooden staircase, dusty and festooned with cobwebs, look more like a haunted house ride. He diplomatically swiped the webs away. Amber decided next time she'd include the stairway in her housecleaning.

"There's the generator. I'll get to work on it!"

"Yup, and I'll open the garage door. We usually roll it over here so the fumes go outside." Amber tugged on the rope to release the door. With a loud click, the door opened. They were greeted by her truck and a lot of snow. It was dark and quiet, which didn't make her feel any safer. Now the killer would have a new access to the house and fuse box—if he wasn't already in the house.

"I usually have two cans of gas filled for snowstorms, but I haven't been as prepared this winter," Amber admitted with a small shrug that no one saw.

Clark stepped into the conversation with an armful of wood, followed by Eli. "No one expected a storm to be this massive this early, Amber. I think we were all caught off guard, like the Donner Party." She shone her light on them, making Clark shake his head.

"Oh, sorry, Clark, didn't mean to hit you in the eyes. You just startled me. Yes, but I should know better and be prepared. We all should."

Eli shifted his load around again. "Sounds like you got this, then."

"We do," Myles confirmed.

"This is getting heavy. I'm gonna head upstairs," Clark announced.

"I'm right behind you, Clark."

As the two men disappeared up the stairs, Britney held the flashlight on Myles as he poured the gas. "Okay. It's almost full. You guys ready?"

"Oh, yes!" Britney exclaimed. Amber wondered if she would have clapped for him if not for the flashlight in her hands.

The generator roared on and sent a rumble through the garage. It blew out a cloud of smoke into the chilled night air. Myles turned the choke off, and it settled into a calmer roar. He plugged it into the outlet and flipped the switch from power to generator and *boom*. They were bathed in light.

"Let there be light!" Myles exclaimed with a huge grin.

"I'm so thankful you were here to help us, Myles," Britney gushed with a silly grin. Amber was starting to feel like a fifth wheel when he returned Britney's grin with a wink.

"Happy to help."

"The fridge is running!" Eli yelled from the top of the stairs.

"Thanks, Eli."

"That went well." Myles wiped his hands on his pants.

"Yeah, it did. Thanks." Amber rubbed her arms, wishing she had worn a coat.

The conversation fell into an uncomfortable lull. Was this love at first sight or lust? Either way, she needed to remove herself from this *National Geographic* mating ritual moment.

"I'm gonna go back upstairs. Um…thanks."

Myles met her gaze with a grin. "Sure, no problem. I'm going to keep an eye on the generator for a little bit."

Britney moved next to him. "I'll keep you company."

"Great." Amber got out of there as quickly as her feet could take her feeling like she suddenly needed a shower. She left the door open a crack in case they needed anything and fully embraced the heat from the woodstove. She loved being greeted by two good-looking men in her kitchen doing dishes. Britney wasn't the only one who had new possibilities.

Clark held up a small plate. "We'll get this cleaned up in no time."

Amber could have sworn Eli rolled his eyes. "Oh, thanks. The generator doesn't run the dishwasher, though."

"I don't mind doing them the old-fashioned way."

Eli picked up a towel and winked at her. Amber felt her face redden. "I can do it later."

Clark rinsed the plate off and handed it to Eli to dry. "I honestly don't mind, and I'm sure Eli doesn't, right?"

"I don't mind at all." He sounded…well, a bit sarcastic to Amber. She held back a smile.

Clark seemed oblivious, much to Amber's relief. She sent Eli a warning look when Clark wasn't looking. Clark handed Eli another dish a little roughly, and Eli almost dropped it. "So we're all set. Go do what you need to with some power."

"Yeah, good idea. I'll get some pillows and blankets I have stored upstairs. One random light in the bathroom works up there with the generator."

She caught Eli's eye, and he winked at her again and held his hand out to Clark, waiting. Clark scrubbed furiously and slapped the pan at Eli, who went into drying mode. She headed upstairs with the sound of the generator filling in the silence that had been lingering in her house. She didn't have to wonder what Myles and Britney were doing, nor did she want to think about it. Clark and Eli continued their dishwashing race.

Tiger was lying on the bed. His eyes caught the light from the bathroom.

"If I were you, I'd stay up here. It's like Grand Central Station down there." Amber smiled fondly, remembering her aunt using that expression when she and Iris had friends over.

Tiger closed his eyes as if he understood.

"At least the sheets are clean if anyone wants to sleep here. Just warning you, Tiger, your space could be invaded."

The cat didn't acknowledge her alert.

"Too bad the spare room downstairs is full of old junk from Iris's garage sales. Oh, well, someday I'll clean it out and make it an office." Amber opened the linen closet and filled her arms with dusty bedding. This room had been untouched for the last six months.

"Look out below!" Amber called and tossed them over the railing. The pillows and blankets landed with a small thump on the couch. She knew from experience they would land far enough away from the stove that they wouldn't get scorched. She and Iris used to make a game of it, throwing things downstairs when their aunt wasn't around. They even had races to see what would hit the floor first.

"Landed safely. I could have helped!" Eli shouted from the kitchen.

"It's a family tradition to toss bedding," Amber called down.

"Oh, well, then, carry on!"

She thought she heard Clark say something, but she couldn't make it out.

She would leave Tiger some food. Hopefully, he would come out later after everyone went to bed. His upstairs cat box needed scooping, so she did that. On a whim she decided to take a quick shower. After rinsing a couple of resident spiders down the drain, she got under the hot water. Using her sister's rose soap made her feel close to her again. As she rinsed the flowery conditioner out of her hair, a feather floated by.

"You here, Iris?"

The small white feather landed on the sink.

"That feather sure gets around," Amber muttered. "If you're here, I hope you stay out of the garage. You know, where Myles and Britney are." Amber shut off the water, feeling silly. She grabbed a clean towel from the cabinet but didn't want to wear the same clothes, so she threw on her sister's bathrobe and hurried downstairs with her hair in a towel.

"Glad you could enjoy a shower." Clark smiled, but it felt more like a leer.

"Yes, it was nice, thanks."

Eli came out of the downstairs bathroom right as she shut her bedroom door. She was glad her room was fully hooked up to the generator. She could watch a movie if she wanted. She threw on some leggings and a sweater, feeling refreshed. Maybe she could stand the rest of the night with a houseful of people. Running a brush through her hair and applying some lipstick, she felt ready.

The feather ended up in front of the spare room. She had to be transporting it around the house somehow. Amber shrugged and peeked into the room. A board game in the beam of the flashlight caught her eye. It was a game she and Iris always used to play as kids —Clue. She grabbed it and shut the door, and a familiar chill shot through her as she stepped over the traveling feather. She'd never been stalked by a feather before, unless this was a different one. Perhaps from one of Tiger's toys, or Tiger had killed a bird for the first time and brought it into the house without her knowing. She placed the game on the kitchen table with a hollow thump.

"Feel better?" Eli asked.

"Yes, just what I needed."

"Do you mind if I do the same? I'm feeling a bit grungy."

"No, please go ahead. Use the upstairs one. I want to hang on to the water in the tub just in case. There are fresh towels in the cabinet, but the only soap is flowery."

"Okay, thanks. I don't mind flower scents, and I'll make it fast so I don't waste water or the generator. Will I be bothering Tiger?" Eli threw a side glance at Clark.

"He likes you, but he doesn't seem happy with me right now with all these people in his house."

Eli nodded and then ran upstairs.

"Who or what is Tiger?" Clark asked.

"My cat. Well, it was my sister's cat, and now mine. He's not a fan of that arrangement, though."

"Oh, right. I saw cat food and a box earlier. Guess I forgot." Clark shrugged under the harsh fluorescent glow of the single kitchen light. She wished every light was on so she'd feel safe.

She heard a giggle come from the garage. She rolled her eyes when Clark wasn't looking.

"You guys need any help up there?" Myles yelled from the garage. "I want to stay here just a bit longer. Make sure the generator doesn't have any problems."

Amber went to the top of the stairs to reply. "No, we're fine. Cleaning up and getting some things done."

"We'll be up in a couple of minutes. I found a can of gas. How long have you had it?" Myles shouted.

"Oh, several months, but we put an additive in it," Amber yelled.

"Okay. It should be fine. We'll be up in a bit."

Amber frowned and added more water to the bathtub and the bucket. That would get them through after the generator ran out of gas until the power came back on. She walked past the door, hearing Britney's giggles again.

When she turned back to Clark, a wave of raw emotion passed over his face. It looked like pain, but he quickly covered it up with a forced smile. "Myles is handy with *things*."

Amber held back her question. Was he jealous, and of whom, Eli or Britney? "Yes, I'm glad he's here. I found Clue. Maybe we should all play it."

Clark's expression didn't match his cheerful tone. "I'm a fan."

"My sister and I loved to play it."

"Figuring out who's the killer seems like more than a game right now."

"Well, yeah, true. But I thought it might be a good distraction."

"Oh, I didn't mean to insult you, just pointing out the obvious, I guess. Sorry, I'm not always very tactful. I haven't played since I was a kid. It should be fun, and I think we're all safe here together, don't you?"

"Safety in numbers—isn't that what they say?"

"They do." Clark smiled broadly.

"I always wonder who 'they' are, don't you? 'They' sure have a lot of opinions." Amber added a log to the woodstove with a loud thump.

Clark gave a small chuckle as he pulled on his boots and coat.

"That's a fantastic question. I've wondered the same thing. I'm going to grab my overnight bag from my truck."

Amber held back a question about why he had an overnight bag in his truck. "Okay."

"I pull a lot of all-nighters at work. I always keep a change of clothes with me. Be right back."

A few moments alone was just what she needed. She ran her fingers through her hair, and some of the water dripped onto the stove with a sizzle. She heard the shower running and tried not to think about Eli in it. She sank in front of the fire and closed her eyes. The next thing she knew, Eli was next to her.

"Rest, Amber. I have a feeling it's going to be a long night."

"I do too. At least we smell good."

"That we do."

Amber glanced over her shoulder. "Where's Clark? He went out to his truck a while ago to get his overnight bag."

"His overnight bag? He's prepared. Maybe he's in the garage with *them* now." Eli tugged the blanket from the couch over them.

"Maybe."

Their gaze locked, and soon their lips did. She felt herself melt into him with the tiny nagging thought in the back of her mind that she shouldn't trust him—or anyone—right now. She heard the front door open and pulled away right as Clark entered, stomping the snow off his boots.

Amber stood up and gestured him over. "You must be freezing, Clark. Come join us by the fire. Safety in numbers, like *they* say."

"Yes, it's very cold out, I give you that, and I'm still wondering who *they* are that says such things." He snickered as he set down a black gym bag with a thump.

Eli looked puzzled. "We were wondering, when people say, 'They say,' who the 'they' are who say such things."

Eli smiled. "Yes, 'they' do seem to have a lot of opinions."

"Perhaps you could answer this mystery in one of your books." Clark grinned, but his words lingered heavily in the room until they were pushed away by more laughter from the garage.

Eli grinned and nodded. "I will consider that."

"Great. You can thank me in the acknowledgments." Clark sounded sincere, but his vibe was sarcasm. Maybe he wasn't a huge fan of mystery books or their authors.

"Will do," Eli's clipped reply almost made her cringe. He caught her eye and added a small shrug. Then he continued in a more Eli-like tone. "Myles and Britney sure seem to be getting along."

"Myles gets along with everyone." Clark's expression tightened as he sat down. Eli and Amber joined him, Amber in the middle again.

Eli glanced at her with raised eyebrows. "Oh, of course he does. I mean, with his job, I'm sure he has to."

Clark crossed his legs. "Well, not all the other senators are as socially skilled as he is. A few can be quite rude."

Eli nodded. "Yeah, like every other job. I suppose people are the same all over."

"Yes, people can be predictable, but Myles is very trustworthy for a politician."

"It's refreshing to hear that what everyone says about him is true." Amber jumped up.

"You are *very* welcome," Clark was turning on the charm with a smile that could melt a glacier. His words dripped sweetness.

Eli frowned slightly. He stood up fast and kicked a plate toward the woodstove right as Clark stretched out more.

"Hey, careful, there, Eli. I like that plate," Amber joked as she picked it up.

Eli offered her a boyish grin. "Didn't see it, sorry."

Clark quietly rubbed his ankle.

"Sorry, Clark."

"Accidents happen."

Amber moved to the kitchen. "I'm gonna set up the table for the game."

Eli was right behind her. "That's why I'm up to help."

"Thank you."

Clark was suddenly next to them, moving quietly like a cat. "I'm here to help too."

Amber shook her head. "You've both already done too much between the dishes and firewood."

Clark held up his hands. "It's the least I can do for your hospitality. Let me know if you need a hand."

Eli stepped around Clark to get to the table and almost tripped over his foot. She saw Clark hide a smile. The tension filled the air like a swarm of killer bees. She wanted to swat it away, but the moment passed quickly when Myles and Britney burst into the room, laughing like children at a joke that included bodily sounds.

"Your friend here has the best sense of humor, Amber," Myles grinned at a beaming Britney. They could use her as a flashlight when the lights went out again.

Britney shook her head. "You seem to bring it out in me. Ask Amber—I'm never this silly. She always sees my more serious work side. You know, because we're job buds."

"Job buds! You are the best!" Myles declared.

"She certainly is," Clark repeated in a tone that shot through Amber like the winter air outside when she didn't have her coat on.

Amber pointed at the table.

"We have Clue if anyone's interested. And we still have some apple pie and what I'm sure is some soft rocky road ice cream, if anyone wants dessert."

Britney's face lit up. "Oh, Clue, I love it! I'll take some of that pie and ice cream first, though. We could share, Myles, if you want. Save a plate."

"Dessert and a game. Perfect, and I think sharing is a fine idea," Myles added.

"I'll get it." Eli was already heading for the freezer.

"You do that, and I'll put on some water for herbal tea or grab whatever everyone wants, like more wine." Clark was right behind, Eli.

"Deal. You want some pie, Clark?"

Clark smiled. "I'm still full from that wonderful meal."

"Me too. I've had enough wine." Eli crossed the kitchen in a single step.

"Me too." Britney chimed in.

"No takers on the wine?" Clark held up the bottle.

Eli and Myles shook their heads.

"Well, for tea, I have Earl Grey, peppermint, or chamomile. The cups are over here, and there's hot chocolate or coffee right above it." Amber pointed.

Clark grabbed the tea kettle. "Peppermint sounds fantastic to me. I'll get the water started. What does everyone want?"

"I'll take some peppermint." Amber got out more cups.

Myles and Britney cozied next to each other by the fire. "I'll take some peppermint too. What about you, Myles?"

"Ditto!"

Clark looked at Eli. "You?"

"I'll have what everyone else is having, thanks!"

"You want dessert, Eli?"

"I'm okay. I've had my share of pie today." Eli smiled at Amber.

Amber handed a big slice dripping with rocky road ice cream and two forks to the smitten couple by the fire. She would have never chosen those two for each other.

Britney took a small bite. "This pie is wonderful! You're lucky to have a neighbor who bakes. And you picked my favorite ice cream, but I'm so full, I know I can't finish this."

"Good thing I can help you," Myles added with a slight blush. Gone was the stern-warning senator. He had been replaced by a giggling schoolboy. If he was so in love with her sister...no, that wasn't fair. He was allowed to be happy after the fact, wasn't he? But this fast?

Amber's face felt heavy behind her smile. "Thanks. Mrs. Jones can make a mean pie."

"It's so nice to have neighbors who are so close to you. It must make you feel safe." Myles offered a bit to Britney which only brought on more giggles.

"Yes, very safe."

The conversation fell into a comfortable silence. Clark was fiddling with the teacups in the kitchen while Eli slipped in next to Amber as she waited for the water to boil. Amber glanced down at

Britney. Her face had softened, and her smile was genuine. Maybe all she needed was to meet the right guy, but did it have to be this guy? The hum of the generator filled the silence of the unsaid words.

After Myles and Britney had gotten their sugar fix, Clark brought the tea to the table. They spent the next hour figuring out who killed whom and with what.

Clark held up a hand "The professor in the library with a rope."

Britney clapped. "It is! You're good at this game, Clark."

"I'm just good at deducing things."

"That you are," Myles added.

"Thank you. I always appreciate your positive comments."

"You are very welcome. They are much deserved." Myles smiled broadly.

"I can imagine how amazing it is working with Myles. Clark, you are so lucky," Britney added.

"You have no idea." He smiled, finishing his tea.

Clark reminded her of a kid opening presents on Christmas morning when he won the first game. Who knew the mild-mannered man would take winning a game so personally? He was cute but would be hard to deal with, Amber concluded as she finished her now cold tea. The flavor was sweet and bitter at the same time.

"This is interesting with the honey added."

"It's my favorite. I hope you all like it. I added a couple of spices too. My secret ingredients."

Myles nodded. "That's the extra kick I taste. It's very good."

"What's your secret?" Eli asked.

"That's just it. It's my little secret." Clark grinned with a slight giggle.

Myles smiled benevolently at Clark. "That's how he cooks. He never shares his secrets with me. But I don't mind because it's all so good."

"Thank you. You are always too kind to me." A cloud of sadness passed over Clark's eyes.

"I only give credit where it's due." Myles set the empty cup down on the table.

"I think I taste cinnamon," Britney offered.

"Perhaps." Clark winked.

Amber set her cup in the sink. "I have everything here for bedding. There are sleeping bags, pillows, and extra blankets, and there's a bed upstairs too."

Amber caught the look between Myles and Britney. Would they try to sleep together here, at her house, tonight? In Iris's bed, no less? Her opinion of Myles was slipping quickly.

Clark smiled. "Thank you. You're quite the hostess, Amber. I'm up for one more game before bed."

"Me too." Britney chimed in. Everyone else quickly agreed, and soon they were back to figuring out who the next murderer was. On top of the fridge in a bag were the clues to help her solve her sister's murder.

The game went by quickly, punctuated by yawns. She glanced at the wall clock in the kitchen and was surprised to see it was only 10:45. It felt like midnight.

"The butler in the kitchen with a knife," Eli announced, winning the final round.

A loud yawn escaped Amber. "I think that means I should go to bed. Please, everyone, make yourselves at home."

"We will, thanks. Where is everyone sleeping?" Britney asked, mainly looking at Myles.

"I thought you should take the room upstairs, and us guys will bunk down here." Myles hid a yawn behind his hand.

"I agree." Eli joined in the chorus of yawns and finished his with a tired smile.

"Yes, that sounds great." Britney added to the round of yawns. "It's been a long day, and these yawns are contagious. Night, all." She headed off to the bathroom.

"It has. Good night, everyone," Amber said from the kitchen. As she headed into her room, she was suddenly glad she had put the knife under her pillow Friday night. It might be overkill with that and a gun, but better safe than sorry, she thought grimly.

Her body felt heavy, and her feet dragged across the floor. She quickly shut her door and locked it, tugging on it twice to be sure. She was comforted by her favorite picture of dancing bears as she stripped off her clothes. Her garments were tossed around her room like she was a carefree exotic dancer. The green flannel nightshirt didn't fit that illusion, though. She sank into bed without even bothering to brush her teeth. Amber tried to read but kept falling asleep, so she turned off her light and dead to the world.

She suddenly woke up and saw the glow of her alarm clock had disappeared. The house was eerily silent. Did the generator run out of gas already, or did someone turn it off? She considered for a moment going into the garage and switching the house back to electricity in case the power came back on, but what did it matter when they were sleeping? She pulled her covers high over her ears just as the darkness began spinning. Eyes closed tightly, everything faded away.

CHAPTER 15

 *N*ester felt like hours had passed—and maybe they had; he couldn't be sure. The house darkened as the humans settled into their beds. He felt helplessly entangled with the other evildwels. The winged ones and the evildwels were in a stalemate. Neither side was backing down. Nester felt weaker and met Zelina's gaze, hoping she understood he was at a breaking point. She raised an eyebrow and then nodded to Thomas, and they advanced. Dark and light surged against each other in waves of sparks.

"This is painful," Nyx cried.

"I can't take it anymore," Xene broke to safety, away from the winged ones.

"Weaklings," Nester muttered loud enough for them to hear.

"I will stay with you. I'm not weak like Xene." Nyx's mist lightened.

Nester felt some relief after Xene's exit but was still racked with pain from being near Nyx. He wished they had both left. He shot a quick look at Zelina, whose face was masked by a grimace. She had linked arms with Thomas and Olive, and Ed was right behind them. His features were squeezed tight in determination.

"We can't fight these winged ones alone. They're too strong, Nyx.

Move away before this horrible light consumes us." Nester moved next to Xene.

Nyx shook her head and stood her ground. She looked like she was going to spin out of control, like Nester had been doing when Zelina reached out. The sparks lit up the room like fireworks. Both the winged one and the evildwel were locked in a scream until Thomas pulled Zelina back. Nyx's eyes were brown, and she was a pale shade of herself. Her eyes met Nester's first, then took in the rest of her audience. Nester could feel her shame.

"I need to feed," she announced and raced out of the house.

"She should have listened to you," Xene's tone was smug.

"Yes, I agree. Well, we learned an important lesson. Those winged creatures are stronger than us." Nester raised his voice just enough so the outside evildwels could hear too. Nyx had just done him and the winged ones a favor.

"This time they are, and Nyx was stupid to do it alone. I still think in numbers it would be different," Xene said quietly.

"The winged one looks fine, but Nyx didn't. I'm not so sure about that, Xene. We need to be careful with these things. Protect ourselves above all."

"I suppose that's true. It's up to Geo now. He might have to fight that Ed thing again. We did our best, and I doubt he'll even thank us for it."

"You know he won't. It isn't our way to be thankful." Nester felt a small surge of hope when this evildwel showed such an uncharacteristic emotion, much like Nyx did when she left in embarrassment. Yet right now, he had to worry that the other evildwels might kill him or even Nyx tonight for their weakness. No guarantee anyone would survive the night.

Ed sneered toward the window where the other evildwels had gathered. They were showing restraint after what had happened to Nyx, at least for now. Ed ran at the host again and this time landed inside comfortably. Nester could see Geo's red eyes glowing. The battle had begun.

"It is up to Ed now. I am going to check on Amber. You two stay here and make sure these things stay away from Ed," Zelina said this out loud so the evildwels could hear her.

"We saw what your touch did to that unfortunate creature. I am sure they do not want to mess with us." Olive smiled sweetly at Xene.

Nester held back his grin. The winged ones were putting on a show for them, and he wished he could do the same thing. But what had happened seemed to keep the other evildwels outside for now. Their red eyes were glowing with self-preservation.

"You are right, Olive. They do not want to mess with us angels." Zelina shot a glance at Nester before leaving in a bright flash of light. Thomas and Olive held hands and stood guard in front of the host.

Nester peered inside the host, watching the battle. Geo was showing a strength that surprised Nester. Ed might not win this battle to remove him from his host. Geo pushed back hard, and Ed was on his knees with his hands over his ears. Nester wanted to get closer, but that would have made the other evildwels suspicious. Geo looked out at him with a huge smile. He might regret underestimating that young evildwel, who he was now sure was worthy of this host. Would he be the one to see what Nester was? Nester suddenly heard the winged one's thoughts.

"I must go. It is time. Stand strong, my love." Olive placed a quick kiss on Thomas flushed cheek, and in a flash of light, she was gone.

"You stay safe until we meet again," Thomas whispered to the space where Olive had been. He ran his fingers through his hair and focused on the host. On Ed.

Zelina suddenly appeared next to Thomas, making him jump.

"That was a bit ahead of schedule. Olive cannot be in two places at once. Those two new evildwels have boldly entered the house. You see them over there? They are waiting for Amber's death like vultures. This host, if it has its way, will not let Amber die easily. But love is stronger than they are, though, so we have that on our side."

"Maybe we should call for help," Thomas suggested.

"I did. Hopefully, some will make it here in time. With all that is going on, we are already stretched thin. Right now, it is you and me, Thomas."

"Can we still save Amber?"

"I hope so. It is too bad Olive had to leave. But she had to be where the other killer is—or another piece to this puzzle. Sometimes this makes my head hurt," Zelina admitted.

"Yeah, I understand. I wish this were not so complicated." Thomas sighed and pushed his wavy, shoulder-length hair out of his face.

"Me too."

"I will do everything I can to help." Thomas squeezed Zelina's arm.

"Stand by me." A smile crossed Zelina's face. "At least I was able to distract the host for a moment, back when it was important."

"I was wondering what you were doing." Thomas nodded with a grin.

Nester listened intently to their conversation. How could he help? Nester felt the two new evildwels studying him. Soon there would be so many more to feed on the moment.

Just then, two bright flashes came from outside, and then two more. More winged ones! They were positioning themselves next to the evildwels. Inside there was a bright flash, and that winged one stood next to the new evildwels. Do they know about me? Nester wondered.

"This is worrying," Xene's eyes narrowed. "Maybe we should go feed, so we will be stronger to deal with this new development."

"I've just fed. I think it is good you feed again. I will stay here for now and keep an eye on things."

Thankfully the evildwel didn't argue. He knew Xene would be back stronger and ready to battle. He felt that undercurrent in the evildwels. For now, though, Nester was peacefully alone in his corner.

He saw Ed pull himself up and slowly moved forward.

"Look out, Nester. These winged ones mean business," Geo called out.

"All you need to do is focus on this feed and avoid touching that winged one next to you. That didn't go well earlier. We will prevail, though. Then we'll enjoy our feast." Nester finished up his lie with a huge red smile, and the winged one next to the young evildwel shook his head.

Thomas glared hard at Nester. "I am going to come at you. Just play the part and look uncomfortable and in pain, and that will show the new evildwels the anguish we can cause before they get too brave."

Nester replaced his smile with a frown and stood his ground as Thomas advanced. "Will do."

"Good. Thanks. Milk it for all it is worth."

Nester let out a huge roar and then screamed as if he was in the greatest of pain. Thomas matched him.

"Perfect. You look like you're suffering. Just a bit more. Great, thanks. I should go back to Zelina. Hang in there, and keep your swirl going."

Thomas threw a scowl as he shouted in his fake pain voice that almost made Nester laugh. He pushed the humor of it down, and kept up his pained face and small grunts, with all the red eyes pinned on him as Thomas moved away.

"Be careful, Nester, you're picking up the winged one's glow," said Geo. "You sure sent some pain back to him. That's what I'd do."

"There is no need to offer advice to your elders," Nester replied firmly.

Geo didn't reply. The winged one next to him reached out and sparks ignited, making the evildwel scream. That shut him up and made Nester look impressive since he hadn't sparked at the winged one.

"Good one, Sarah," Thomas thought to the new winged one.

"Thanks, Thomas. Zelina confided in me. I am trying to help you, Nester. Have you tried feeding on the good?"

"Sometimes, but I still need the bad too," Nester thought back.

"Well, just a thought. You know, see what happens."

"Maybe someday, in different company, I—"

"Let us not communicate unnecessarily. I do not think—" Zelina warned.

Thomas interrupted. "Ed is in trouble, Nester. Scream as loud as you can and run at me. It might be the distraction he needs."

"I, ummm...okay."

Nester rammed into Thomas as hard and as loudly as he could.

There was no expected bolt of pain or the usual sparks. He just bounced off Thomas like he was a piece of furniture. But his performance was on a level with the human movies he'd caught glimpses of. Their acting had always fascinated him.

"Stay back, you evil mist monster!" Thomas shouted, grabbing his head. He made sure the other evildwels could hear.

Nester added in another shriek for good measure. You would have thought they were both in excruciating pain, but it was more like the satisfaction he used to feel when finding the perfect host. He glanced at Ed. Unfortunately, the performance hadn't helped him. Instead, he was being picked up and thrown. He landed on the floor under Thomas's feet again.

"He's the toughest evildwel I've ever met, young or not. I'm not sure I can pull him out of his host. It doesn't help there are so many evildwels adding to his power." Ed's thoughts were breathless.

"Then we fight this host as it is. Get ready," Zelina warned.

"I'm gonna try one more time."

Ed made a run for the host. He disappeared inside, but they could see him screaming again. There was little hope he'd have much success. But a little hope was all they had been going on for a very long time.

Nester tried to focus on the feelings the winged ones sent to each other. He felt a small tingle run through him. He lightened up more and felt stronger for a moment before feeling completely drained. He could feel the eyes of the evildwels on him now. They sensed his weakness. Xene returned and was approaching him. Nyx was still gone. Xene's red eyes narrowed, and her mouth turned down in disgust.

He felt his swirl going out of control. He didn't need a mirror to know he wasn't dark anymore.

"You should feed, Nester. You are losing your darkness. That winged one took it from you." Xene's tone bordered on insolence.

Nester returned the stare but didn't have the energy to respond. He tried to focus on control but had none left. He was changing, and there was nothing he could do about it. He wasn't sure how he'd end up, but he felt like a butterfly coming out of his cocoon. Too bad his time to fly would be cut short with all the evildwel attention on him. It would soon be a feeding frenzy. He didn't look forward to that, but if his death could mean something, it might not be all bad. If they were focused on him, maybe they would leave the winged ones alone. Maybe even Geo would get distracted. It was the perfect plan for maybes. He hoped he could bring himself to let go when the time came.

"Hang on, Nester." He heard Zelina's thoughts in his mind.

"I don't think I should," Nester responded.

"Yes, you should."

Nester didn't reply. It didn't matter because he knew what was coming from the evildwels.

"You have so many here to help you. Olive will be back soon— Eve's time is limited. Please, try to hang on," Zelina encouraged with a gentle smile.

Nester froze as a bolt of dread shot through him. "Who?"

"Eve. Amber's mother." Zelina turned to face Nyx as she returned. "It is time."

Nyx shook her head at the winged one. "Nester! You are weak." Nyx moved closer. Xene never took her gaze off Zelina.

Ed let out a scream that vibrated through Nester. He grabbed Geo in a lock between good and evil. Geo's cry matched Ed's. Nester felt the evildwels gathered around him, with Nyx in the lead. Her mouth was twisted in a snarl as her red eyes filled with hunger.

"We will be feasting here soon, Nyx, and the winged one's damage will be gone."

Nyx glanced at Xene, who nodded. The group pulled back from Nester, but only slightly.

CHAPTER 16

$\mathcal{E}$ve lay face down on the cold white marble floor, unable to stand. She painfully turned her head. "Why did you push me down the stairs?"

Bo smirked. "Jeb loved you, but you turned on him. What did you expect?"

"What are you talking about?" Eve pushed out between short gasps.

"You cheated on Jeb."

"I what? No, I didn't."

"Of course you did. He'll believe me."

"He won't."

Bo smiled at her and patted her head right as Jeb walked through the door and froze. His face turned white. "What happened, Eve?" He raced to her side and took her hand.

"Jeb…" she called out. Bo pushed a finger hard into her side. She almost passed out from the pain and gasped loudly.

Bo shook his head. "Don't try to talk, Eve. Jeb, she's hurt badly after taking a tumble down the stairs. But don't worry. You won't mind after what she did."

Jeb tightly grasped her hand. "It's going to be okay. An ambulance is on its way, right, Bo?"

Eve focused on breathing until the wave of pain passed. Her words couldn't make it past the curtain of pain.

"No. Not after I saw her in a hotel with Neil earlier, and they weren't playing golf or practicing her golf swing."

"Hotel? What are you talking about, Bo? You owe me, and calling is the least you could do." Jeb sneered and pulled his cell phone out of his pocket.

Bo shook his head, grabbed the phone from him, and tossed it on the floor. "You're right. I do owe you, many times over. I can't let you make this call. You're too upset. Let me handle this."

Jeb's face dropped. "Yes, please call for help. We can figure the rest out later."

Bo patted Jeb's shoulder. "Of course we can. Please comfort her if you need to, but it won't change the outcome. She cheated on you. She's no better than the rest of them. She's a liar. A bad woman like all the others."

Eve tried to shake her head as Jeb dropped her hand. His face was that of a stranger. His empty eyes looked down on her and sent a chill through her body—at least the parts she could feel.

"Outcome? You pushed me," Eve whispered. It was as if she was leaving the room but still there at the same time, and everything echoed inside of her.

Was she going to die at the hands of their so-called friend, Bo Wright? She couldn't bear to watch Jeb's mouth turn downward in an expression she'd rarely seen from him. It reminded her of a conversation they'd had years ago. If she cheated on him, he said, he'd never forgive her. That was the only line she could cross and not come back from. She hadn't. She needed to convince him, but the words weren't coming out as she wanted, and Bo's were. "Jeb, please…he's lying."

Jeb looked back and forth between his wife and best friend.

"Are you sure it was her, Bo?" he asked quietly and stood up.

"I'm positive. I saw it with my own eyes and have proof. I was shocked when I saw them kissing and him groping her and her hand

—well, never mind, Jeb. You certainly don't need that image in your mind. I came to confront her, and well, then this happened. Unfortunate, but it does make things easy for you now."

Eve shook her head as much as her battered body would allow. She couldn't move her legs or hips. Did she break her back? Her right arm worked, but the left one hurt with every attempt to move it. Each breath took effort. Maybe if Jeb got help… "Please, Jeb. I love you. He's lying. He pushed me."

Bo shook his head with the practiced politician's smile she had come to hate years ago, "Even dying, she still lies to you. That's how these women are. I'm sorry, Jeb. I hate to see you in so much pain because of a woman." Bo changed his look to include sympathy for Jeb.

How did Jeb not see how fake this all was? Eve wondered. Bo turned his steely blue eyes on her, removing any hope of survival she had. He was crazy.

Her only chance was getting through to Jeb. "Neil Ramsey? You know he couldn't make time for me in his schedule. I always went to the old guy, Sam. Besides those phone calls, I've never even talked to Neil. Help me, Jeb. Bo's crazy."

"Eve, he wouldn't lie to me. Not after all we've been through together. He's the only person I've ever trusted besides you. But even though you crossed the line and deserved this, I can't let you die like this." Jeb had tears in his eyes.

"You can trust me always…I love you." Eve tried to reach out for him.

Eve felt optimistic for a single second when Jeb's face softened and he started to lean forward. Then Bo interrupted. "She's lying. You know I'd do anything for you after all you've done for me. You helped me out of a jam and have always been there for me. Let me help you back."

Jeb straightened up and looked between Eve and Bo before he shook his head and that mask appeared again. It was frightening.

"I believe you, Bo, thank you. I was stupid to think I'd found the one woman who I could trust."

"You can!" Eve called out.

"Shut up. You're lucky you fell down the stairs. A much easier death than the others—"

Eve gasped. "Jeb...what?"

"I clean the world of bad women, right, Bo? Helped you out when that girl died. That death would have put a crimp in your political aspirations. And she was bad too. You know that."

Bo looked away. "It was an accident, though."

Jeb smiled. "Of course it was. No one would have believed it."

Eve tried to sit up, but the pain washed over her again.

The clouds began to lift from Eve's mind. "My drinking..."

Jeb nodded slowly. "Yes, I accepted your little hobby. It made my life easier. I was very fond of you, Eve, but Bo's right. I can't let you live now."

Bo smiled. His bright white hair matched his teeth. "Pitiful thing drank so much she fell down the stairs is one way to spin this. Really too easy. I can't be here, of course, not with my presidential campaign and all. When she takes that last breath, be the grieving husband. Simple."

Jeb shook his head. "She's not one of my kills. This isn't simple."

"It is. The biggest issue is you don't want them to think you killed her. You know, like you found out about her affair and pushed her down the stairs. Happens all the time, you know."

"I know."

"And your son—you must protect him since he's just like you."

Jeb's face was stark white against his graying hair. "He's my priority. He's helped you too. He's helping me right now. I hope you aren't threatening him."

Eve felt the pain lessen. Maybe that was a good sign. "Are they almost here? Your voices are so faint. I can't hear what you're saying." Maybe if they thought she hadn't understood her husband had just admitted to killing women...

"You can hear us just fine, Eve. See? A liar. Your eyes are very expressive. No, Jeb, I would never threaten you. I only offer my concern for your family." Bo smiled at her.

161

Jeb frowned. "I know, I apologize. Did you cheat on me, Eve? Please tell me the truth, and I'll make sure you're okay." She saw no love in his eyes. How could he turn on her so quickly?

"No, I didn't. I promise you." She held his gaze, hoping he'd hear the truth in her words.

Jeb sighed and bent closer to her. She twisted to see him. A tear dropped from his eye onto her nose, ran down her cheek, and dripped off her ear. "If you had just admitted it, I might have had some empathy left for you. You know, I've heard Neil's had affairs with some of the wives, but I never thought it was you, Eve. This all makes sense. You've been working out more and gone when I get home. Yes, this does make sense."

"No. I work out…" Eve took a breath and pushed the pain down "to look good for you is all. Don't listen to him. I love you, always."

"At least she's staying true to her lies. She'd make a good politician, I give her that," Bo added, tugging on Jeb to stand up.

"I put you above all women, Eve. I even killed your loser first husband and took care of his brats. We were perfect together until now."

"You…don't—" Eve coughed, barely able to catch her breath. It wasn't an accident. She had married a killer and had been too drunk to know it. It was the first clarity she'd had in years.

Bo sneered. "I agree—*don't*. Here, you go sit down, Jeb, and I'll handle this. We're in this together."

Eve tried to catch her husband's gaze, but he avoided looking at her. "I did warn you not to cheat on me. That was the only rule I had for us."

"That rule is still intact," Eve choked out.

"If you cheated on me, then you don't love me. I will always love you in my own way, though. I will always think of our good times, Eve." Jeb covered her gently with a plaid blanket from the couch and sank into a green silk chair with a sigh.

"Come back," Eve whispered.

Jeb shook his head and looked away.

Bo smiled and looked down at her. "All that blood you're coughing up isn't a good sign, my dear."

"Jeb?" was all she got out.

Jeb sat in the chair with his head in his hands. He looked so far away.

"Old Jeb here had a bad childhood, as you know. When I accidentally ran over Nancy with my dad's boat in our senior year, Jeb helped me out. Her body was never found. As they say, don't drink and drive. I owe him, and now we're even. Right, Jeb?"

Jeb nodded, spinning his wedding ring. "Right. We are. Thank you."

"I hired a detective to follow Eve. She took polishing clubs to another level." Bo smirked. "The report is full of her indiscretions, but now isn't the time to share that with you. I think you'll understand when you see it. Only we'll know."

"Where is this report, Bo?"

Bo put a hand on Jeb's shoulder. "I have it. Remember, she did the same thing to her first husband too."

Eve tried to sit up, but she only got her head slightly off the ground.

"Not true..." Eve whimpered.

"She's going to say anything to survive. That's what this type of woman does. I honestly thought she would be dead by the time you got home. Her internal injuries are extensive. Soon she'll be with her daughter and that man who loved her as you did."

"Help me, Jeb...I've loved only you..." Eve pleaded again.

"The report."

Bo snorted. "Here, look at this picture the detective got." He pulled a snapshot out of his back pocket.

Jeb nodded. "It's you, Eve. I recognize the mole on your back and those black high-heeled shoes. You're doing for him what you used to do for me." He held the picture so she could see it.

"Not me," Eve gasped through gurgles of blood. "A back with a painted-on mole. Fake."

Jeb shook his head and threw the picture at her.

Bo bent down and picked it up. "Oh, Eve. You are funny. You never loved Jeb. All you've loved is money and booze. You were a joke as a mother. Did you know your daughter, Amber, was in love with Jeb? He turned her down for you. Pathetic."

"Amber…" she spit out blood.

"Yup. She wanted you to make love to her, didn't she Jeb?"

Jeb nodded but wouldn't look at his wife.

"Oh, my God. She tried to tell me, but I didn't believe her." Eve felt like a useless rag doll, her only working parts her hands.

"Let me take out this trash," Bo said with a leer.

"Trrr…asshhh?" she repeated as her tears became blood-tinged and streaked down her face. She felt them drip off her face and watched them land on the white floor. For some reason she was reminded of an abstract painting as they spread out in bloody patterns covering her sterile existence.

Jeb nodded. "Yup. Trash. I agree."

The truth rushed through her like a hurricane and opened her eyes. "Oh God! Please forgive me for what I did to my girls and what I did to their father. He was a good man, and I should have tried to stop drinking." She felt stronger again, like she was going to survive.

Bo shook his head. "God doesn't take kindly to women like you. You were aptly named. I'm not so sure your daughter will forgive you, dear, or your dearly departed husband. You had to know it was Jeb who killed him. Pathetic. Does Jeb know you changed your mind at the last minute and were going to stay with your dead husband?"

Her eyes widened as she struggled to catch her breath. "How did… I was going to stay for the girls. But I loved Jeb."

"I know a lot of things. Did Jeb ever tell you his son was with him?"

Eve just stared at Bo as each breath became more difficult.

"No? Little Deanie was the one who checked on him. Like father, like son, huh?"

Bo bent over her. "She still breathing?" Jeb asked.

"Unfortunately." He smiled and pushed his finger into her neck out of Jeb's sight, making her choke. She tried to push him away, but she didn't have the strength left to fight. He pulled away the moment her eyes shut. She thought he would be the last face she'd see, and then the pressure let up. Bo smiled brightly and straightened.

More blood gushed from her mouth as she continued wheezing, trying to catch her breath. She saw a flash of bright light to her left, where Jeb's cell phone was. If she could only get it and call the police.

"Please...." she choked out.

"Nice to use manners. But you are a fibber. I'd love to stick around and watch you take your last breath, but I want to help. Picture this outcome, Jeb. You will be the grieving widower when the lover kills your wife. I have him in the truck. Did I forget to mention that part—or a better plan? I'm starting to think like you, old man, and had your back covered the whole time. Come on, Jeb, I could use a hand. If you hang on a moment, Eve, I'll reunite you with your lover. He's going to shoot himself in grief after you die."

Heartbroken, she painfully crept her way to the phone, dragging herself with her arms. Her legs trailed uselessly behind. She was worried that she felt no pain now in her lower half. Her vision was blurry, and she had to blink hard before she could read there was 8 percent battery left. She dialed 911.

When they answered, she whispered into the phone, "I'm Eve Cadwell at 3455 Maple Land Drive—" The call dropped. She quickly dialed again. "Please help me, I'm badly hurt." Her call dropped again, and she blacked out. She woke up with a painful start, confused, and finished her conversation, unaware she wasn't talking to the police anymore. "Neil Ramsey has been kidnapped. Bo Wright did it, and my husband killed my first husband and others. Bo pushed me down the stairs. Hurry." She couldn't remember hitting end after she blacked out a second time, but she was pleased to know justice would be served.

Eve wheezed, determined to get one more message out before... She hit the record button on the video camera, and with her final burst of energy, said to the phone, "I love you, Amber. I'm sorry for everything and not listening to you years ago about Jeb. I hope you can forgive me someday. I love you and wish I had never hurt your father... I should have been a better mother... Be happy, baby. And I told the police what—" It stopped recording and began to shut down. Eve heard footsteps approaching. She used the last of her strength to push the cell phone under the hall entry table, hoping the police would find it.

Fear shot through her broken body when Bo started talking.

"Here's your lover!"

Neil Ramsey, the golf pro, stumbled in behind Jeb. "Eve? What happened? What is going on, Jeb?"

"You drank too much, my friend, remember? You pushed your lover down the stairs after a fight. You must have blacked out." Bo held the man up.

"My lover? Is this a joke? Besides, I could never hurt anyone, and you know that. You know me, Bo. I thought—" Bo shoved Neil down, knocking the breath out of him.

Neil shook his head as his mouth dropped open. He looked like the victim in a slasher movie and was clearly drugged.

Eve tried to warn him, but only a squeak came out. Bo smiled. "*Shhh*, don't try to talk, Neil. I'll take care of you."

Neil stared at Bo with a silly, grateful grin.

"Why don't you head up and take a shower, Jeb? You have some blood on you."

"I wish this had been done in the killing shack. I could have cleaned it up nicely. Oh, well. You're right, I need to clean up. Thank you, buddy. This one hurts me, though, inside."

"My pleasure. Now don't go killing yourself, Jeb. Well, I would if the police showed up, but that's just me. I mean, jail would be a bitch. But no way they'll know until you call them, right, old friend? I'll be here to help when you get out. We'll make this look so good no one will question you, but as it stands now, they might blame you." Bo smiled.

Jeb shrugged and headed up the wide marble staircase.

Neil's head fell to the side. He had passed out. Bo placed a gun in Neil's hand, but he didn't awaken.

"I…" Eve tried to make her mouth smile but had no luck, and she was quickly running out of breath, making it impossible to say any more to this monster. She wanted him to know she'd told the police he was a murderer. He would find out soon enough.

"I what Eve? *I* must wrap this up is what *I* must do. You should have heard my call to the sheriff. I had a prerecorded digitally altered voice that hysterically reported a murder at the Cadwell house. So I know they're on their way here. It will take them a good twenty-five minutes to get here. A big benefit, living so far out in the country. Don't worry, I'll be careful leaving, and I'll throw the phone away. Jeb showed me a shortcut through the woods. No chance I'll run into the police, even if I hear them coming.

"Tomorrow's headlines will be Jeb killed his wife and her lover and then himself. If not, I'm sure the police will shoot him. I left a gun in the bathroom under his towel and one in the shower. I'm finally free of him, and no one will find out I was best friends with a serial killer because I'll clean up after him. I've taken care of all those pesky forensic details. I'll promote mental health care when I'm elected." Bo clicked his tongue as Neil put up a weak struggle and added, "Here are some quick fun facts to take with you to your grave, Eve. Jeb doesn't know he has another child. He has no idea I had the affair with Neil, who wanted a relationship. I couldn't have that, could I, since I have a wife. And one more thing." Bo smiled brightly at her. "Little Deanie is killing your daughter as we speak. That's on Jeb, though. Well, tick-tock. I have to finish up. Rest in peace, Eve," Eve opened her mouth to scream, but nothing came out. The last thing she heard was Bo's laughter and then a gunshot. Then everything faded away.

CHAPTER 17

$\mathcal{I}$ was the only one awake as everyone was asleep in a drugged haze. The house was quiet except for the sound of my feet gently meeting the hardwood floor and the wood snapping in the woodstove. The snow continued falling as I made my way through the residence that was soon to be these people's tombs. Silently and with the practiced proficiency of a professional killer, I tied up the sleeping beauties. No one stirred as the drug coursed through their bodies, leaving them unaware of their danger. Finally, I had them all where I wanted them, except for Amber. With an extra bit of joy in my step now, I found myself at her bedroom door. The gentle snore indicated her blissfully unaware state, but I was still careful when turning her doorknob. It was locked, as expected.

"That won't stop me, Amber," I whispered with a slight chuckle.

This was going to be fun, and we had all night. Each one would scream when it was their turn. Never had there been such a wonderful opportunity to try out a few new things. To draw it out. I was glad now that none of the other attempts on Amber had worked. This was perfect, nothing anyone could plan for.

I inserted the knife into the lock and soon was next to Amber. The hope was to surpass the fear that had been in her sister's eyes right before she died. I wanted it to last for hours—if she lived that long. Sometimes it was hard to hold back. But there would be three other bodies to play with, so a small mistake wouldn't matter.

The only thing that could make this more perfect was if the *annihilation associate*, what we liked to call each other in private, was here to experience this. Sometimes we got to work together. It was nice to share those memories. But for now it was all about satisfying some important needs. Because after this, I would have to lay low. More killings might attract attention.

I could wait, though. I've learned patience. But right now it was time to focus on the present and tie up Amber. I felt that familiar tingle in my jeans. Although sex never compared to a kill, tonight would be my first attempt to combine them. I slowly bent over the sleeping woman, binding her hands together in front of her. I felt some satisfaction wrapping her ankles with the rope and tying it off tightly. She was quickly secured like the rest of them. That sedative always did the trick. Now to bring them all together and start having some fun when they woke up. Yes, it was going to be the perfect evening, thanks to a huge winter storm.

* * *

AMBER WAS DREAMING about a large red-and-black snake that was slithering around her room. She watched it with interest, thinking about how beautiful it was. Then it came for her. It wrapped itself around her legs and arms, and she realized it was going to choke the life out of her. Her heart was racing as her eyes popped open. What started as a dream became very real when she found she couldn't move. She blinked rapidly as her vision cleared, and she saw a dark figure next to her dresser. The rope cut into her skin as a scream tried to escape her throat. She swallowed back her fears while she took in air and pushed it out slowly. She closed her eyes and focused on that. In and out like the waves. Yes, everything was going to be just fine.

She carefully opened her eyes again and watched a feather float behind the person, buried in the shadows, who didn't belong in her room. The feather quietly landed on her clock. The dimly lit face, operating on backup battery power, showed it was 1:07 a.m. Seven was her sister's favorite number. That had to be a sign not to give up. She started twisting her hands to free herself, but the rope was securely bound. A glimmer caught her eye. Laid out neatly on her dresser was a row of wicked-looking knives, a camera, and two guns. The knives terrified her. What about everyone else? Were they still alive? She stifled a yawn. She couldn't allow herself to fall asleep. *Come on, Amber,* she told herself. *The feather is telling you to try. Pull yourself together and think.*

Amber tightly closed her eyes and flashed back to a memory of making dinner with Iris. They were celebrating Amber's new job at the newspaper. Iris began chopping up a carrot with a butcher's knife, much like one of the knives on top of her dresser.

"Why don't you peel the potatoes?" Iris suggested.

The memory vanished, and all she was left with was the realization that she would soon be that carrot if she didn't figure something out, but what? She gulped and slowly opened her eyes. The intruder was gone, but the knives weren't. The feather was on her pillow now, a small flash of light bursting around it. Yes, of course, the knife. Hopefully it was still there under her pillow.

She almost smiled when she heard the intruder's footsteps moving away from her, and she inched her hands toward her weapon. Luckily, they were bound in front of her, making the motion much easier, but a dragging sound was coming her way. She got back into the position she'd been in and closed her eyes tightly. Then she heard a loud thump next to her and the footsteps retreating. She forced her eyes open when all she wanted to do was fall back to sleep. On the floor was Eli.

He was tied up with the same yellow rope she had seen in the parking lot and at the scene where Iris was killed. Was this the rope she had brought home? Not that it mattered now that the killer she had been looking for had found her. With Eli next to her, she felt a renewed strength. That left either Clark, Myles, or Britney as the killer—unless it was someone else. She wiggled her hands under the pillow and retrieved the knife in her right hand. Never had the dry wooden handle ever felt so good on her skin.

Using her thumbs and fingers as best she could, she bent them toward the rope and started making small cutting motions. This might take a while. She worked as quickly as she could, with a strong will to live.

"Eli!" she whispered as she kept the knife moving. Her muscles started to fight the bent position she was holding them in. "Wake up!"

No response. She could see his chest rise and fall, so he was still alive. His hands were bound in front of him, and his feet were tied together. She was surprised that they didn't have gags, but who would hear them if they screamed, anyway? Mrs. Jones certainly couldn't— did the killer know that?

She yawned, and her eyes began to droop. No, she couldn't fall asleep, but her body felt so heavy. Amber bit the inside of her cheek, drawing blood, to help her wake up. She shook her head back and forth right as a loud thumping sound began on the stairs leading down from Iris's room. Her time was running out. Furiously, she kept at the small strokes of the knife against the rope. Her muscles were cramping, but she was making progress, so she ignored the agony.

She heard a loud thud coming from the living room. Would someone else be thrown in the room with them next? She had sawed her way through the first yellow rope, but the other one was still tight on her wrist. She kept cutting until the sounds were coming down the hallway. She quickly repositioned and closed her eyes.

She peeked when she heard a slight grunt next to Eli. The shadowy figure was wearing the same mask as in the parking garage, and she could see the same inhumanly glowing red eyes. The killer was focused on the pile of victims on the floor. The new person next to Eli was Britney. She was breathing, but unconscious. The killer had on baggy black clothes, and she couldn't tell who it was. Whoever it was didn't even glance her way and headed right back out the door.

Amber went back to work on cutting the rope around her wrists.

She heard footsteps going up the stairs again. That didn't leave her much time before the killer came right back. The second rope broke, and the knife slipped, almost slicing her hand. She let out the breath she'd been holding. The blood from a cut might have alerted the killer she had a knife, but relief shot through her as her hands were free. She shook them out to get the blood flowing again.

She began freeing her legs. It wasn't going to be a fair fight with the killer armed with her gun and, she assumed, everyone else's, but at least there was a fight to be had. Anything would be better than finding out what those knives did. In the glow of her small nightlight, she could see the blades were dirty, like they were stained with blood. They were dealing with an obvious serial killer. She sliced faster as adrenaline rushed through her body, amplifying every sound.

She heard more thumping coming from upstairs. Was it Myles or Clark next? She kept working on her feet, which had an extra loop of rope. Sweat poured down her face in the icy room. She cut through the first two knowing she would soon be dealing with the person who had brutally killed her sister.

She shuddered and almost dropped the knife when she finally severed the last strand of rope around her feet. The thumping had stopped, and there was silence. Was the killer checking on her? She froze and forced her breathing to remain calm and study. Time went on forever in that moment. Then the thumping continued toward her. Amber wondered why the killer was bringing everyone to her room.

She made the rope look like it was still tied around her legs and lay back down under the covers that the killer had so nicely replaced after tying her up. She wound the rope around her wrists and resumed her position, eyes closed tightly right as the dragging sounds entered her room. She did her best impression of sleeping.

Another body was dropped on the floor, and the killer left again. She opened her eyes and saw it was Myles. That meant Clark would be next, or else he was the killer. She heard the woodstove opening and more wood being added. There were no more thumps when the killer entered the room again. She held her breath.

"Too bad you're even here." Like a snakebite, the voice's venom entered her bloodstream, leaving her in pure shock. She had welcomed him into her house. He wasn't talking to her, was he? "I'll make you comfortable in the meantime. I mean, we have the same father, but you weren't on my list to be killed since he didn't know about you. You can blame your so-called best friend here for this, not me. Now, if you don't mind, I have a room full of people to kill, Britney." Clark exhaled loudly.

Amber almost fainted. Britney was related to Clark, and Clark was the killer. Oh God! Her mouth filled with her dinner, and she pushed it back down. She knew she needed to get this psycho talking before he started.

"What's going on?" she mumbled, like she had just woken up.

"Do you really have to ask?" Clark spun around and pulled off his mask.

A chill cut through her like a knife. Pretending might be her best option. "Clark? What's happening? You need to untie us before the killer comes back."

Clark smiled, running his fingers through his hair. "You are truly the definition of a dumb blonde. And if you're smart enough to wonder about my mask, it's become a ritual to wear it until I have my prey set up, as you saw in the parking garage and at the other near misses that provided me with this opportunity. You understand, don't you?"

"I don't." Amber gave up on playing clueless. She needed to hear him say it. "Did you kill Iris?"

"Now, that's a smart question for someone so dumb. Of course I did. I waited a bit to take you down next. You know, so it wouldn't be so obvious, not that I put much confidence in the police force. As for your group here, they're all going to die with you."

Amber felt the room spinning around her. "Who do you think you are, deciding who lives or dies? You are lower than bear shit!"

"You do have bears around here. I ran into one twice. I decided it was time to leave, but nothing could keep me away for long. And I prefer you to speak respectfully to me, or you'll pay for it later. Understand? After all, I have all the power here, and you have none."

He added a smile as he bent down until he was directly in front of her face. He raised his hand and slapped her hard. Pain filled her, but she managed to hold her hands and feet in place so he wouldn't know she wasn't tied up. He grinned broadly.

She tasted blood from her lip. Her skin stung, but nothing was broken. If it had been a fist, it would have been a different outcome. He stepped back and rubbed his hands together.

"Well? What do you say? Gonna be good?"

She nodded but didn't reply.

"What was that?" he repeated, pushing his glasses back.

She could barely get the words out. "Yes. I will be good."

Her body was trying to rebel. She could barely suppress her urge to lunge at him with her knife. The man who had been hiding behind those glasses, trying to appear timid, wasn't. He didn't turn into a superhero. Instead, he was a supervillain. The feather tickled her nose, and the clock indicated it was 1:27. *Okay, okay, I get it—seven again.* She took a deep breath and held her rage inside. She would try another approach with the psycho, buy some time until he let his guard down.

"I'm sorry. I'm sure you have your reasons. I was just so surprised, and well, I didn't mean to upset you. I guess I deserved that." Boy, were those words hard to get out, but maybe she could make him think she was weak or completely stupid. "I thought we were hitting it off. I mean, I hoped you'd ask me out." She felt her stomach contents trying to exit again. Would he believe she would come on to her sister's killer? Couldn't hurt to try to stroke this insane person's ego.

"Yes, well, I'm flattered, and a bit surprised the way you were throwing yourself at Eli. I suppose you're just that type of girl my poor mother warned me about. You know, like your mother? You aren't my type though, sorry. Myles is more my type. He never understood what we could have had together. Too bad he came here tonight after I told him to stay home. It wasn't his time yet, but I suppose it was inevitable." Clark bent over and sharpened a long, brutal-looking knife.

"Oh, well, I didn't know. Sorry. You misunderstood what was

going on between Eli and me. It was nothing really—but you...well." Amber gave up. It sounded fake even to her ears.

"If I misunderstood, then I'm sorry. But my gut tells me you're a harlot."

"A—" Amber bit back her fury and swallowed it whole. "I don't even date, but I can understand how a man could misread a woman's intentions. I know my sister was...well, demanding. I can almost comprehend why she drove you to that point with your feelings about Myles. She always took things from me too." Amber rambled on as if she was writing a story. It was the only way those words would ever come out of her mouth.

She slowly positioned the knife. She was thankful for her yoga practice, but she still struggled to move without him noticing. At least the blanket was still over her, or he'd see what she was doing.

"You understand? That's rich. No, you don't. You're way too stupid. But if you want to know the story, we seem to have some time."

"I would like that very much." She smiled encouragingly.

"Your mother must have dropped you on your head as a baby. How did you ever hold a job as a writer?"

Amber pasted a huge fake smile on her face, even though it hurt her swollen lip. She shrugged and played the dumb woman to a tee.

"I thought you might fight me or be angry. I expected to be compared to bear shit and was hopeful for a bit. I'm kind of disappointed in you. Well, I can work on that later. As for what happened, you should know who I am. I don't look anything like my father— well, except for one thing, but no matter. I used to be fat, with braces, and well, very awkward, as they say. I didn't go by Clark, that's my middle name. Can you guess who I am?" Clark asked as he arranged his tools on her dresser.

If she survived, she would throw away everything he had touched, she decided. She would only get one chance, so she had to get Clark to let his guard down. She heard her own pleasant voice ask, "Guess? Did I go to school with you?"

"Nope. One guess down. You have two more."

"Did I know you?"

"We never met, but yes, you know who I am."

"I know who you are?"

"Yes, I answered, and that was your final question. Now you pay for not guessing correctly." He pulled back her blanket and ran a knife down her arm, drawing blood. It wasn't deep, but it hurt.

"Stop!" Amber cried.

"There's always a consequence to your actions. That is minor compared to what I'm going to do to you."

He held up the long knife and licked it. She couldn't think of anything else to say to this animal as her throat tightened and her mouth went dry.

"What? No more guesses, my sweet stepsister?"

"You're…" Amber racked her memories. She remembered seeing a picture of him once as a child.

"Yup, little Deanie, as my father used to call me. You can still call me Clark—I prefer it over Dean. He told me about that night when you tried to sleep with him—well, I was there already, in a guestroom, until he told your mom of my visit. I saw how disappointed Dad was, and that cost a girl her life later—my first kill with my annihilation associate after I followed him that night. Great nickname Dad and I had for each other after that."

Amber grasped the knife and slid forward bit by bit. "You and your father killed a girl. Who?"

"I have no idea who she was—a hitchhiker, though, which is asking to be killed. Dad was so impressed with my natural skills. Like I said, my first real kill, except for helping your dad pass after my dad ran him off the road. I knew what I was at that moment. A chip off the old block is what 'they' call it. Not that we know who those people are, right?"

Amber's jaw dropped, and she almost forgot to pretend she was tied up. "Hey…you…my dad?"

"My dad swerved into your dad's lane. Your dad reacted to our oncoming car by running into a tree while I was in the backseat, supposedly sleeping. I wasn't. It was a thrill watching the car crash. I raced out the minute Dad stopped with my car pillow in hand. I smothered your dad, although I think he would have died anyway. After Dad yelled at me, he realized I was just like him, but he warned me not to do it again. Of course, I didn't listen, but then killing became a family business. Nice, huh?" Clark smiled, setting the knife down.

Amber held back the screams inside, knowing he would cut her again. She focused on breathing. In and out. She managed a nod.

"I see you've learned your place quickly. Good. Well, then I'll finish the story. As you know, my dad left my pathetic mother for yours. Not much of an upgrade other than that she had money—lots of it. My mom wasn't much of a mother, either—a drinker like yours. She did share a bit of interesting information right before her apparent suicide from pills. Want to know what it is?"

Amber could only stare at the monster before her. How did she ever think he was cute? He hid behind that timid disguise, and now it was removed. There was a dark mist swirling around him, along with that red glow in his eyes. What was he?

"I'll take that as a yes again. I do expect you to respond when asked a question next time, or the next cut will be deeper and on your pretty face. Understand?"

"Yes, I understand."

"Great. Here's a part you'll enjoy. Not sure if you overheard me talking, but my mother let it slip about Britney, and I managed to get her to share the rest with me. You see, my father's mistress had a baby when I was only five years old. The harlot gave up Britney for adoption when my father wouldn't leave my mother, but he had no idea about the baby. That bit of news had shocked me, I admit, learning I wasn't an only child. Do you want to hear my mother's parting words?"

"Yes, Clark," Amber responded.

"Apparently, she'd found my collection of small animals buried behind our house over the years, but it crossed the line for her when she found a human body out there, along with my knives. Her exact words were, 'I feel shame for what you've become, Dean. I hope you seek God's forgiveness and repent your sins.' See, I told you she was crazy. Then she willingly took the bottle of pills that I poured into her hand. Her gaze never left my face as she drifted off. I finally forgave her though. I mean, she was crazy—what could I do, right?"

"Right, Clark."

"Glad you see it my way. Any other questions before we get started? Because you should have a couple more, and I'm going to enjoy answering."

"So you helped your mother kill herself?" Amber asked, unable to believe what she was hearing. She quickly closed her mouth when she saw the rage in his eyes.

"I had to kill her, I already told you that. That isn't the question I want you to ask. One more chance."

Amber glanced down at Britney as her chest rose up and down. Thankfully, she didn't hear this. Amber didn't know what he wanted to hear from her. "Why did you kill my sister and want to kill me?"

"See, that's a really good question, Amber. Very simple. Your mom changed her will, leaving her money to you and Iris and only leaving Dad the house. Can you believe that? I couldn't remember when he told me. He was insistent he could change her mind. Poor sap. Then he finally gave in and decided it was time for the twins to go. See now?"

"Yes, I see it was all about the money that I didn't want."

"It didn't matter if you wanted it or not. It was yours and Iris's money."

Amber's eyes filled with tears. "Eli, Myles, and your sister don't deserve to die along with me. They don't even know. Kill me and let them go. They won't know it's you."

Clark smiled and grabbed another knife. "Gee, isn't that noble of you to offer to die for everyone. But I'm certainly not going to give up an opportunity to have this much fun, especially if I can't do it again for a while. You know, keep a low profile. Plus, I'm doing the world a favor, killing you and Britney. The guys here—well, wrong place for them. Of course, no one will think it's me. I will be so devastated when I get the news. 'They' will hear my story—that I was here but left right after I checked on you. Plus, I have a fantastic alibi. Aren't you curious to know what happens?"

"What happens, Clark?"

"Your house burns down from a gas leak and some candles after you've all been killed. 'They' should conclude that the killer was cleaning up when it happened, and the fire killed him. Rather funny if you think about it. Your bodies will be unrecognizable after that event. I'll leave some choice evidence for those idiots to find their killer. Who do you think that will be?"

"Who, Clark?"

"Crazy Eli, of course. Author brings his writing to life, so to speak. He will have to be alive when he burns, which means I'll have to be careful with him and keep him breathing. Anything else you'd like to know before we get started?" Clark smiled down at the pile of bodies at his feet and then licked the knives again and shivered. Amber trembled.

She shook her head. Her sister was dead because he wanted money that she didn't even have, and now Myles, Eli, and Britney were involved. Amber tried again. "I'll sign anything you want relinquishing the money. I won't say a word, and they won't know. Please don't do this."

"Like I would trust you. You're kidding me, right? You do have a wonderful sense of humor, but with your mom out of the way, Dad and I are in the money once you are dead."

Amber gasped as her gentle tears turned into a storm of fury. She would feel no remorse when she plunged a knife into this monster. He looked at her expectedly, with narrowed eyes. So, she played along, "My mother is dead?"

"Yes, that is a question I'd been hoping to answer! Good job!" Clark smiled deeply at her, but it looked more like his lips were trying to escape his face. "No, it wasn't Dad; someone else helped out. Dad had no idea that was coming. And I just got a text a moment ago. It's a done deal. Dad was only involved in me killing you and Iris for him. But he'll be better off without your mother."

"Who killed my mother?" Amber's voice trembled.

"I'll share that information with you later, when you're begging me to kill you. Unless you want to know now. Do you, Amber?"

"Yes, Clark."

"Well, it's a fun story, but a long one. Short version is our illustrious presidential candidate, Bo Wright, had a long overdue favor to pay back to my dad. Give Dad control of all that money so he could live in peace. Nice to have the man who will be our next president helping out, don't you think?"

"Bo Wright killed my mother?" Amber whispered.

"I can barely hear you, Amber. You must be so tired after my peppermint tea with that extra ingredient. To answer your question, yes. Although the police will believe it was her golf pro lover. Bo is a loyal friend to Dad and me. He's not a true killer like us, but still a good man." A warm expression crossed Clark's face and was gone as quickly as it came. In its place was a mask of insanity. "Question time is up. Let's get started." Clark turned his back to her and picked up a knife sharpener.

Amber tightened her grip on the knife. "Yes. Let's."

Eli groaned, stopping her from saying something she'd regret. She watched him turn on his side and look up at her. She shook her head slightly as he saw who had tied him up. She had to do something before he lashed out and got hurt. She mouthed *wait*, hoping he'd understand. He frowned at her and nodded before closing his eyes. Good, he would play along. Myles and Britney were still motionless. She could only tell they were alive by the motion of their chests. Amber focused on her breathing to keep her inner squall from bursting through. Clark had to die, and it had to be her. She couldn't think about what he'd said about her mom. She hoped it was all a huge lie.

Clark smiled. "So eager to die. That's refreshing." He glanced down at the three bodies and then kicked Britney in the side, getting no response. He winked. "She'll feel that later. I could wake the guys up. I find when you open up their skin to breathe, it always gets their attention."

Amber gulped loudly. "Let them sleep," she whispered.

Clark put his hand to his ear with the knife pointing up. He reminded her of a rabid bat. "What was that? Are you losing your voice? You want me to wake them up?"

Amber's tears had dried up. She would show no more weakness. "No. Please don't do that."

The mist around Clark blackened, and his eyes grew redder. What was he turning into? "Oh, yes, well…sure, I do want to keep my stepsister happy, but I'm really looking forward to settling a few things with my real sister too. You know, sibling issues." Clark lit a couple of candles and threw the match on Britney while it was still burning. It went out before doing any damage.

"She did nothing to hurt you."

"You keep defending a person you so clearly dislike. You're a lot like your father, always giving the wrong people chances until it's too late—your mom, for example. I will do to you what I did to him at the very end. Smother the breath out of you—well, once I've had my fun, that is."

Amber swallowed the words that crept up into her throat and took a deep breath. He turned to his knives and continued. "Good control. Might I suggest if you have some sort of religious belief, you make your peace now? You know, get that last prayer in before I get started. Then you won't be thinking about anything but me. I wish I'd had more time with Iris. That was a simple kill, but I can make up for it with you."

"I would prefer you didn't do that."

"I'm sure you would." Clark laughed.

Amber used all her control to not ram her knife into him immediately. "Who have you killed, besides my sister?" She saw her gun tucked into Clark's waistband in the back. She didn't have time to wonder where Eli's gun was. She didn't think he'd forget about it, so that left her with one chance to act swiftly or die.

Clark spun around and put his hands on his hips, shaking his head. "Are you trying to keep me engaged in hopes someone will save you?"

"I think I deserve to know before this happens." Amber kept all emotion off her face and held her body still, playing the tied-up victim. The candles shed light on his knives, but not on her. The mobile feather floated down and landed next to his killing tools. She felt a rush of calm knowing she wasn't alone. Maybe Iris really was watching over her.

Clark rubbed his hands together and then cracked his knuckles. His gray eyes narrowed. "Deserve is such a strong word, but I'll play along. Alone I've killed…well, I'm not sure that one counts. It was an accident. But well, you will be number nine. If I include the ones I've helped with, that increases the number to fifteen. My annihilation associate always rapes his victims, but only after they're dead—you know, necrophilia. That has always fascinated me, but of course, I never did it myself, although I plan on it tonight. Pretty nice of him to wait until they're dead, if you ask me." He paused, waiting for Amber to respond.

She absorbed the information and shoved it into her rage. The man her mother loved raped dead women. After he'd killed them. How had she not known? Something flickered on the wall behind the candles. It looked like…wings. She saw a faint outline of a woman with green wings, a silvery dress, and long black hair. It wasn't Iris. It looked like an angel, and then it disappeared.

"No response to that? Interesting. You won't be very quiet soon, though, when we get started. My annihilation associate and I hold the same belief: get rid of nasty women, of which you are one. But you'll have to wait a bit—I have others ahead of you. At least you can watch."

Amber felt like she was watching a poorly done horror movie. He didn't seem real to her, but those knives were. She had to keep him talking. "Why do you kill, Clark?"

He set the knife down. "Well, I'm not sure I have an answer that you would like. It gives me pleasure, much like what you get from between your legs. It's that simple. Don't look so shocked. I guess I inherited my kill gene. Maybe my dad did too. I feel like you're going to suggest I get help and say you'll be there for me, so don't bother. Oh, yes, there is the thrill I get watching the life pour out of someone. I wish I could bottle that. You'll see what I mean soon."

"I don't want to see. Just kill me and leave them alone," Amber choked out.

"And back in a circle we go. So we're done now. I need to get started. The question time is up. Think about your death, but keep it quiet—I'm working." He smiled and selected a knife. He ran it slowly over the sharpener. The sound of metal on metal lit up every nerve in her body.

Amber's heart was pounding. It was now or never. She glanced over at Eli, who was studying her. She looked at her hands and feet and nodded. Then, while Clark had his back turned, she lifted her blankets, showing Eli the knife. His eyes lit up and he nodded.

"Could I have some water before you get started?" Amber tried.

Clark stopped. "Water?" He glanced over at Eli, Britney, and Myles, who were all unmoving. He shrugged. "Last request, huh? Well, step-sister, I do want to hear all your screams later, so why not?"

He left the room with a wave. She could hear his feet padding down the hall. He started to whistle off key, a tune she didn't recognize. She quietly crept out of bed and started cutting Eli's bonds. She heard Clark bump into the kitchen table and grunt in pain. Good. The whistling stopped, and she froze.

"I've got your water, Amber, but I'm going to finish off the pie. I need my energy. Wait for me," Clark called from the kitchen. He giggled. Amber went back to cutting furiously.

"Hurry," Eli whispered.

Clark spoke around a mouthful of pie. "Too bad lover boy has to die and have his reputation ruined. Yum! This pie is wonderful. It's a darn shame that old lady had to perish too. So nosey, though. My only real regret will be killing Myles." He laughed. "No, I'll find another pretty face to admire. Hang on." She heard the water running.

Amber went numb as she cut Eli free. She met his gaze and shook her head. Her eyes filled with tears. How could he kill that sweet old lady? That was why she didn't answer the door. Tears rolled down her cheeks, and she wiped them away impatiently. She didn't have time for that. She felt a hand on her arm as Eli grabbed her knife. He gestured to get another one from the dresser. The killing knives.

Repulsed, she grabbed the biggest one and then a second one that looked like it could cut through anything and probably had.

Amber turned back to Eli as he reached over Britney to get to his legs. She knew if he tried to push her off him, it might create an unwelcome sound. Eli was sweating and almost free when they heard footsteps and that horrible off-key whistling coming down the hall. Amber got in position at the door with a glance back at Eli. It was up to her. He caught her eye and mouthed to her *you can do this* as he cut through the final rope. Eli carefully began to pull his legs from under Britney, but she grunted, and he froze.

Amber clenched her teeth, frowning. She nodded to Eli grimly and held her knives tightly, one in each hand, high over her head.

Clark stopped that horrible sound and asked from down the hall, "How do you feel about your fingers, Amber? Attached to them? Ha ha ha…."

Amber began to pray. There was a brief flash of light by her nightstand. She saw a male angel come out of the flash alongside the female angel from the wall. Clark's camera moved. No one would believe her if she told them what she was seeing. Well, maybe Eli.

The female angel held Amber's gaze and nodded toward the door. "We will help, but you must be the one to stop Clark, Amber. Stay there, Eli." The angel's gentle voice floated in her head like a dream.

Amber nodded, planted her feet, and tightened her grip on the knives. She threw a glance at Eli, who was motionless, his mouth hanging open.

Clark entered the room with heavy steps. "Here's your water, Am—"

The camera crashed to the floor, drawing Clark's attention. He pulled his gun out, his back to Amber. She advanced on him, raising the knives right as Clark started to turn. The first knife went into his side right as his gun went off. His mouth formed a small O as he reached for the knife. She pushed the second one in, aiming for his heart. She met little resistance as it slid in, like she was cutting a chicken. Her stomach flopped as the blood started to flow. Then she held her breath, hoping that was enough to stop him. She saw Myles beside her as Clark's mouth flew open with unsaid words. His hand released the gun, which landed quietly on the bear-patterned rug, outlined with red. He collapsed on the rug, driving the knives further into his body.

She saw more blood puddling on the floor. It wasn't from Clark.

CHAPTER 18

*E*ve found herself at peace, standing next to a beautiful, smiling angel. "Can we stay here for a moment?" she asked.

"Yes. We can. I am Olive."

"Thank you, Olive. Is there anything we can do to help Jeb? He was always good to me until tonight—well, I thought he was."

"No, unfortunately, there is not. I am sorry. He is a killer."

"I know, but I can't imagine it right now. Will he come with us?"

"I am not sure what will happen to him. If an angel comes for him, he will be reviewing his life for eternity. You have much to atone for, yourself." Olive shrugged.

"I do. What if an angel doesn't come for him?"

"I never stay around to watch that. I hear it is unpleasant, and his soul is destroyed. I hope that is not the case."

"Oh, yes, I understand."

Another angel entered and held out his hand to Neil as he left his body.

"He will take care of him?" Eve asked.

"Yes." Olive nodded at the new angel.

Neil and the other angel were suddenly gone in a flash of light.

"Ready to go too?" Olive asked, taking her hand.

"What about Bo?"

"He has gotten away, Eve. There is nothing we can do about that right now."

"I told the police. I called them."

"The phone cut out before you told them who killed you. But at least you got to leave a message for your daughter. Know that Bo will have to face what he did."

"I thought...sorry. Can I...can I see Jeb one more time, please? I know it's dumb, and perhaps I never knew him, but I feel like if he had feelings, he gave them to me."

"Love is never dumb. Yes, he did have feelings for you, even with the evildwel inside him."

"The what?"

"I will explain later. I do give him slight credit because he cared for you, but that does not cancel out all the women he has murdered."

Eve shuddered as they watched Jeb in the shower. He was frowning as he scrubbed his skin. She glanced out the window right as Bo's car sped down the driveway and disappeared into the thick forest.

"Has Bo killed anyone else?"

"No, not intentionally. He wanted to get out from under Jeb's grasp. This is what he came up with. He is a weak man who made bad decisions that Jeb took advantage of."

"He won't be president, will he?"

"That is up to your daughter now."

"My daughter?"

"Yes, I wish I could show you."

"So she isn't dead like Bo said?"

"No."

Eve smiled. "Good. I didn't want to believe him."

Olive looked away but didn't respond.

Eve lightly brushed her hands over her silky, pristine white gown. "So, can I wait to see that Jeb's arrested? It will offer me some...relief to know that no one else need die at his hands. The very hands that made love to me..." She shook her head.

"Making love is never a bad thing, Eve. Do not forget that."

"Maybe it was only sex."

"For you it was not. I know that."

Jeb shut the shower off, stepped onto the bath mat, and set down the gun he'd found hanging in the shower. He saw another gun under his towel.

"I wonder how they got here," he frowned, pulling on his bathrobe. A siren blared, coming toward the house. He froze.

"Bo set me up." Jeb shook his head. "He outsmarted me and took away the one person I actually loved besides my son."

He picked up the gun.

"You knew I'd clear my head and realize what you did. You're free now, Bo, but my son will take care of you once he learns. You were right, old buddy—I will not go to jail." Jeb smiled and put the gun in his mouth as he heard the police enter the house.

"No, Jeb. Don't!" Eve screamed.

"He cannot hear you, Eve." Olive put a gray wing tipped with black around Eve as Jeb pulled the trigger and a black mist left his body.

"No," Eve whispered.

Olive pulled her out of the room and back to her body before Jeb had crumpled to the floor.

"What was that thing that came out of him?"

"The evildwel. It feeds off fear and anger."

"Oh, so this wasn't really his fault."

Olive shook her head. "He is fully responsible for his actions. They only feed and encourage what is there."

"Did an angel come for him?"

"I am not completely sure."

"I wish you had let me talk to him." Tears flowed down Eve's cheeks. "I have to know why he did what he did."

"This is not the time for a conversation between the two of you. You have much to learn first, like what his mother did to him. It was a miracle he trusted you. In his own way, he kept you safe up until now. But those women who looked like his mother paid for it. Come on. It is time now. You have some things you need to review, but I will let you know what happens to your daughter."

"Is Amber still in danger?"

"I hope not. She is not dead, though."

"So Bo wasn't lying about Dean... Can I go to Amber?"

"No, we cannot go there. So you know, Dean is a killer like his father, only worse. He kills for fun, not like Jeb did to wash away the memories of his mother. Your time here is over. As I said, I will let you know the outcome."

Olive took her arm, and then there was a bright flash of light right as the police burst through the door with guns drawn. They checked the bodies as Eve left her life behind her and peace filled her completely. Soon she found herself seated with her life before her, painful moment after painful moment. She couldn't imagine what Jeb was feeling and seeing right now if he was doing the same thing. Not that it mattered—she had to atone for herself. She wished him luck and kept watching as tears tumbled down her face.

CHAPTER 19

The room lit up as Olive entered it. Blood seeped around Clark like a sluggish river as he gasped for air. Geo evacuated his host, lugging Ed like he was taking out the trash. He tossed Ed on the floor next to the winged ones. He smiled smugly at Nester, who had finally pulled back his swirl, but Nyx was still watching him with the look of a tiger hunting its prey. Nester knew one wrong move would be his last. Geo frowned and moved away when another winged one appeared next to Clark. Nester wondered how bad it would be for Clark. The things he had to atone for were so horrendous that even a seasoned evildwel like Nester couldn't imagine enduring that.

He felt everything spin out of control as he observed the scene in front of him. Amber's face was devoid of emotion. Her mouth snapped shut and curved into a frown as she kicked Clark's body with her red-painted toes. He didn't move. Myles put his hand on her shoulder. She glanced up and looked behind him. Eli was on the ground holding his arm. Red oozed through his fingers.

"I'm okay. It's just a flesh wound, like yours. Make sure he's dead." Eli's face paled as the blood continued to flow unchecked.

Amber grabbed the gun and a knife. She bent over Clark and touched his neck.

"His pulse is so weak, barely—" She ran to Eli, crying, letting the weapons fall on the bed. Britney was sitting up, looking like a child awakened from a nightmare. She immediately clung to Amber, and Myles joined them.

Nester pulled his attention back to the winged ones and evildwels, pleased to know the humans were now safe. The winged ones had prevented so much evil from happening. Nester watched Thomas's response to Olive and waited for Ed to wake up.

The evildwels weren't leaving. Their attention was on Nester.

"I am glad they are all okay," Olive said.

Thomas nodded. "Yes, but Ed is not."

Nester felt Geo's eyes locked on him, but he still thought to the angels. "Why isn't he waking up?"

"The evildwel hurt him somehow," Zelina said, glancing over at Geo, who gave her his full attention. He smiled brightly.

"Is he dead?" Nester asked.

"He is already dead as a human, but this? I do not know. My touch is not working." Zelina didn't break eye contact with Geo.

Nester felt a pain shoot through him. He had never felt anything like it. In a panic he cried out, which brought Nyx closer.

Zelina shot Nester a warning look and approached him, keeping her eye on Geo. Her face darkened like a storm, but her voice was gentle as a light rain. It was a confusing combination for Nester to unravel. "Any ideas, Nester?"

"If you don't know, how would I?" Nester replied, noting the strange look passing between Thomas and Olive. He remembered seeing that expression before when...when what? Nester couldn't remember now as more pain shot through him.

It suddenly hit him. "It came from my kind. Only my kind can heal it."

Zelina frowned and shook her head. Thomas responded with a loud sigh, and Olive had tears in her eyes.

"No, Nester, that is not what I meant!" He heard Zelina's voice but ignored it.

Nester swirled out of control. He glanced back at Geo and was hit by a scowl and narrowing eyes, right as Xene moved next to him. The other evildwels kept their distance along with the winged ones, at least for the moment.

Nester tore his gaze away from what he used to be and turned it to what he wanted to be. He didn't know if this would work, but he had to try. He drifted to Ed's side without thinking.

"There's nothing left to feed on, Nester." Geo's voice was heavy with sarcasm.

He ignored Geo's taunt. He felt the residue of the evildwel lingering on Ed from Clark's fear and anger. It filled him with familiar feelings of feeding. Nester felt his mist darken. He wasn't going to be able to help; he was too much an evildwel.

"Focus on love, everyone, and they will leave. Then maybe we can give our love to Ed to try to heal him." Zelina's honeyed voice cut into his despair.

Then he felt Zelina's love. It shot through him much like a feeding did but without the weight. He felt light and free. It was a wonderful feeling, and when his mist lightened and spun out of control, he didn't fight it but embraced it. With no idea what he should be doing, he poured these new feelings into Ed. His swirl contained itself and lost all the darkness that held him in the shadows. He was completely white now, like the sun, bright and warm, as he heard Clark gasp his last breath. Nester was surrounded by his three winged friends. They were protecting him.

He had a flash of understanding. When evildwels died, they faded away because they didn't know the strength of love. Death no longer scared him, but first he had to save Ed. Could this new love do it? Nester pushed all thoughts from his mind and thrust more of his new energy into Ed. He saw Ed's hand twitch and felt encouraged. He doubled his efforts and was rewarded with Ed's eyes opening. He stretched out his legs and sat up, smiling at Nester.

"Thank you." Thomas helped him up. Ed was barely able to stand.

Zelina smiled. "Thank you."

"I had to save him."

"I know, and you did it through love." Her gentle smiled turned into a frown as Geo advanced, shaking his head.

"Great show, Nester. You've been talking to these winged ones. Your color has changed, and you helped this Ed thing. You are extremely sick. We are going to help you now. Fellow evildwels, please join me."

Nester started swirling out of control, and he welcomed it. "No, Geo. You don't understand. We can change. We don't have to feed on the evil. We can feed on love, and we can give love too."

"I knew Nester was off." Nyx's mist darkened.

"If you will excuse us, winged ones. We have an evildwel matter to resolve."

"You aren't getting through us." Thomas squared his shoulders.

"I beg to differ. There are many more of us than you." Four more evildwels pushed into the room.

Olive grabbed Thomas's hand. "Not getting through us."

"Have it your way." Geo grinned.

All the evildwels pushed forward into the winged ones. Sparks and screams flew.

"Hold on!" Zelina yelled, "I've called the angels back."

"I cannot!" Olive screamed as she was thrown back against the wall.

Thomas reached out for Zelina, but they were both thrown away from Nester.

"Make a circle. That will keep them out," Geo commanded.

"Are you okay?" Nester asked his friends.

"Yes, Nester. We will get you out of there."

"It's okay, Zelina. I know love now, thank you."

"No, the other angels are almost here. Please hang on."

So are more evildwels, Nester thought.

"Dinner time!" Geo led the attack as they jumped on top of Nester. The pain was immediate. Two more evildwels poured into the room in a frenzy while the others fought outside with the few winged ones who had stayed.

"Get away from him!" Thomas shouted. The winged ones advanced on the evildwels again, with Ed standing behind them.

Thomas screamed at the evildwels. A few turned to attack him, pushing him away. Two winged ones appeared, and they almost seemed to be making progress until five new evildwels entered the fray. The winged ones were pushed away, and a dark cloud encircled the evildwels. Their dark mist was blending, as Nester had feared. Nothing was getting through that. The pain intensified, and the evildwels turned their attention back to Nester. He saw another winged one appear, but they were sorely outnumbered this time.

"Thank you!" Nester called out to his friends.

"I am sorry," he heard Zelina say. "Forgive me."

"I have. I'm okay now," Nester whispered as he met her eyes. She was crying. Olive tried pushing again but was thrown into Thomas's arms. Her bright red hair splashed against his chest like blood.

They couldn't get through with their love because there was too much hate.

Pain and fear shot through his body as the evildwels ripped away at his layers of life. They had saved Amber, and he saved Ed. He tried to contact the winged ones again, but he was too weak. He focused on the love the winged ones had given him in the end and what he'd given to Ed.

As each rip came, he saw a life he'd been responsible for taking, and he was filled with regret, yet he felt no shame as he screamed. He suddenly felt lighter and filled with hope for their kind. What could they become someday if they learned to embrace this change? If he had only gotten through to Geo, the strongest evildwel he'd ever seen.

Everything started to fade away, and Nester realized with some satisfaction that he had become love.

* * *

THOMAS WATCHED in horror as the evildwels grew darker and Nester went from white to clear. Then nothing was left. He didn't think he'd ever get the sound of Nester's scream out of his mind, or the sound of ripping and chewing of the mist. It was like tigers tearing through their prey's flesh. At least he had somehow saved Ed and found love. Ed looked fully recovered.

"Misty-man died for me," Ed said weakly. "He shouldn't have."

"I want revenge for the very first time." Thomas shuddered.

"Yes, I understand. All this bad can even affect us. It will pass since that is not our way." Zelina met Thomas's eyes with a firm gaze as she wiped her tears away.

"We need to avenge our misty friend," Ed insisted as several angels arrived.

Geo interrupted. "You didn't win like you thought, winged ones. This sick traitor who became your pet is dead. His illness won't be a stain on our kind."

"His illness is your salvation," Zelina responded as more angels stood next to her.

"I disagree. He was sick. You winged ones ruined a grand feeding. Everything is changed now that my host is dead, and I've grown weary of your interference. We are evenly matched now, but we still can't kill you. It's time we move on. We have an entire universe to feed on. Good luck with your boring little planet. I'm going to find a better one to feed on without any pesky winged ones." Geo whirled away before anyone could reply.

Nyx and Xene boldly grinned at the angels. "Yeah, you can have this planet. Wait for us, Geo." The other evildwels followed.

"Is it over?" Thomas asked.

"Almost. The rest is up to Amber and Myles and a little bit of help from us. I pity the place the evildwels find. I had hoped they would all change and not need to keep feeding on fear. Maybe someday."

Ed shook his head. "That misty monster Geo absorbed all my energy, and then Nester gave it back to me. I felt his regret and pain. He really wanted to help us, you know."

"I know. I will always feel remorse for not being able to help him and see what he could have become. We did our best, though, and that is all we can do."

"It is," Thomas admitted, pushing his hair back. "And I agree I would have liked to see what he was becoming."

Zelina shook out her wings. "Yes, well, at least Amber has done what she needed to do right now."

"She saw you, though. Will she remember?" Olive asked.

"She will remember seeing me but not what I will instruct her to do. Of course, humans always doubt themselves and their perceptions if any memories do try to come back."

"Yes, that has always been a weak point for them." Olive rested her head on Thomas's broad shoulder.

"What instructions?" Ed asked.

Zelina gave him a sad smile. "What she needs to do. And I am glad you are okay, Ed."

"Yeah, I've never felt that much power from an evildwel. It scared me," he admitted.

"It scared all of us. Imagine if they had stayed. Their power…" Zelina didn't finish.

"Yes, well, things are changing. Maybe we will too." Thomas reached out and put a hand on her shoulder. "I put all my faith in us and you."

"Thank you. Well, we had better finish up."

"Right," Thomas agreed as Olive and Ed nodded.

CHAPTER 20

*A*mber wound a towel around Eli's arm tightly to try to stop the bleeding. Myles was helping Britney up when a bright light flashed in the room.

"Amber," Zelina called out gently.

"What is that?" Britney cried.

"It's an angel." Amber smiled.

"Those shadows...they were real." Eli shook his head and wiped his eyes.

Myles patted Eli's back gently. "Very real. I hope this doesn't mean we're dead."

"I feel alive," Eli said.

Zelina smiled and opened her wings for full effect, "You are all very alive, do not worry. I will not keep you long since you need to alert the authorities. You will all forget that it was Amber that saved you."

"What? Why?" Eli interrupted.

Zelina held up a hand. "Because that is what is needed. Amber is a hero, but for the good of your world, you need to forget that. You will recall that it was Myles who untied himself and saved all of you. The evidence will support that. It is necessary for his political career, so he can win this election."

"What? That makes no sense," Eli murmured.

"Oh, it does. You see, if Bo Wright wins, he will be the cause of war and death on a large scale. So it is necessary that Myles becomes president. This scenario makes Myles a hero, and a hero wins by a landslide, thanks to Amber."

"I don't understand," Myles said. He glanced at Britney, who just shook her head.

"What have I got to do with him becoming president?" Amber's mouth fell open. Eli reached out to her with his wounded arm and winced as more blood flowed.

"Eli, please try to remain still. I repaired what could kill you, but you must wait until the doctors fix the rest. I am leaving some damage to satisfy the press and authorities. You are Amber's soul mate, so take care of yourself, please."

"Um, soul mate? I will…um…thanks." Eli shook his head as his face reddened.

"He could have died?" Amber asked, her eyes wide.

"Yes, the bullet hit more than his arm. You are welcome, Eli. Now, Myles, you have the first lady right next to you. This is more than flirting. This experience has triggered the good inside you, Britney. Love will fill that empty void. There will no longer be the need to try to get attention for yourself all the time. Amber, this woman cares for you, and you will have a friend like you had in your sister because you will both learn to love yourselves again."

"First lady?" Britney repeated.

A puzzled look came over Amber's face. "What about her being…"

Zelina held up a hand and cut Amber off. "That will be forgotten. No one needs ever to know. That is for the best."

"Forgotten what?" Britney demanded.

"Sweet Britney. It is all going to be well for you. You are loved, by your man next to you and your best friend, and that is all you need. You will be a great first lady—helping children will be your focus."

"This is crazy," Britney muttered, looking down.

"How do you know all of this?" Myles shook his head.

Zelina smiled. "I am an angel."

"Of course, but who I marry and all...I mean, I'm attracted to Britney and wanted to date her, but—" Myles broke off.

"I know. Do not worry about all the details right now. They will come to you. To answer your question about your part in his election, Amber, you will write the article about this that will ensure he wins. Then there will be two famous authors in your family. That is all you four need to know. If things work out as planned, your mother's killer will be caught soon."

Amber shook her head, tears running down her face. "Wait. So he was telling the truth about who killed her?"

"Yes. This will come out later, and you won't remember what Clark told you about Jeb or Bo." Zelina gently wiped away Amber's tears.

Amber felt serene as Zelina started fluttering her wings as Eli's gently placed a hand on her shoulder.

"What about my sister? Can I see her?"

"Oh, Amber. I am sorry, you cannot. She is not here with us. But she is happy and watches over you from where she is. She works with the animals, you know, like cats and birds. And bears. She loves you deeply."

"Bears? Was that her sending that bear?"

Zelina shrugged without making eye contact. She wore a slight grin as she twisted her long black hair into a loose ponytail that she draped over her right shoulder.

"I think it was. Please thank her for me and tell her I love her."

"Yes, I will, but she already knows. And Myles, Iris wants you to be happy too. She approves of your upcoming marriage, and yours too, Amber. I must go—I have run out of time. You have all the new memories you need. You will see. You all will forget I spoke to you, but you will remember what to do. Oh, with one tiny exception. Amber and Eli will remember seeing an angel appear in the shadows." Zelina smiled and added a wink.

"What about my—" Amber wanted to ask about her dad, her aunt, and her mother, but the angel was gone in a brilliant gold flash. Then they were alone in the dark room with a lifeless killer.

"Thank God it's over!" Britney cried, her tears flowing.

"Thank you for saving us, Myles," Eli said. "I can never repay you."

Myles shrugged. "I got lucky. He didn't tie me as tight is all. I'm glad everyone is okay, but keep your arm still—it's bleeding pretty badly." Myles put an arm around Britney.

Amber hurried into the living room. The landline was working, so she dialed 911.

"They're on their way. I'm going to check the fuse box. You know, in case he shut the power off."

"I'll go with you." Eli tried to stand up, but Myles guided him gently into a chair.

"You aren't going anywhere." Amber shook her head. "You need to sit. You got shot, remember?"

"Yeah, guess you're right, but don't forget your arm too."

Amber shrugged. "It's fine."

"I'll go with her." Myles held his hands up.

"Thanks, Myles."

Soon the lights were back on, and Amber shut her bedroom door. She'd never be able to sleep in there again. Not after what happened. She would have to completely redo it someday.

Red lights and a siren blared outside. She watched the emergency vehicles pull up in front of her house. Across the street stood a bear. Her bear. It dipped its head and ran into the woods. She felt like it had been watching over her.

She glanced at Eli, who was sitting in the kitchen chair with Tiger in his lap, stroking his fur. He was pale, but she knew he'd be okay. She heard footsteps running up the stairs to her door. It wouldn't be long before the press knew, and then her privacy would be gone. But at least she finally had some peace from knowing who had killed her sister—and why. She got up to answer her door with a quick glance at Eli. Yes, maybe she did want more with him, she thought.

* * *

ZELINA LOOKED pleased as she watched the other angels leave. Thomas and Olive remained.

Ed sighed loudly. "I'm glad this worked out and all, but you know I'm gonna miss my first misty friend."

"We all are."

Thomas pulled Olive closer as they watched the police enter. The look of surprise registered on their faces when they saw Myles standing there.

"This is going to be quite a story for Myles," Thomas commented.

"It will not inflate his ego like it would for some. He is very grounded for a human," Zelina replied.

"Yes, he is." Thomas nodded.

Ed wiped a tear away, and the angels pretended not to notice. They were all going to miss Nester.

CHAPTER 21

ONE YEAR LATER

*I*t seemed like a lifetime ago when she had met Myles and almost lost her life to her stepbrother. Luckily, Myles had stopped him. She never mentioned the angel she'd seen or the feathers and warnings, except to Eli, who had seen the shadowy figure too.

Jeb murdering her mother had hit her hard, but Eli had been there for her. Amber felt blessed that they'd found her mother's last message to her. She couldn't see her mother's face in the video, but she did see her blood on the floor. She would never forget that image of her mother's life puddled on the cold marble, but her message healed a lot of wounds. It gave Amber closure and peace, hearing the words of love and regret, something she had needed for a long time. The police didn't put much stock in anything in that recording as her mother lay there dying, but Amber believed she was trying to tell them something before she died. She would never know what that was.

At least her sister's murder was resolved. She wasn't sure if she bought the police's theory that Clark/Dean had killed Iris because she found out he was skimming money from the campaign and gone after Amber because he was afraid Iris had told her. They did have a money trail, but Amber believed it was more likely he knew about Iris being with Myles and was jealous. One of the few things she remembered from that night was him confessing to being interested in Myles. Yet if that were true, why her? She had considered seeing a hypnotherapist to relive that night in case she'd repressed something, but in the end, she decided to leave well enough alone. So far, no one knew about her sister's relationship with Myles except Eli, and she wanted to keep it that way.

A small smile touched Amber's face when she thought about Bo Wright's landslide loss. Right after the election, he went into seclusion. She was proud her article had kept that snake out of office while Myles soared into the country's hearts like a real-life Superman. The man who walked through drifts of snow to save the sister of his murdered employee who he believed was in danger. Too bad he couldn't have saved Mrs. Jones too.

She sighed, which triggered a comforting hand squeeze from Eli. He hadn't left her side since that night. After he moved into her house last summer, they had remodeled the upstairs bedroom and made it their own. She moved out of her old bedroom, where Clark died, the next day, had it professionally cleaned and remodeled, and then shut the door. Too many bad memories between those walls that no amount of sage smudging could erase. Eli used the spare room as his office.

Lately they had been talking about adding on to the house or converting the garage into two offices. After her very successful article, she quit the newspaper, jumped on board Myles's campaign, and even started working on that book Iris had pushed her to finish.

"You okay?" Eli whispered.

"I am," Amber replied, spinning her new engagement ring.

They hadn't set a date yet, but the plan was to rent a boat in the fall and get married on Lake Tahoe.

A young man behind her tried to suppress a cough, with little success. Britney had met his mother on the campaign trail. She had just lost her daughter, Carrie, to cancer but wanted to help with the campaign. Her son, Robert, had started helping and become one of Myles's biggest supporters.

"Your article saved him, Amber," Britney had confided. "He was hanging out with some bad people after his sister died. You gave him hope and something to believe in."

Robert's mother was going to Washington to work in Myles's cabinet, Britney had shared, with the warning "Don't tell anyone yet."

Amber turned around and smiled at the young man whose shining brown eyes were pinned on Myles.

Her phone vibrated. She had planned to ignore it until a feather landed at her feet. Seeing it was an email from Steve, Myles's old bodyguard, filled her with unease. She had been surprised that he and Marsha, who had recently married, weren't there. She opened the message.

MYLES IS A TREASURED FRIEND, and I wish I could be there to share his day with him, but something came up that I need to stay on top of. I wouldn't be sending this email now if it wasn't important, and some of this information will soon be all over the news.

Authorities found Bo Wright's body early this morning after an apparent suicide. A call had come in from his ex-wife requesting a safety check after she received a strange text from him. He was found hanging from a rafter in his cabin and pronounced dead at the scene. A lengthy and detailed note was found. I will send you a copy when I can obtain it, but here is a summary from a trusted source.

AMBER'S REALITY spun out of control as she read the summary. That night smashed into her so hard she felt like she couldn't catch her breath. The image of Clark telling her what she was reading now—how did she forget that it was Bo, not Jeb, who killed her mother and the golf pro? Yes, it was to implicate Jeb. It had worked perfectly, but apparently Bo couldn't live with it. Amber felt like she was going to throw up, and she swallowed hard. She did her ocean breathing, in and out, as she recalled Clark bragging that he had personally finished killing her father after Jeb ran him off the road. She blinked hard as she scanned the summary. That part wasn't there. They didn't know—

yet. More memories hit her as she envisioned Clark's smug smile and all those knives as she had desperately struggled to cut through her ropes.

Had she repressed all of this because it had been so traumatizing or…wait a minute. The angel. She wanted them to forget, but why? So many had died because of Jeb, Clark, and even Bo, including sweet Mrs. Jones, who had done nothing. Amber forced herself to remain calm as everyone's attention was on Myles. She held back a frown as she read the last words:

To MAKE up for his silence all these years, he left a map to where the killing shack is located on the Cadwell property, which Wright purchased after their deaths. He also left a map to find the grave of the young girl who died in the boating accident so her family could finally have closure. He ended this note with a plea of forgiveness for his role in all of this, but he wanted to be remembered as a good man who did the right thing by providing the information and that he would have served his country well if he had won the election.

That ends the summary. This note was from a man who wasn't much different than the serial killer he protected all these years. The killing shack Wright spoke of was found this morning. Your stepfather kept detailed records that will give some closure to the families of these missing women. Your mother's real murderer has been found. Your stepfather's crimes have become known, along with his son's involvement. I will update when I can. Please give Myles my highest regards and congratulations.

TEARS FILLED her eyes as she handed the phone to Eli. Her mother's message now made sense, and she knew the truth about how her father died. Eli handed the phone back to her with a look of pure disbelief.

He whispered, "I remember."

"Me too."

His arm tightened around her. She wished she understood why the angel had taken away her memories only to return them now, but she wasn't going to try to figure out an angel's motivations. Maybe it would have changed things. No need for Myles and Britney to ever know if they didn't remember what really happened. She sighed, and Britney looked at her, questioning. Something nagged at her about Britney. What was it? She smiled at her best friend and passed the phone down to her. The same feather flew by, and Amber knew her sister was smiling down on her, along with the angels. She felt a calm spread through her like she was wrapped in love. It was really going to be okay now.

* * *

"WILL they find out Britney is related to two serial killers, Zelina?" Ed crossed his arms as he leaned against the railing.

Zelina had her wing wrapped protectively around Amber. "No. And before you ask, Ed, if they had remembered, it would have changed things. If they could not prove Bo had done anything, well, it could have been spun as a plot against him by Myles. His fans would have rallied behind him at the injustice."

"Fans? The voters?"

Zelina nodded. "Same thing, it seems."

"He could have gotten away with murder?"

Zelina sighed and disengaged from Amber. "It was one possibility. We could not take that chance."

"Will the other two remember what happened too?"

"No. It's best they don't. Amber and Eli will do the right thing by not saying anything."

"Then it is over." Thomas hugged Olive.

Zelina nodded. She was satisfied Amber would be okay now with Eli and Britney by her side and the information now out there.

Olive tugged Thomas away from the group. "Excuse us. Now we can talk about an event we should start planning."

"Do you think they're finally gonna tie the knot?" Ed asked.

"That has always been such a strange expression. Yes, they will join together."

"Well, I didn't make it up."

Zelina grinned as Thomas's face reddened. "I know you did not."

Ed followed her grin and gently nudged the angel. "I wonder who's asking who."

Zelina gave his offending arm a look, with a bit of affection thrown in. "A love like that takes both. You will like angel weddings. They are quite beautiful. They have a different meaning since it is truly forever, you know."

Ed smiled sweetly at Zelina. "Yeah, that's a pretty big commitment, I'd say."

"It is. I have never been in love, you know. Maybe someday, who knows? Most angels do not fall in love, so it is a rare and lovely thing, like a blooming desert flower."

"That would sound good as a toast in their wedding, Zelina."

"We do not eat toast...oh, yes, the speech they make."

Thomas picked Olive up and swung her around, and Zelina knew they would be very happy. The familiar glow sparkled next to Ed. It had been there since that night when they had almost lost him, the night they did lose Nester. She had hoped it might mean that part of the evildwel had survived and that someday he would be more than just a sparkle. She sent the sparkle some love.

She turned back just in time to see everyone standing and clapping for President Stroud, who had just removed his hand from the bible. The sparkle grew brighter and brighter next to her. Thomas put Olive down, and soon they were encircling the glow.

"Is it...?" Olive asked.

"Send love—lots of it!" Zelina commanded.

"I am," Thomas replied.

Blue eyes appeared in a white mist that slowly changed into a male human form.

"Can you hear me?" a weak voice called out.

Zelina's mouth dropped open for a split second before she spoke. "Yes. Nester, is that you?"

Nester's white mist was becoming solid. The angels and Ed watched in awe as it split at the bottom, making legs, and the sides lifted to create arms. Finally, the head formed, with the ears and nose popping out last. "It is."

"That was amazing!" Olive reached out and grasped Nester's hand. Startled, he pulled back.

"Sorry, Olive. That felt weird. I've never had my own hand before. Only my hosts had them."

"No need to apologize to me." Olive looked up at Thomas.

"Where have you been, dude?"

"I've been right here. I've been trying to communicate with you guys, but you couldn't hear or see me. It got kind of lonely."

"You will never feel that way again." Zelina put her wings around Nester, who was beaming in his male human shape.

"I wonder why now," Olive said.

"Because good won?" Thomas's eyes filled with tears as he put his arm around Olive. She rested her head on his shoulder.

"Yes, I think that is it. They have Bo Wright's body. A new president will guide them wisely through a major crisis, and now our friend is back with us physically."

"Well, welcome back, Nester." Olive glowed. Thomas broke into a huge grin as he wiped a stray tear off his cheek. "I am so happy to see you again."

Ed held his hand up and went in for a high five, which Nester tentatively held up his palm to receive. "The misty-man is back!"

Zelina wiped away her happy tears. "This has brought me the greatest joy ever, my friend Nester."

"Thank you. I have stayed close almost the whole time. Your presence has comforted me."

"I am glad of that." Zelina patted his shoulder.

Nester stood next to Zelina, smiling broadly as the group took in the moment. "Did I hear right that there was going to be an angel wedding?"

She glanced at Thomas and Olive, who both nodded with huge smiles. "Yes. I am pleased and happy."

"Thank you," Thomas replied.

Olive beamed up at Thomas. "Yes, we are very happy."

"There is so much joy right now, and my heart is full. Nester is here with us again, Myles is president, and you two are getting married."

Ed grinned. "It's the best, I agree. I owe you, misty-man, although I can't call you that anymore with that body you're sporting. You kind of look like Brad Pitt now."

Nester clasped his hands together and then held them out, studying them. "You can still call me that. I have no idea who Brad Pitt is, but I will take it as a compliment. I only did what any of you would have."

"Well, thanks, dude. Being compared to Brad Pitt is a compliment, according to human females. You're the best."

Nester smiled as he held up a foot and moved it in circles before he lost his balance. That only made him giggle. "So are you."

Ed grinned. "Yeah, whatever. Are you doing the Hokey Pokey, misty-man?"

"The what?"

"It's a kid's game."

Nester shook his head. "I don't think I am."

Zelina had a slight grin as she embraced Nester. "All of this good is spreading. Think of all we can do together now."

"Zelina, I almost gave up hope I'd be able to communicate with you again."

"There is always hope, and you have proven that. I think you were in something like a cocoon, and you hatched finally. You are a butterfly now."

Nester pulled away from Zelina and spun around. "I wonder what butterflies eat?"

Zelina laughed and shook her head. "Have you been eating?"

Nester stopped spinning and rubbed his chin. "No. Although when things feel good, so do I."

Zelina nodded and put a hand on him. "Now you feed on love."

Nester nodded as he squatted down and then jumped up. "I have a body now, like you do, Zelina. This is what we're meant to be, I think. I'm not an evildwel anymore."

"No, you are not. And yes, like us, but lacking wings. Who knows, maybe you will get those later, or be more like Ed?"

Ed had a lopsided grin as he patted Nester's back. "He can only hope to be as cool as me, Zelina. And slow down, misty-man. You don't want to break your new body."

"Break?" Nester's blue eyes widened as he tentatively touched his blond hair. His skin had a golden tone to it like he had spent the summer in the sun.

Ed chuckled and winked. "Just kidding, misty-man, you'll be fine. You know you're a pretty good-looking dude now. But we gotta come up with a name for what you are. How about a happydwel?"

"Isn't that kind of cheesy?" Nester winked back.

"Do you have a better term for it, Nester?" Ed smirked.

Nester shrugged and then stared in surprise at his shoulders. "This will take some getting used to. I suppose I don't have a better term for it…yet."

"We will come up with something," Zelina said. "You are the first of your kind that we know of on Earth, and maybe anywhere."

Nester nodded with a broad smile. "Okay. I can accept that."

"If you are going to spend time with us, then you will need to be educated on our ways. Are you willing, Nester?" Zelina asked.

Nester bowed his head. "Yes, I'd be honored."

"Good."

"There is one thing. I spent some time away from you for a bit looking for another evildwel who met my fate. I told you about Arius. Unfortunately, I haven't found any traces of him…yet. I want to resume that search again soon."

"Yes, of course. We will help you."

"Thank you."

Zelina held up a finger. "First, though, you need some training. We will start tomorrow, but now let us enjoy this moment."

Nester nodded. "Agreed."

"Good!"

"Cool! Now back to names. What about lovedwel?" Ed threw out. "Angeldwel?"

Zelina frowned. "No, Ed."

Ed put his hands up. "Well, I'm going to keep trying."

Zelina laughed. "I would expect no less from you. When are you going to, as Ed puts it, tie the knot, Thomas and Olive?"

The couple were wrapped around each other, lost in their bliss.

"Olive? Thomas?" Zelina repeated.

Thomas blushed. "Oh, sorry, Zelina. I am listening, but I guess I'm so happy I wanted to feel it and forgot to talk, if that makes sense."

Olive glanced at Thomas, who nodded. "We want to do it at Christmas, when we met."

Zelina hugged them both. "Good, that gives us several months."

"Yes, lots to plan!" Olive pitched in.

Nester held up a hand. "I'd like to help."

"I would like you in it," Thomas replied.

"I'd be honored."

Thomas smiled broadly. "So would we."

"Another happily ever after, Zelina." Ed grinned.

"Yes, it is. This time, the happiest of them all."

"Gooddwel, or how about Heal*Ed*wel?"

"Maybe."

They stood together, watching and listening as Myles gave the speech of generations. There is a lot of hope now. Zelina smiled, knowing love had won in the end.

POEMS

it dwells in thick dust
a paradise forgotten
underneath your past

* * *

the angel's gift shone
like a rainbow umbrella
in a vile gray world
I saw through her eyes of love
possibilities revealed.

* * *

the bear
with a black coat
lumbers through the forest
scrounging for its next tasty meal
alert

it never misses the garbage can
noise sends it up a tree
where it's safe
watching.

AUTHOR'S NOTE

Thank you for reading, "This Last Chance." Reviews are vital, and each one left is an appreciated gift to the author. I've tackled abuse in many forms in the previous books. Although in this story there is the loss of a loved one, a dysfunctional family, murder, greed, and hate. I wanted to show that perhaps there is still good in the world and maybe, just maybe a time when good finally wins over evil.

Many thanks go out to my amazing beta readers, John, Jan, Sandra, Mae, and Mark. Your input was invaluable! A huge thanks to my editor, Denise, from *The Artful Editor*.

All my love goes to my husband, family, and friends for their patient support and encouragement.

Finally, to my readers, you are my inspiration!

ABOUT THE AUTHOR

D. L. Finn is an independent California local who encourages everyone to embrace their inner child. She was born and raised in the foggy Bay Area, but in 1990 she relocated with her husband, kids, dogs, and cats to Nevada City, in the Sierra foothills. She immersed herself in reading all types of books but especially loved romance, horror, and fantasy. She always treasured creating her own reality on paper. Finally, surrounded by towering pines, oaks, and cedars, her creativity was nurtured until it bloomed. Her creations include children's books, adult fiction, a unique autobiography, and poetry. She continues on her adventure with an open invitation to all readers to join her. You can learn more about Ms. Finn at her website www.dlfinnauthor.com or email her at d.l.finn.author@gmail.com.

EXCERPT FROM THIS SECOND CHANCE

ANGELS & EVILDWELS BOOK 1

CHAPTER 1

They hovered over the familiar woman in the wedding dress. She looked terrified, and on the day that she should be at her happiest.

"You are getting a chance most do not get. You understand that, right?" Zelina asked.

He meekly nodded at her. Her brown eyes narrowed, piercing his soul. She clearly didn't like him—not that he blamed her.

"Good. We are clear. You give Rachael her happy ending. Then you can move on and let go of *some of* that bad you did," Zelina said, pursing her lips tightly together.

Her pale silver gown flowed around her like an ocean wave ebbing in and out. He never understood how angels' clothes did that yet, at the same time, kept their form enough to cover them modestly.

"I understand, and I'm grateful I've been given this second chance. I won't let you, or Rachael, down. I'll do whatever it takes to make it happen," he replied, more confidently than he felt.

Although it confused him that he was being given this chance, he'd never question this angel. He certainly didn't deserve it and hadn't had a moment's peace since his death. Everything he'd done flashed before him—over and over. He was relieved to have a break from it and a chance to finally do some good, but he was merely a ghost—a soul, or a man without a body. What could he do to take away that expression on Rachael's face?

"Yes, it is a break from your much-earned reflections." Zelina crossed her arms, obviously irritated at him.

He felt his face redden as he nodded back at her. In this form he felt all the physical and emotional reactions he had when he was alive, but stronger. He needed to remember that angels always knew what he was thinking. He had no privacy now.

"I had to watch Rachael make some bad mistakes. I will not do this again; this is too important. You must figure out how to fix this and make your atonement. You know the rules. If I see you doing any harm, I will send you back. This is your *only* chance to do some good. I will be watching if you need some guidance, but I think you will figure it out," Zelina finished, suddenly seeming taller to him.

Her black hair glowed as she put her hands on her hips with her wings fully extended. He never tired of seeing the shimmering, feathered wings that reminded him of a peacock tail. They were beautiful. Under all that splendor, he knew, there was a ferociousness akin to a bear protecting her young. Rachael was her cub.

When her wings were tucked behind her, unseen, Zelina seemed perfectly ordinary. She could walk among the humans unnoticed. She turned her gaze on him again and scowled. She oversaw people like him—the tough cases. He sighed. Zelina responded to his sigh with a smirk. On Earth that look would have infuriated him, coming from a woman. Now it scared him.

A sudden chill ran through him. "Is someone else here?" he asked.

"It is not a someone; it is more of a thing, and it is what you are up against. It has no conscience, unlike even someone like you; your conscience peeked out after your reign of terror. This thing has no empathy, no love—only hate. I cannot hear what it thinks. It is the purest form of evil and is called an *evildwel*. This one has consumed its human—even in death. You had one in control of you, but a part of you remained. Death might have saved you, or you might have fought it off someday. I do not know things like that. What I do know is that this evildwel means Rachael harm. Be careful, and do not disappoint me," Zelina warned, and then she vanished.

In the corner of the room, there was no form for him to make out, only thick, dark mist. Did the evildwel know he was there? He suddenly wished Zelina hadn't left him. He was afraid, yet he was going to do what Zelina requested—not because he had no choice, but because he had a lot of things to make up for. It was time to get to work.

CHAPTER 2

Rachael's detachment from the image in the mirror smoothing the satin, off-white wedding gown puzzled her. After all, this was the same scalloped three-quarter dress, showing off her newly trim waist, that she'd pictured herself in after seeing it on a *Bridal* magazine cover over twenty years ago. Frowning, Rachael adjusted the tiny yellow roses and baby's breath in her Gibson-styled, lightened auburn hair with her set of pink, acrylic nails.

"Not bad for age thirty-seven and three kids," Rachael tried to reassure the pale image in the mirror.

It didn't work. The urge to rip off the dress and fake nails and make a dash out the back door was even stronger now.

"Why?" Rachael asked the woman staring back at her in the mirror, unaware of her unseen visitors.

Rachael couldn't have asked for a more perfect day. The weather, the gazebo Tony had built for their ceremony, the dress that her mother had spent hours making for her—everything in her life had finally fallen into place. It was perfect. Maybe this was just a very delayed reaction to her first wedding. That was when the strong urge to run out the back door would have come in handy. But if she'd done that, her kids wouldn't be here. Besides, Rachael couldn't compare this June morning to that snowy December day nineteen years ago when she'd stood holding a stale bouquet of faded satin flowers at some nameless chapel in Reno.

Rachael sighed and felt a chill shoot through her, even though the room was over 75 degrees. Stress, she concluded. Careful not to wrinkle her satin dress, she sat in the old maple rocking chair and pulled the handmade pink comforter over her. The comforter had been made by Tony's mother, Nora. She raised Tony alone after his father, Wayne Battaglia, died in a horrible car crash when Tony was barely a year old. Tony knew very little about his father, and his mother had never talked about him to her son. Tony was convinced this was due to grief and never pressed for information. Rachael thought his mother's response, not to tell a son about his father, was strange. One thing Rachael was positive about was that Nora had done a fantastic job raising Tony into the man he was.

Unlike her first mother-in-law, who'd raised (well, at least given birth to) Ed. Tammy kept food on the table and a roof over his head by helping make meth in a lab next door to their trailer. When she finally walked away from that addiction, she turned to others: drinking and pain pills. Tammy always had a man in her life. Some of them helped raise Ed; others didn't. Ed hadn't been sure if one of them was his father. He wasn't sure if his mother knew, either.

After Rachael gave birth to their first son, Eddie, Tammy had confided to her in an emotionless tone, "Al, this man I was seeing, fooled around with little Ed, if you know what I mean. I think he was eight or something like that. I didn't stand for that crap. I kicked Al right out on his ass, I did. I'm glad Ed grew up to like women. Never know which way they'll go after that. You keep an eye on little Eddie Jr., here, so you can have grandkids someday too," Tammy added with a nod, as though she had imparted some heavy wisdom to Rachael. Tammy then brushed her frizzy, bottle-blond hair out of her face and took a long drink from her vodka-scented orange juice.

Rachael had been horrified and tried to talk to Ed about it. He'd refused and made sure his mother knew to never bring that subject up again. Rachael understood he had good reason to be angry. What she didn't understand was why it was directed at her and not at the people who'd hurt him. The one good thing Tammy had done for Rachael and her kids was to stay out of their lives after the divorce. Tammy had even left the planning of her only child's funeral in Rachael's hands. Rachael had been shocked when her ex-mother-in-law didn't even attend Ed's funeral because it fell during happy hour.

The motherly rhythm of the rocking chair wasn't easing Rachael's anxiety. The turmoil she had thought she was rid of when she signed the divorce papers still haunted her. After Ed's funeral a couple of years ago, she thought she had *finally* found closure—guess not. Images from those dark days slammed at her like Ed's fist used to do when he drank too much.

The most predominant image was falling snow. Snow was something Rachael had only seen on TV (until her first wedding) because it didn't snow in the Bay Area, where she grew up. There was one exception, of course (because there always is an exception with everything, Rachael learned quickly), when she was in junior high school. It had snowed for five minutes and melted in even less time.

So when her first soon-to-be husband, Ed, suggested, with his best smile, "What do you say to going to Reno, building us a snowman, and tying the knot?" Rachael had quickly agreed. To be a bride *and* see the snow seemed perfect. Neither Rachael nor Ed had much money; they were both freshly out of high school. So Rachael bought her wedding dress off the discount rack at the local department store. She found a light-silver prom dress at 75 percent off that covered her already bulging belly. They got into his old, beat-up, red Chevy pickup and drove. The snow at the summit was beautiful and magical. When they got to the "biggest little city in the world," it started to snow. She had been convinced this meant they would have a long and happy life.

Ed had a fake ID so he could gamble, and he won big. They went out for a steak dinner at a fancy restaurant at the casino to celebrate and got a room that overlooked Reno. She'd watched the snow fall from the eleventh floor with Ed by her side. She was completely at peace. The next morning, they went to the chapel in the hotel and got married.

Things went downhill the moment they returned home. A few

years later, Rachael (who had just found out she was pregnant again) grabbed her two small children and escaped when her husband wasn't home. They only had the clothes they were wearing when they found safety at a local women's shelter.

"What am I doing?" Rachael exclaimed, jumping out of the rocking chair. "This is going to be the happiest day of your life, Rachael, whether you like it or not! This just has to be those prewedding jitters they always talk about." The wide-eyed figure in the mirror didn't look convinced. "Besides, all the important people in your life are waiting for you downstairs! Well, not everyone..." Rachael sank heavily back down into the chair.

Eddie wasn't going to be there, all because of a comment Rachael had made to his girlfriend a couple of months ago.

"If you need *anything*, you can always come to me, understand? My door is always open to you. You have a place to go." Rachael hugged Sasha goodbye before going down to bail Eddie out of jail.

He'd gotten into a brawl at a bar where he shouldn't have legally been. She promised herself this would be the last time she'd help him until he helped himself.

Unfortunately, when Eddie finally got released (and later put on probation), Sasha repeated what Rachael had said. Eddie didn't see it as a sweet gesture, like Sasha did. He caught the intended warning. He cut his family out of his and Sasha's lives—just like his dad had done.

Ed had moved Rachael away from her family right after they eloped. Los Angeles was a seven-hour drive from her family and friends. It was a place Rachael had never got used to living in. But Rachael could be wrong about Sasha and Eddie. He certainly didn't move her away from her friends, and she had no family to cut out of their lives after her parents died, although Rachael could see Eddie becoming more like his dad every day, with drugs, drinking, and stealing, which worried her.

Just over two months ago, Rachael still believed Eddie would change his mind and come to the wedding. He hadn't. Rachael's calls were screened by an answering machine, and her messages were never answered. In one final attempt last week, Rachael tried dropping off a birthday gift to Eddie at his apartment. To Rachael's surprise, Sasha opened the door.

"I'm sorry, Rachael. I must honor Eddie's wishes and not let you in or take the present. It's his birthday, and I don't want to upset him. You understand, don't you?" Sasha asked with a weak smile.

Sasha looked like she was coming down with the flu. She was as pale as her white-blond hair. Rachael held back her questions on Sasha's health. It wouldn't help the tensions between her and Eddie if he thought Rachael was suggesting more than the flu.

"Yes, Sasha. I understand perfectly. But if you would just tell Eddie—well, maybe don't tell him I came by. I'll try coming back when he's home. Thank you, Sasha."

"You're right. I don't want to spoil his nineteenth birthd—I didn't mean it to come out like that! It's just that Eddie is cleaning himself up. He wanted one more celebration tonight. Eddie's gonna quit drinking. He brought home some catalogs from colleges to go through. Tomorrow we're deciding where he's going to school. Oh, I forgot about Eddie's cake in the oven. I hope you have a wonderful wedding day. Sorry we can't make it. We'll be in touch soon, but maybe you shouldn't drop by anymore unless you talk to him first—sorry," Sasha said, quickly shutting the door.

Hurt, Rachael climbed back into her blue SUV. She prayed Sasha was right about Eddie cleaning up. Rachael had tried to help him, as had her mother, the counselors, and Sasha—but only Eddie could overcome this. What if that therapist at the women's shelter was right? She said that Eddie, at six years old, couldn't be helped—he was too far gone. Rachael thought the woman was not only rude but completely wrong. Eddie had been in therapy for that first year, after she left Ed. It was fine for a while, until Rachael began to see signs that he might be taking after his dad. By that time Eddie was refusing all help. Ed was coming around and playing the victim card with his oldest son.

Rachael finally had to change the child visitation rights. Ed was only allowed to see the kids on supervised visits, twice a month. She always felt Ed found a way around this with Eddie, but she could never prove it. Eddie was as good at lying as his father. More therapy followed Ed's death, with no results, even with the medications. Eddie always slipped back into his bad behavior, until he was kicked out of school in his senior year—then he moved out.

It was painful to have her oldest son push her out of his life. Rachael sighed as a single tear flowed down her cheek. She quickly wiped it away, right as her mother burst into the room.

"I finished Kelly's hair," Mae announced. "She looks like an angel, and so does her mom."

"Thanks-s, Mom," Rachael said, hopping up from the chair and rushing to check her hair again. *No more bad thoughts. Today marks the wedding I have always dreamt of,* Rachael thought, staring at the bride in the mirror, who returned her look with a phony smile. "Where's Kelly?"

"She's in the bathroom. Probably fixing her hair exactly like you used to do after I styled it. Like all girls do, I guess." Mae grinned.

"Well, I could use some help. Do you think we should put more flowers in my hair, or less? Should I put the back down, or leave it all up?" Rachael was relieved to be back in action.

"I think you look perfect. I wouldn't touch a thing, except for this," Mae said as she held out a box.

"What is it?" Rachael asked.

"Open it," Mae encouraged with a smile.

Rachael ripped through the pink paper. It was a ring box. In it was the 1.5-carat, square-cut diamond set in white gold that her father had given to her mother on their thirtieth wedding anniversary. When he died five years ago, her mother had put it away and started wearing her old gold wedding band on a chain around her neck.

"Oh, Mom! I can't take this!"

"You can, and you will. Tony and I had this conversation a long time ago when he asked me for your hand in marriage. Besides, the Lord only blessed me with one daughter and one son. I plan to spoil them both as much as their father spoiled me. So you have your wedding ring, you are wearing the blue garter, which is also new, and your pearl necklace is borrowed and old. You're set. Now all I have to do is deliver you to that gem waiting for you in your gazebo."

Rachael smiled. Her mother had loved Tony the minute she met him. The fact that he was Italian, like Rachael's father, was a big selling point for Mae. For the last four years, she had fussed over Tony like he was her long-lost child. It was such a relief to Rachael that she had fallen helplessly in love with Tony—her mother would have been lost without him.

"Is Stevie dressed?" Rachael asked.

"Yes. I already got some wonderful pictures of him and Tony—I mean, Dad, now. They look so handsome. Oh, I forgot. There's a small box that came for you this morning. A note on it said, 'Open Now.' Bet it's something from your husband-to-be. I'd better get it."

Rachael's mother seemed to float out of the room. Rachael grinned when she noticed a similarity between cotton candy at the fair and her mother in her long, pink gown. That shade of pink was Mae's favorite color. Rachael's dad always said that when her mother wore pink, he always had good luck. Rachael hoped this worked for her, too.

Kelly pushed past her exiting grandmother and straight into Rachael's arms. "Mom! You look so beautiful!"

Thank heavens Kelly had her dad's dark looks, but not his dark moods. She was the most even-tempered of her kids, and also the most stubborn. She tugged impatiently at her pink, rose-covered dress cuffs, which were too short. Rachael's mother swore that Kelly had grown an inch just last week, and she couldn't let them out any more before the wedding. Rachael and Kelly knew the dress was too small. Mae thought of Kelly as perpetually ten years old, but she was fourteen.

"Thank you, Kelly. You look good, yourself. I don't know if I should let you out there; you might take away all my attention," Rachael teased.

"No one will be looking at me today." Kelly shook her head.

"I hope you're right." Rachael beamed at her daughter.

"I am. Where'd Grandma go?" Kelly asked, checking her hair one more time.

Rachael glanced at the doorway. "Grandma went to get a package that came for me this morning."

"Here it is," Mae said, coming back with a small box and handing it to Rachael.

"This isn't Tony's handwriting," Rachael commented. No return address, but it had been sent to Tony's house. No—it wasn't going to be Tony's house anymore; it was going to be *her* house now, too. That was what Tony kept telling her over and over. It didn't seem real yet.

"Well, another wedding gift to add to the rest. Kelly, you'd better go downstairs with your brother for a few pictures. It's almost time for you to lead your mom down the aisle," Mae said as her soft doe eyes teared up.

"Why don't you open the present first?" Kelly insisted.

"No time. Besides, you need to get downstairs and get things ready. You have a bigger job to do as flower girl since the sick twins had to stay home. Those dresses were so cute on them, too! Can you believe that *both* sets of twins have the chicken pox?" Mae paused for a moment, so Rachael shook her head. Satisfied, she continued. "They should have gotten the shots for it. Oh well, at least Kathy, Patrick, and the boys made it, right? Now scoot, Kelly, and don't forget your flower basket," Mae finished breathlessly, making shooing motions with her hands.

"Okay," Kelly replied with a glance at her mom. She rolled her eyes. Yes, she was too old to be a flower girl, but she was playing along for her grandmother. At least she was head flower girl, they'd joked. "See you downstairs!" Kelly dashed out the door.

"Stay clean," Mae warned, but Kelly was, thankfully, long gone. "What else do you need, Rachael?"

"Nothing. I think I'm ready," Rachael said, but her eyes kept returning to the package. "I can't wait. I have to open this and see who it's from." She tore through the brown mailing paper and found a beautifully wrapped box underneath. "Isn't this paper pretty? Look!

There are tiny gazebos on the paper. It must be from Tony! Maybe someone else addressed it for him."

"That would be like him. What is it?" Mae asked, trying to peek in the box.

"This isn't from Tony," Rachael quietly informed her mother. Her icy hands shook as she took the gift out of the box and handed it to her mother.

"A snow globe? Who'd send you this? Why, it's—" Mae said.

"Yes, it's the same snow globe Ed gave to me on our wedding day. It was the snowman he promised me. I thought we got rid of this years ago." Rachael shook her head in disbelief as her heart started racing.

"We did. I helped you take it to the charity myself. It must be another one just like it, a coincidence. Who sent it?" Mae asked, putting her hand on Rachael's arm.

Rachael quietly shrugged and took back the snow globe, studying it.

"Mom, something is written on the bottom of the globe. 'Remember'," Rachael whispered and dropped the globe onto the hardwood floor. It cracked open on impact and rolled into a small wooden table next to the bed, decapitating the snowman, and the severed head rolled under the bed. Shimmering goo splattered all over the satin mauve comforter.

"Don't walk in it, honey. You could slip. Thank my pink luck this didn't get all over you! I'll clean this up." Mae sprang into action. "Here, you'd better touch up your lipstick. Your brother, Kathy, and the boys just pulled up—late, as usual. It's eight forty-five already. The wedding starts at 9:00 a.m. sharp. We'd better get down there. Hurry."

Rachael numbly did as she was told and spread pink lipstick over her lips. But her feet wouldn't take her out of the feminine room with its lace doilies cradling the mauve lamps. This gift was a bad omen; her mother's "pink luck" wasn't working. Limp, Rachael sank back into the rocking chair. She watched as her mother dabbed up the last of the fake snowflakes on the floor and bundled up the comforter. Her mood had darkened and filled her body with a foreboding that she hadn't felt in years.

"I'll run this comforter through the wash later to make sure it doesn't stain. Now, you put this strange prank out of your mind. Don't let anything ruin *your* day. Please!"

"But Mom, it's as if Ed..." Rachael couldn't say the words she'd been thinking, that Ed was reaching out from the grave.

"Ed's gone. I saw him myself, in that coffin, where he belonged. But you know, little Eddie might have something to do with this."

"No, Mom. How could he know about this globe? I put it in the top part of my closet after he was born for safekeeping. I didn't see it again until I got out of the shelter and picked up those boxes that Ed left in the apartment. Then we got rid of everything that Ed hadn't ruined, and the snow globe was in one of them. We only took the kids' clothes when we flew home with you," Rachael said, feeling like her whole world was crashing down on her.

"Yes, we did get rid of all that stuff. Oh, Rachael, if you hadn't been so far away from me, I could have—you—but..." Rachael's mother faltered for an uneasy moment. "But now isn't the time for all of this! Shame on both of us! There must be a good reason for this. Right now, I don't care what the reason is, or who sent it! No one is going to ruin your day! And none of this 'reaching out from the grave' nonsense. Now, give me a hug, and let's go get you married!"

Rachael smiled and held onto her mother, taking in her floral scent. It was soothing. Mae was right; this wasn't the time. And after today, it would *never* be the time for it again. Rachael and her matron of honor, her mother, hurried downstairs. It was a family wedding, including Ava (who was like her sister), whose job was to play the song Tony had written for their wedding on his new Martin acoustic guitar while Rachael walked down the aisle. Ava began playing the song the moment Rachael stepped on the last stair and entered the kitchen to make her grand entrance out the back door.

Rachael's second wedding began with the oldest flower girl on record (that term had become a personal joke between her and Kelly) leading the procession. Rachael walked slowly down the aisle, covered

229

in red rose petals, with her mother at her side. Not proper—the matron of honor should have led Rachael down the aisle—but Rachael wanted to do this *her* way today. Her brother, Patrick, could've taken their father's place at her side, but he was Tony's best man, and his sons, twelve-year-old Paddy and nine-year-old Sammy, were serving as ushers. At least Rachael hoped they were; she hadn't looked up yet. Couldn't. She felt that if she did, everything would be taken away from her.

"Isn't Kelly sweet?" Mae whispered to her as a couple of *oohs* and *ahhs* came from the guests.

"Like her grandma," Rachael whispered and forced her eyes to look up.

Kelly didn't disappear as Rachael watched her stroll ahead of them. Each step was perfect as she left a trail of rose petals. Rachael's eyes watered. Now that she had overcome her fear, tears were going to be the new problem. Rachael was *not* going to cry and ruin her makeup, not with all the cameras trained on her!

Mae squeezed her arm, sending a shock down her body. That was just what her father used to do when he was trying to cheer up Rachael or Patrick. She could clearly picture her father beaming down from heaven in approval at his family. He would have an extra twinkle in his eyes for his beloved wife in her pink dress. Rachael was smiling as they came to a stop at the gazebo.

She sent a silent message. *I love you, Daddy.*

It was time for Mae to hand her over to Tony. She tenderly kissed Rachael's cheek and put her cold hand into Tony's outstretched, warm one. Rachael immediately locked eyes with Tony. Everything disappeared but him.

She felt no qualms about doing this; love flowed through the rose-covered gazebo, the twenty guests, family members, and the priest. Her anxiety forgotten, Rachael had never felt safer in her life, except for when she was little and her mother or father could take her into their arms and make all the bad go away. Before Rachael knew it, she was saying "I do" and kneeling before the priest for the final blessing.

After they shared a shy kiss in front of the guests, Father Michael made the introduction: "May I present Mr. and Mrs. Battaglia."

This was met with clapping and whistles. Tony kissed her again, not as shyly as before. Suddenly, they were crushed by hugs, with Rachael's mother leading the way. Ava got the last hug in.

"I'm so happy for you, Rachael. You deserve all the happiness in the world," she said, sniffling.

"It almost seems too good to be true—" Rachael started to say.

"It isn't. You've earned this one many times over. And don't forget me, now that you've inherited an opal mine named Tony," Ava said with a laugh.

"I did," Rachael agreed with a grin. Opals were Ava's favorite stone; their fiery colors reminded Rachael of her best friend's personality. She added, somberly, "I'd never forget you. Only you and my parents were there for me when I reached out."

Ava shrugged and then added, with a wink, "Well, it looks like you'll be reaching out tonight and doing some mining." She pulled Rachael into another quick hug and then broke away and grabbed Kelly, who grinned at her mom, into her embrace.

"I believe you owe me a dance, Mrs. Battaglia." Tony claimed his bride.

"I believe I do, Mr. Battaglia," Rachael said. Boy, it sure felt good to be called "Mrs. Battaglia."

Tony nodded to Ava, who rushed back to the guitar. She quickly began playing the song Tony and Rachael had shared their first kiss to, *Before You*. Ava's honeyed voice carried over the microphone and silenced the party. Tony held Rachael tightly, making her feel like nothing bad could ever happen if she was with him. They slowly glided over the backyard's freshly cut grass to the rhythm of the guitar. Rachael couldn't wait to get her high heels off, but for her wedding, she could stand it another hour or so. She was almost as tall as Tony at five feet ten inches in her heels (or "hells," as she liked to call them). Ava had run across these shoes, which went with her dress, last week, and they looked perfect—painful or not.

Tony nuzzled her cheek with his strong, Italian nose, and their eyes met. He was the most beautiful man Rachael had ever seen. His sloping, golden-brown eyes rarely flickered with anger; instead, they were creased at the corners as a sign of someone who always had a smile on his face. His wavy hair was under control today, thanks to some hair gel and Ava, even with the slight ocean breeze. Usually, his hair was endearingly tousled. The only imperfection Rachael could find was a small scar above his right eye, a reminder of a trip over the handlebars on his mountain bike on their third date.

"I love you, Rachael Battaglia," Tony whispered.

"I love you too," Rachael choked out.

Suddenly Tony dropped Rachael into a deep dip. The clicking sounds of cameras filled the air. Rachael caught her breath as she came back up and laughed, only to be dipped again. This time, Rachael had time to look around and noted how nice the house looked with its newly painted white trim from their sprucing-up party a few weeks ago. She was about to pull her glance away when she saw a shadow in the window of the bedroom where she'd just gotten dressed. No, it wasn't a shadow. It looked like a bearded man, but his facial features were darkened or perhaps blocked, like he was taking a picture. Unsure of what she was seeing, a sudden chill shot through her just as her husband pulled her upright.

"I think someone is taking pictures from your bedroom," Rachael commented, glancing around the backyard. All the guests seemed to be accounted for.

"That's because we're such a good-looking couple. They want to get all our angles, and it's *our* bedroom now," Tony added and twirled her around while the photographer snapped picture after picture until their song ended.

The morning was going by fast under a perfect June sun that pleasantly lit up the worn, dark wood of the two-story house that was to be her new home. Tony's mother, Nora, had been fond of mauve and dark brown, while Rachael had always leaned toward yellow and white. Tony had already suggested a redecorating party when they got back from their honeymoon. He didn't care if the whole house was bright pink, like everything in her mom's house, as long as Rachael was in it. She was so lucky.

When Ava finished her set of songs for dancing, the caterers served brunch. It was a huge spread of eggs, bacon, sausages, pancakes, waffles, French toast, potatoes, egg casseroles, and fruit—all of Rachael's and Tony's favorite foods. Soon it would be time to leave, after a delicate exchange of cake (cramming cake into someone's face wasn't the best of ways to start a life together, Rachael and Tony believed).

The wedding was ending, and the honeymoon waited to begin, even if it meant getting on a plane. Rachael's doctor had given her a prescription to help her through the flight. Her last flight had been to come home with her mother and kids after leaving Ed. She would have drunk her way through the trip if she hadn't been pregnant. Even though it was only an hour and a half, she was almost crawling out of her skin by the time they landed in Oakland. This trip out of San Francisco would be different, Rachael hoped.

Patrick made the toast. "May my baby sister and new brother, Tony, live happily ever after."

Kathy, her sister-in-law, piped in. "At least until you get home from the honeymoon and pick up your kids!"

Kelly loved going to her aunt and uncle's house. She and Kathy both had a love for all things paranormal, especially shows about ghosts and hauntings. Rachael knew they'd have a ghost movie marathon this week. Stevie, on the other hand, had bonded with his uncle. They both loved building things, just like Rachael's father. Kathy had assured her that she wouldn't notice either one of them mixed in with their six kids, who ranged in age from three to twelve years old, especially "whatshisname"—Stevie. Kathy loved to tease Stevie, who was the spitting image of Rachael's dad. He always played along.

They were amazingly tireless parents. Rachael didn't know how they did it, and they made it seem easy, too. She hoped it was something that would rub off on her and Tony. At least Rachael wouldn't have to worry about being away from her kids for the first time since she'd had Kelly.

The next toast came from Tony's only living relative in America, his mother's sister, Lee, who lived in San Francisco. Tony had only been around his aunt during the holidays when he was growing up. She was distant but made a point of making it to their wedding. Her blessing was in Italian, so Rachael didn't understand a word of it.

Aunt Lee had two boys around his age. Tony warned Rachael they wouldn't come to the wedding, and they hadn't. Tony hadn't been invited to their weddings years ago—nor had his mother. His aunt's explanation was that they'd had small weddings.

Tony confided once to Rachael that his cousins acted like he and his mother had a contagious disease.

"Jack and Steve were always polite, but they seemed like they wanted to leave the moment they walked in the door," he told Rachael and shrugged. "I haven't seen them since they graduated from high school. But we do exchange Christmas cards."

Well, with a strange mom like Lee, how could anyone expect the kids to be normal? Rachael thought, studying the woman. *Who wears black to a wedding, anyway?* In addition to her style choices, Aunt Lee sat apart and kept glancing at her watch. She would be the first to leave, Rachael determined. What really held the woman's attention, though, were the upstairs windows. Did she see someone up there too? Maybe it was time to introduce herself and ask. Rachael started making her way to her table.

She smiled and nodded as she passed by guests. She wondered if Tony's father's family had been as odd. They were killed in a helicopter crash right after he graduated high school. They were both teachers, like his father. It ran in the family, even though that was all she knew about that side.

Rachael had almost made her way to Aunt Lee when the woman suddenly stood up and rushed into the house. Was she avoiding Rachael, or did she suddenly have to use the restroom? Rachael sighed. It felt like Aunt Lee was avoiding her, and she understood

Tony's comment about being treated like they had a contagious disease. Fine.

Rachael spotted her only other family members. Her mother's rich brother and his wife had moved to Arizona from San Diego (where Rachael's family used to spend vacations at the beach, visiting them). Her uncle and aunt were too busy eating, as usual, to join in the toasts. The remaining people were from work, except for Ava and her husband number two, Tim. He turned out to be the husband who had Ava talking about wanting children. Right now, though, Ava sat, surprisingly quiet, next to Mae. Rachael had thought Ava would say something at the toast, at least a quick joke, but instead, she had smiled with tears in her eyes and raised her glass to her. Rachael reciprocated.

Rachael made her final rounds through the rented banquet tables covered with pink flowers that, of course, her mother had helped pick out. Rachael smiled when she saw that Tony was in deep conversation with Patrick. From the way Patrick was demonstrating air fishing, she knew they were discussing their upcoming trip at the end of the summer. Rachael would then be in this house without Tony, the house his mother had bought after inheriting some money from her late aunt, who had left nothing to Aunt Lee. Maybe that was the issue? Nora had moved her seventeen-year-old son from San Francisco to Rachael's hometown, Pacifica. Tony said once that his only regret was leaving all his friends behind, but his mother was happy from the day she moved in, so it was worth it to him—once he got over the move. It was too bad they hadn't met earlier in life. He went off to school, and she got married, but finally they'd found each other.

Tony said he had never been married because he'd never found his soulmate until he met Rachael. At least, that was the story he told her, and Rachael chose to believe it. Luckily for Rachael, Tony had been a very devoted only child to his mother, and now that devotion passed to her.

Rachael knew she was the luckiest girl on Earth, even if she did have to walk through fire to get to this point. Speaking of fire, Rachael finally released her feet from her hells and watched Aunt Lee leave the party. She already didn't like one of her new relatives. She quickly headed back to her table and sat down next to her husband, who had another glass of champagne waiting for her. She didn't drink it; she'd already had two glasses during the toasts.

Ava came up behind Rachael, startling her.

"Time to throw that bouquet, Mrs. Battaglia," Ava said.

She heard Tim telling Tony the very same thing about the garter. As soon as Kelly caught the yellow roses and Bob, a teacher colleague of Tony's, caught the garter, their morning wedding came to an end.

Rachael and Tony ran to his truck through a steady rain of birdseed. Tony's truck had been decorated with a "Just Married" sign in the back window and pencils and erasers tied to the back. Rachael was sure she had Ava and Kelly to thank for that.

She had spent the last few years getting her teaching degree at night while she worked in an elementary school office during the day. She'd met Tony in a night class, but he wasn't a student; he was her math teacher. Now there would be two teachers in the house. She had a job waiting for her at the same junior college where Tony worked and would be putting her English degree to use next fall.

Rachael turned to her kids, who were lined up at the door of the old green pickup.

"I love you guys," Rachael said, with tears in her eyes. She gathered Kelly and Stevie (who was way too big to be called Stevie since making quarterback for the varsity football team this year, but old habits were hard to break) and pulled them into a group hug.

"Hey, don't leave Dad out of a hug," Tony protested.

The new Battaglia family clung together until Rachael's mother cleared her throat.

"You'd better get going so you don't miss your flight. Don't worry, everything will be just fine. I'll keep an eye on things. Now go have a wonderful honeymoon, you two. I love you."

"We love you too," Tony said. Another hug.

"Hey. Don't forget me!" Ava said, throwing her arms around them.

"We'd never forget you," Tony said.

"Better not, or I may keep Tootie," Ava said.

"Thanks for watching her."

"What are friends for but watching each other's cats?" Ava said and laughed.

Tootie had been Ava's cat to begin with, until they found out Tim was allergic; then the little spoiled cat became Rachael's. Ava planned on introducing Tootie to her new house while Rachael and Tony were on the beaches of Hawaii. Patrick's job, while they were gone, was to move Rachael and the kids' stuff out of her apartment and into their new home. Kathy and the kids were going to clean up the apartment for the next occupants. Mae was going to help not only with fixing up the kids' rooms and getting them settled in, but adding Rachael's stuff to Tony's room. No, no—it was *their* room now.

All Rachael knew was that everything was going to be ready for them when they got back. She didn't have a say in this part, and this was one time when she didn't mind.

"Have a great time, and don't worry about anything!" Kathy yelled.

"Thanks, Kathy. Let us know how the girls are doing," Rachael responded.

"They're almost better. A few more days, I think. The boys had it at their age, and so did your kids. I couldn't bring them here and take the chance of anyone getting it who hadn't had chicken pox. And I couldn't expose the newlyweds before their honeymoon, since you don't know if Tony's had it."

"Yeah, don't worry, sis, we've got this. Just enjoy!" Patrick added.

"Thanks, guys!" Tony waved.

Kathy's attention had shifted to her phone. *Checking on her girls,* Rachael thought.

Rachael looked for her nephews but didn't see them. They were probably playing video games. Rachael couldn't imagine having two three-year-olds, two six-year-olds, plus the boys, too.

Tony grasped Rachael's hand and winked at her. Time to go.

"Goodbye!" Tony and Rachael said together before he helped her into the truck.

"Goodbye, Mom. Goodbye, Dad," Kelly yelled over her brother. They had accepted him as their father, but not Eddie.

Tony pulled away, honking his truck horn, and then slipped in a CD: *Before You*. Settling her head on Tony's shoulder in contentment, Rachael closed her eyes. This was going to be a perfect honeymoon to top off a perfect wedding. There was that word, "perfect"—only now, unlike her first wedding, she knew what it meant, and she dozed off with a smile on her face.

Her dreams should have been peaceful at this point, but they led her back to her first wedding. She saw herself standing in that pale silver dress, so young and hopeful, next to Ed. She'd only known him for six months but thought she had met her Prince Charming. Then her dream took her to opening the package with the snow globe and watching it break. She opened her eyes, but kept her head rested on her new husband's shoulder as they passed the beach she'd always taken her kids to so they could chase the ocean waves.

Thinking of good times didn't rid her of that knot in her stomach. She'd thankfully forgotten about the snow globe during the wedding. She hadn't even told Tony about it yet. Rachael wondered who would send it to her. And why did they write the word "remember" on the bottom? Then there was that face she thought she'd seen in the window when they were dancing.

She was almost positive everyone was watching them dance. How strange—but not as strange as the snow globe. She wasn't going to tell Tony about this until they got back. She didn't want him to worry. Nothing was going to spoil this week for them. She fell back into a fitful sleep as they left Pacifica and headed for the San Francisco airport.

Rachael was woken out of a dreamless slumber with a gentle kiss.

"Naptime's over. Let the honeymoon begin."

"We're here already?" Rachael asked, sitting up and running her fingers through her hair. She pulled it out of the bun and shook it free. She glanced in the truck mirror and smoothed it down so she didn't look like she'd been in a wind tunnel.

"We are, and, might I add, you look amazing," Tony said, helping her out of the pickup into his arms. Her bad thoughts floated away as he began kissing her; gently at first, then more urgently. His hands began to slide down past the small of her back.

"Careful, Mr. Battaglia. You could get us arrested if you begin our honeymoon too soon," Rachael said, pulling away with a smile.

"We have a little time before we need to check in," he said, guiding her back into the pickup. They were rolling around on the truck seat like teenagers when a car pulled into the parking space next to them.

"Now, that's enough! There will be plenty of time for that later," Rachael scolded, sitting up and dabbing lipstick off Tony.

The sour older couple looked at them as though they'd never seen people kissing before. Rachael thought it had to have been a while—like maybe a decade or two—since they'd even held hands. The "Just Married" sign didn't seem to soften them toward Rachael or Tony.

"Maybe we can finish this in the restroom on the plane," Tony said, loud enough for them to hear.

Rachael stifled a laugh and replied in a fake Southern drawl, "It's a long flight, so when the movie starts, so can we. We don't need that cramped bathroom, honey."

The man was as red as his wife as he slammed down his car trunk and hurried away with their luggage. They heard the woman say to him, "I sure hope those two animals aren't on our flight!" The man nodded as they left.

Rachael and Tony burst into laughter, which they ended with one more kiss.

"I bet those two haven't had that much to talk about in a long while. I sure hope we don't get like that," Rachael said, smoothing her hair down again and grabbing a bag as Tony checked the pickup to make sure they weren't forgetting anything.

"We'll never be like that, I promise. Besides, we're starting out with more sparks than those two have probably ever seen in a lifetime. No man with a hot chick like you would ever turn into such an old sourpuss as that."

"Hot chick, really!" Rachael huffed like the older lady and walked off in a snooty fashion, with Tony closing in behind her.

"That's why I love you so much, Mrs. Battaglia," Tony breathed in

Rachael's ear.

"I love you too, Mr. Battaglia, but look at the time. We'd better get moving so we don't have to run through the terminal to our plane. Truck locked?"

Tony nodded.

They hurried to the shuttle, through screening, and to the airplane that was waiting to take them to Hawaii. Unfortunately, they never got their date on the plane. Rachael's nerves got the best of her when she sat down in her seat. She took the anti-anxiety pill the doctor had given her. She was skeptical, but it knocked her right out, and she fell asleep in Tony's arms. She didn't wake up until he nudged her.

"Rach, look, there's the island through the clouds."

They'd made it! Rachael hoped her mother's pink luck would get them safely on the ground. It did.

* * *

ED WAS WATCHING over Rachael like he was supposed to. He could even see her dreams. How he'd treated her was something he had been reliving since the day he died. He knew the day he married her that she was too good for him. Why hadn't he told her that? Tony seemed to be totally in love with her. Ed understood that, or at least he thought he did. Ed truly wanted Rachael to find happiness, but he had a job to do first. What if Tony wasn't what he seemed? *Could he be part of the problem?* Ed observed the dark entity following along behind Rachael and Tony. It kept its distance from them, but it was never far away.

Ed followed the newly married couple from the airport to their hotel. He pondered over who could have sent that snow globe to her. He knew that figuring that out would help him. Would one of their kids do it? Stevie and Kelly had certainly turned out well, thanks to Rachael. That was apparent at the wedding. That only left Eddie, who wasn't there for his mother. Ed's heart ached when he thought of his oldest son. He had not only failed his wife, but his son. Ed wasn't sure how he was going to make this right.